The Wicked Stepdaughter

In the dim light of the bedside lamp, I saw a sight that transfixed me. Gervaise was standing naked, with his back to me, at the foot of the bed, but all I could see of Holly were the tips of her toes peeping over his shoulders and a single flailing arm.

I hardly noticed what he was doing to her because I was staring so hard at him, my mind blown completely away by the sheer magnificence of his body. It was Herculean – a mighty physique that radiated strength and virile masculinity.

This was no posing, muscle-bound freak with overblown biceps; this was Mother Nature's concept of male beauty and no amount of hours in the gym could emulate a body like this. He was the real thing and, as I looked at him, my reverent gaze delighted in the glorious breadth of his shoulders, the muscles that rippled in his flanks like a stallion's and the sculpted sinews of his powerful legs. Viewed from the rear, he was Superman, Batman, He-man, Ben Hur, Spartacus, and all seven of the Magnificent Seven.

Other books by the author:

The Bitch and the Bastard

The Wicked Stepdaughter
Wendy Harris

BLACK LACE

Black Lace books contain sexual fantasies.
In real life, always practise safe sex.

First published in 2003 by
Black Lace
Thames Wharf Studios
Rainville Road
London W6 9HA

Copyright © Wendy Harris 2003

The right of Wendy Harris to be identified as the Author of
the Work has been asserted in accordance with the Copyright,
Designs and Patents Act 1988.

Design by Smith & Gilmour, London
Printed and bound by Mackays of Chatham PLC

ISBN 0 352 33777 x

1

Time was moving at different speeds for Miranda and me. I had much more than I needed and was running out of fingernails to paint, whereas she was whizzing around like a blue-arsed blowfly that had snorted a line of cocaine.

For her, the minutes were ticking away like heartbeats. But, for me, even the second hand on the clock was dragging itself forwards with the painful slowness of a dying man crawling across a desert.

No doubt Einstein would have had something to say about it but, frankly, as a student, I'd been far more interested in the physics of my lush-bummed science teacher's trousers than in the mind-numbing theories that had mumbled from his lips. If but one of those theories had touched upon the mystery of how a rumoured nine-incher could dwell and survive within the pressurised environment of skin-tight denim, I might have paid greater attention. But, as it was, I could only speculate that such converse perceptions of time had more to do with Sod's Law than with physics.

The facts were these: Miranda had a plane to catch, and I just wanted her gone. But the stupid bitch *would* keep faffing around and fretting over nothing. It was driving me doolally!

Checking her handbag for the umpteenth time, she cried, 'I haven't got a handkerchief!' with the same abject horror of someone discovering, all of a sudden, that they'd mislaid an eyeball or had a foot missing.

'Selina, dear, could you possibly hand me some of those tissues,' she begged, as if appealing for one of my kidneys. It irked me, the way she said 'tiss-use' and not 'tishoos' like everyone else. Her uppity refinement and sock-ironing fastidiousness were just two of the things that I loathed about my stepmother. If she'd just dropped an aitch or uttered a swearword now and then –

I waved my wet fingernails. 'Sorry – can't help you.'

Tutting, she pulled some tissues from the box in front of me and stuffed them into her handbag.

'Got your passport?'

At the sound of Matt's voice, I glanced up to feast my eyes on him. He was leaning against the doorframe: floppy blond hair falling across his eyes as usual. He looked so delectable that I felt like jumping on him right then and there. But I had to be patient.

'I think I have everything,' Miranda declared, 'but I'd better do a wee-wee before I go.' She hurried past him into the hall.

Glancing across at me, Matt gave his head a little shake. 'She'll miss her plane at this rate.'

'Then she'll just have to fly on her broomstick,' I muttered, lowering my nailbrush because my hands had become jittery with nerves.

A car horn tooted impatiently outside. 'That's John again,' Matt said. 'She really needs to get a move on. He won't wait forever.'

When Miranda came back into the kitchen, she had put on her jacket and shoes. 'How do I look?' she asked us both.

'Immaculate,' I said, but haggard is what I thought. Her face was too thin and, at thirty-five, age had begun trenching into the skin around her eyes. I made a mental note to mention her crow's feet to Matt.

'Beautiful,' was his own verdict, but I consoled myself

that he was only being smarmy because of the row they'd had last night.

Oh, he was still *her* Matt at this stage, but it wouldn't take me long to get my newly painted crimson claws into him just as soon as she was out of the way.

'I'll miss you,' she said, bending down to plant a maternal kiss on my forehead.

'Yes, me too.' *Bugger off!* I was down to my last fingernail and my whole plan would be wrecked if she didn't go now.

Poor Miranda: she had no idea how much I hated her or how I wanted and adored the man that she'd replaced my father with. She wouldn't be going to America if she knew, and she certainly wouldn't be leaving Matt with just a chilly peck on the lips to remember her by.

I saw the hurt in his eyes when she pulled from his embrace far too quickly. 'I have to go,' she said. 'I'll call you.'

As she cast a final look at me, I managed to squeeze out a smile and say, 'Take care.' *What a hypocrite I was!*

Then, just like that, she was gone. As I heard Matt closing the door behind her, my heart did a flip. It was time to begin.

He came back into the kitchen, his soulful brown eyes looking troubled. 'She's still angry with me,' he said.

I nodded. 'That's Miranda: she bears malice. What was the row about?'

'You heard us?' He sighed. 'I didn't want her to go. I was trying emotional blackmail, but it backfired on me.'

'That was pretty dumb of you,' I said. 'You know how important her job is to her. And three weeks is hardly a lifetime.'

'I know, I know.' He waved his hands. 'I'm an idiot.'

I lowered my voice to a purr. 'Personally, I don't know

3

how she could leave you so long.' I didn't look up because I wanted him to digest what I was saying. 'I could never do that.'

He didn't know how to respond. 'Do you want some coffee, Selina?'

Now I looked up. 'Love some.'

The last fingernail was finished and, as soon as his back was turned, I lifted the brush and daubed some of the crimson polish on to my blouse, just above my nipple. 'Damn it!' I exclaimed. He swung round. 'Well don't just stand there,' I told him. 'Get a sponge!'

He snatched up the water-soaked sponge that I'd planted on the drainer an hour ago and held the dripping thing out to me, confirming my estimation that it wouldn't occur to a man to wring it out first or question the wisdom of using water on nail polish. 'Wipe it off,' I implored him. 'I can't do it myself, my nails are still wet.'

Obligingly, he rubbed at the stain and, according to plan, the cold water immediately shocked my nipple into hardness and made the cotton blouse that I'd chosen for the occasion transparent. I knew full well that it would cling to my bra-less breasts like a second skin. When he lifted the sponge and saw its effect, his mouth plopped open.

That's right, I thought, take a good long look: compare my youthful breasts to Miranda's sagging pancakes.

While he stood there gawping, I checked my face in my make-up mirror. I looked innocent enough. My wide blue-green eyes were as guileless as a child's. 'Try again,' I pleaded, pretending to look despairingly at the sprawling stain. But this time he hesitated.

'I don't know if I should, I mean . . . you're not wearing a bra.'

'Don't be stupid,' I scolded him. 'And don't look so shocked – I don't always wear knickers either!'

He needed no further persuasion and once more began to rub ineffectually at the stain. I started gnawing my lip as if growing suddenly conscious of a sexual sensation. His fingertips grazed my breast but I couldn't be sure if it was accidental or not.

'I'm just making it worse.' His voice sounded thick.

'No, you're not.'

He rubbed a little harder, but this time there was no doubt in my mind that his thumb had touched my nipple on purpose. When I let out a breathy gasp, he withdrew his hand abruptly. 'I'm sorry.'

'Oh, it doesn't matter,' I said lightly. 'I didn't like this blouse anyway.' His eyes looked everywhere but at the wet patch. I laughed. 'I'm soaking wet.'

He grabbed at the double entendre. 'You're easily turned on,' he said jokingly.

'So they tell me.'

My comment fazed him. He threw the sponge into the sink and reached for the coffee jar.

While he filled the cups, I smiled at myself in the mirror. The first phase of my plan had gone well. I had instigated an atmosphere of sexual awareness between us, finally waking him up to the fact that I was no longer the sullen sixteen-year-old that Miranda had introduced him to five years ago.

Determined to show him how attractive I'd become; I loosened my long copper-bronze hair from its ponytail and applied lipstick to my full, sexy mouth.

When he handed me my cup, I saw him looking at me properly and then sneaking a peek at my prominent breasts. *Excellent!*

He leaned back against the counter, sipping his coffee. 'Does Miranda know that you leave off your underwear?'

'What's it got to do with her?' I asked fiercely.

He blinked his long eyelashes. 'Not much, I guess.'

5

'Not anything,' I insisted. 'I was twenty-one last year. You remember, don't you? You gave me this necklace.' I dangled the little cupid he'd given me from my finger-tips. 'Put it on for me, Matt.'

After handing it to him, I pulled my hair forward to bare my nape and as he threaded the chain around my neck, he fumbled clumsily with the clasp. 'It's just that I wouldn't want you catching cold,' he said.

'Thanks for your concern, *dad*,' I answered sardonically.

Suddenly his fingers were digging into my shoulders. 'Don't call me that. I'm only seven years older than you.'

'And seven years younger than Miranda,' I pointed out, brushing my cheek against his hand. 'Have you noticed she's getting crow's feet?'

His fingers moved round to encircle my throat. 'She'd strangle you for that.'

His touch was making my heart flutter and my breath quicken. It would have been the easiest thing in the world to take his hands and steer them to my breasts. But I mustn't rush. My plan was not to seduce him but to make him aware of my willingness to be seduced by him.

As he moved away again, I commented, 'Come to think of it, my father was seven years older than Miranda. Whoever said it was a lucky number? I think it's poxed.'

He heard the bitterness in my voice. 'My God, you're not still blaming her, are you, not after all these years?'

'She killed him,' I uttered flatly.

He looked at me sadly. 'You know that isn't true. He died of a stroke. It was a fluke; a rotten stinking fluke, but that's all it was.'

Hot denial flushed in my cheeks. 'He'd still be alive if she hadn't forced that fitness regime on him. She took a couch potato and tried to turn him into superman.'

He got angry with me. 'A man in his thirties isn't supposed to die, Selina. It was precisely because Miranda loved him that she worried about his health.'

'It didn't take her too long to get over him though, did it?' I snapped back vehemently. 'He was barely cold in his grave when she moved you into her bed.'

He lifted his shoulders. 'Sometimes things just happen that way.' Then he looked at me searchingly. 'Do you hate me too?'

Nothing could be further from the truth. Oh, I'd wanted to resent and despise him, but he'd been much too gorgeous for that and I'd developed a hopeless crush on him instead: immature feelings that had faded for a while during my experiments with other men and sex. But gradually I'd returned to the belief that he was the one I wanted.

I got up and took his hand in mine. 'Of course I don't hate you.' Then I let my eyes reveal just a little of the hunger I felt.

Confusion furrowed his brow. 'Selina?' he queried, half-jokingly. 'Are you coming on to me?'

Letting his hand drop, I tilted my head. 'What a question.'

'Will you answer it?'

'Certainly not,' I replied, lightening my voice with humour. 'I prefer to keep a man guessing.'

But then he did something that wasn't in my script. He grasped my chin roughly and gave me a steely look that I'd never seen before. Then, with jaw clenched tightly, he chillingly warned, 'Don't fuck with me.'

2

Later that day on my way to work, I tried to convince myself that I'd imagined what I'd seen in Matt's eyes. For, after living under the same roof for so long, it didn't seem possible that my stepmother's partner could have a darker side to him that I knew nothing about. I must have seen him in all his moods. Or had I? Suddenly, I realised that I had no idea of what his sexual proclivities were. He could be kinky, a fetishist perhaps? Beneath those kittenish brown eyes could lurk a tiger or some other such beast with the appetite and wherewithal to eat me alive. Improbable though it seemed, the notion sent a shiver of excitement down my spine.

I was still deep in thought as I entered the small factory unit, converted into offices, that I owned in partnership with my friend and former lover, Harry Lambert.

Harry had started the company, called Masquerade, as a strippergram service from a small rented office, and I had joined him straight out of school. He had always wanted to expand the business into costumed product promotion, so when, on my eighteenth birthday, I'd received a modest inheritance left by my father, Harry had offered me a partnership and Masquerade had grown. But it was still a long way from being successful and was currently languishing in the doldrums of financial instability.

Typically, Harry's first words to me as I entered his office were, 'Have you seen these fucking figures?'

It was always my side of the business in trouble. Harry's strippergram service was thriving as usual.

He smacked the sheet of paper he was holding. 'Do you want to bankrupt me?'

I moved round to his side of the desk and tapped his forehead with my fingertip. 'That's a blood vessel throbbing, Harry. There's no need for a coronary, is there?'

'You're late,' he grumbled.

I sidled behind him and dug massaging fingers into his shoulders. 'I can feel reef knots, granny knots, and this little tendon's got itself into a sheepshank.'

'Don't try getting round me,' he cautioned. But when I lifted my hands, he lolled back his head. 'No, fuck it – try getting round me.'

'I told you I'd be late,' I reminded him, drilling my fingers into the tense muscles around his neck. 'Miranda flew out today.'

'It took you all morning to say goodbye?' he queried doubtfully.

'I had an accident with some nail polish. Stop being the boss,' I scolded him. 'We're partners, remember?'

He slapped the sheet of paper again. 'How the fuck am I supposed to forget?'

Driving my fingers into his crisp brown hair, I noticed some new streaks of grey and felt responsible for them. I made my touch sensual. 'Ahh, you bitch,' he groaned and reached round to grasp my bum.

I didn't mind him touching me. I still adored him, and although he'd seduced me and broken my heart, I felt closer to him than to anyone. And I still fancied him.

Age was adding character to his roguish good looks, giving him a dissipated sexiness that I occasionally found impossible to resist. It was my own fault that the attraction persisted, for I'd ended our affair too abruptly and therefore several fucks short of the finishing post.

Added to this, Harry's uncanny knack of tuning-in to my libido was something that he caddishly exploited.

Ever alert for signs of receptiveness, Harry whispered seductively, 'Feeling horny, babe?'

'Down boy,' I told him, kissing his cheek before stepping out of reach.

His heavy-lidded, lecherous green eyes travelled lazily over my body. 'Well, some lucky bastard is in for a treat.'

'I don't know what you mean,' I said.

'Yes you do. I know that look.' He put his hands behind his head. 'You've got your eye on somebody's fly. Is it anyone I know?'

I tapped the side of my nose. 'That's my little secret.'

'Don't pucker those pouty lips at me,' he moaned. 'You know it gives me a hard-on.'

'So, anyway, back to work,' I said quickly, snatching the paper from his desk. 'I'll go through these figures with Holly. Where is she?'

'Little girl's room,' he replied. 'Playing Russian roulette with her lungs, I expect. We ought to dock her pay for all the smoke breaks she takes.'

'She's an addict,' I said. 'She can't help it. If you'd just relent and let her smoke in the office now and then –'

He rolled up his sleeve to reveal a nicotine patch. 'I'm not spending a fortune on these pissing things only to have my lungs polluted by stealth. All I'm saying is that if she wants to kill herself, let her do it in her own time.'

I pulled a face. 'Is it obligatory for all ex-smokers to become Nazis?'

'Who's a Nazi?' Holly enquired, striding into the room. She was a tall willowy blonde in her early thirties, but looked much younger. Her face was cutely pretty, with wide grey eyes and a turned up nose, and her short feathery hairstyle suited her perfectly.

I nodded towards Harry. 'The ex-smoker from hell.'

'Oh, not that again!' She spun round to present her bottom to him. 'Kiss my butt!'

He wagged a finger at her. 'Don't think I don't know what you were up to yesterday.'

She recoiled in mock disgust. 'Ooh, you dirty old man, were you spying on me?'

He rolled his eyes. 'I mean smoking in my office, you slack-fannied tart, I could smell it as soon as I came in.'

'That's funny,' she said, 'I can only smell dog breath.' She leaned forward to sniff him. 'Must be your aftershave.'

His mouth was frowning but I could see a twinkle of amusement in his eyes. 'I'll bloody sack you if you do it again.'

She turned to me. 'You're right,' she said, 'he *is* a bloody fascist. Harry, give up giving up,' she pleaded. 'Come back into the fold.'

He made a cross with his fingers. 'Get thee behind me, daughter of Satan.'

'Holly, you should quit too,' I advised her, 'if only to rob him of the satisfaction of outliving you by ten years.'

She snorted disdainfully. 'Who needs ten years in an old folk's home pissing through a catheter? No thank you, I'd sooner die tragically young. Besides, I don't want to give up; it's the only non-fattening pleasure there is, apart from the obvious. And just look at Harry – haven't you noticed what a miserable git he's become? And that's on top of the miserable git he already was!'

'Keep it up,' grunted Harry, 'and you *will* die tragically young – any minute now!'

She pouted at him. 'Suck my tit, you beast.'

He grinned. 'I will if you wank my dick.' As usual, their squabble ended in laughter.

Their often-tempestuous relationship had me baffled at times, for I had seldom seen two people so determinedly at odds with each other. They seemed incapable of agreeing about anything and, although their disputes generally took the form of good-humoured banter, I had witnessed the occasional fiery spat that had made my hair stand on end. I had also lost count of the number of times that he had sacked her or she had quit.

She'd been one of the first strippers that Harry had hired when he'd started the business. But I'd been the one to discover the 'A' level maths she'd been sitting on, and had coerced her into the office to do our bookkeeping and generally assist. A move at first disparaged by Harry, but later applauded when he'd realised how invaluable she was. Yet we couldn't afford to pay her more than a pittance, so she still stripped occasionally to supplement her income.

I knew that she'd had a fling with Harry sometime before his marriage to Alison, but how and why it had ended remained a mystery. When I'd questioned her about it, she'd been surprisingly close-mouthed for a thoroughbred Essex girl who, in all other respects, was as frank and open as they came.

On finding Harry just as reticent on the subject, I'd arrived at the conclusion that one or both was harbouring some deep-rooted hurt, which had scabbed over but never quite healed.

Holly had cautioned me, in advance of my own love affair with him, that it would 'all end in tears', but she had never reproached me or 'told me so' when it had. Instead, she'd given me her shoulder to cry on and we'd become fast friends.

She was the only one I'd confided in over my plan to seduce Matt and, in her eagerness to find out if my campaign had begun, she grabbed my shoulders and bulldozed me into my office.

Snapping the door shut behind her, she asked, 'Did it work?' The idea of the nail polish had been hers.

'Put it this way,' I chuckled, 'he's now aware that I have breasts.'

'You little minx!' she cried. 'I can't believe that you actually went through with it.'

'I told you I was serious,' I said. 'By the time Miranda gets back in three weeks, he'll be mine.'

'I pity the poor bastard,' she rued, 'he won't even know what's hit him. You can be downright ruthless when you want something.'

I rubbed my cheek thoughtfully. 'I don't think it'll be a cakewalk,' I surmised. 'I've been warned off already.' I told her what Matt had said.

'Don't fuck with me?' she repeated. 'I don't think I like the sound of that. Are you sure you know what you're doing?'

'Do any of us?' I countered. 'All I know is what I want. Personally, I think it adds an element of danger to the chase.'

'But what if that element turns out to be fire?' she asked soberly. 'Has it crossed your mind you might get burnt?'

'Didn't we have this conversation about Harry once?' I queried laughingly.

'We did,' she agreed, 'and look what happened. Watch your step: that's all I'm saying.'

Once we'd taken our seats on either side of my desk, I handed her the sheet of figures. 'Tell me this isn't as bad as it looks,' I beseeched her.

'It's worse than it looks,' she confided. 'I've had to leave a couple of things off. We can't have Harry blowing all his gaskets at once.'

'Is he right to be worried about bankruptcy?'

'That all depends on Luca,' she said. 'He's already cut off supply and could start proceedings if he doesn't get his money. But that's the least of your worries. Luca isn't known for his subtlety with debtors. He's more likely to put a horse's head on your pillow than take you to court.'

Luca Verdici owned a chain of dodgy sweatshops that, until recently, had supplied costumes to Masquerade. I had run up a debt of three thousand pounds with him and now he was threatening to pull the rug. However, unlike Holly, I wasn't convinced that all Italians had links to the Mafia, or that the scar on his face from a glassing incident was down to anything more sinister than a Saturday night pub brawl.

'Holly, you're letting your imagination run away with you again. I can handle Luca. For one thing, he fancies the pants off me.'

Even though I spoke with confidence, I wasn't sure if it was still true, for Luca had long since given up bombarding me with blood-red roses after I'd gone out of my way to convince him that I had no intention of mixing business with pleasure. As far as I could tell, he had pretty much rolled over and accepted my decision, presumably moving on to pastures new.

'Well, you'd better start thinking about which bits of him you're willing to handle,' Holly said, 'because he telephoned this morning. He's coming in on Friday to pick up a cheque.'

'Shit,' I growled. 'Surely we can scrape together enough money to keep him off my back? We have debtors, don't we?'

'Not many,' she said. 'Most are simply refusing to pay because we fucked up the job.' She ran her finger down the list of names. 'The Diamond Palace, for example. They ordered Mother Goose and we sent them a six-foot mongoose.' She looked at me accusingly.

I pulled a wry face. 'I had a dreadful hangover that day, but I'm sure that's what they said.'

'Then there's Brimingtons,' she continued. 'They've agreed to pay for the frog costume but not for Andy's time, which is quite reasonable considering he spent most of it on his back.'

'Have they no sympathy?' I asked. 'The poor sod fainted.'

She shot me a look that asked if I was kidding. 'The poor sod "fainted" because he was pissed as a newt,' she commented blandly.

I giggled. 'OK – so he was the wrong kind of amphibian. How was I to know he had a drink problem?'

'The list goes on,' she said, handing it back to me. 'There's a few I can chase: Stratton Publicity have no reason not to pay. But it's like squeezing blood from a stone. Everyone's having cash-flow problems these days.'

I checked the name on the paper. 'They owe us over a thousand!' I exclaimed. 'Do you think Luca will wait if I take them to court?'

Holly looked up at the ceiling and started humming the theme to the *Godfather*.

I leaned back and exhaled a deep breath. 'Can Harry bail me out?'

She shook her head. 'Not this time. The bank won't even lend him the money to finance this costumed waitress scheme of his. I happen to know that he's using his own cash.'

'I didn't know that,' I said. 'What the hell am I going to do, Holly?'

'What are you asking me for?' she said. 'I'm just someone who strips for a living and turns a trick now and then to pay the gas bill.'

'You've got "A" levels,' I pointed out.

'Not in business studies.' She patted my arm. 'Besides,

I don't need an "A" level to recognise when someone's in a hole. The way I see it, Selina, you've got four options: beg, borrow, steal, or fuck your way out of it.'

'Who do you have in mind?' I asked. 'The bank manager?' She smiled non-committally. 'Do me a favour,' I moaned. 'He's five stone overweight and has a head like a buttock.'

'Well then, what about Matt?' she suggested. 'Can't you borrow the money from him?'

I was about to tell her this was out of the question when, unexpectedly, the door flung open and Harry swaggered in like John Wayne. 'Got room in here for a sex bomb, girls?'

Holly threw him a withering look. 'Sex bomb?' she queried. 'I hate to disillusion you, Harry, but at best you're an indoor firework.'

He crumpled as if she'd shot him. 'You heartless bitch – that one got me right in the nuts!'

She held out her hand. 'Give them here and I'll kiss them better.'

'Oh, sure,' he said, 'and right after that I'll stick my head in a shark's mouth.'

I laughed, but I was itchy about the interruption. 'What do you want, Harry? We're in the middle of something here.'

He effected his 'little boy lost' look. 'You know the school reunion dinner–dance tomorrow? Well, I'm a couple of waitresses short. They've gone down with the plague or something and I can't find anyone to replace them at short notice.'

'Too bad,' I said. 'You're in Shit Street, Harry.'

He looked pleadingly at Holly. 'Can't help you,' she said. 'Tomorrow night I'm being Madonna.'

He tutted. 'So you are, I'd forgotten about that gig. Selina ... sweetheart?'

'I don't strip,' I stated firmly.

'It isn't stripping,' he insisted. 'It's just dressing up as a schoolgirl and serving bangers and mash to a bunch of nostalgic tossers.'

'And getting my arse pinched black and blue,' I predicted grimly. 'I'm not doing it, Harry, it's degrading.'

'Oh, come on,' he said. 'Last week you dressed up as an Italian tomato for that spaghetti sauce promo. What's more degrading than that?'

'That was different,' I declared. 'I was standing in for one of my own people.'

Harry threw up his hands. 'So would I if I thought I could get away with it. But I don't have the fucking legs for it, do I?'

'A tomato doesn't need good legs,' I pointed out. 'I didn't notice you rushing to help *me* out last week.'

'You didn't ask me.'

Holly giggled. 'Perhaps she doesn't see you as a tomato; perhaps she sees you more as a withered old prune.'

'Oh, piss off,' he told her. 'I'm begging, Selina. You know how much this means to me.'

I looked at Holly who nodded towards the sheet of paper on my desk as if to remind me that I owed him this much. 'Oh very well,' I relented. 'But you'd damn well better get some backup on your books because there won't be a next time.'

'I will,' he said, cuddling me. 'You're an angel.'

'I wouldn't mind,' I told Holly after he'd gone, 'but I don't even know how to waitress.'

'You get some food and you plonk it in front of someone,' she said. 'Oh, and if they twang your suspenders, shove their face in the mash.'

We went back to discussing the figures.

* * *

I was still mulling over my options when I got home that night.

Matt noticed my furrowed brow. 'Is there something wrong, Selina?'

Holly's suggestion that I ask him for money flashed through my mind, but I dismissed it. I knew that he and Miranda were saving up to buy my half of the house and I was so desperate for a place of my own that I wasn't prepared to compromise either his or her savings. Not that Miranda would have loaned me a penny in any case, for she had thoroughly disapproved of my investment and, on several occasions, had accused me of squandering my inheritance. Pride alone forbade me from seeking any help from that quarter.

'It's been a long day,' I sighed, dropping on to the couch in a way that rucked my skirt up. I closed my eyes and stretched my arms luxuriantly, conscious of him watching me. 'What about you? How did the interview go?'

'Pretty shitty,' he grunted sourly. 'I was turned down again.'

Matt had lost his job as a graphic designer several months ago and, because he had failed to embrace computer technology, he was finding it difficult even to get an interview.

'Poor Matt,' I murmured. 'Why won't you accept that people don't want drawing board skills anymore? They think you're a dinosaur.'

'I know you're right,' he admitted. 'You, Miranda, everyone – you all say the same. I *will* start looking at courses. It's the bloody mouse that puts me off. It'll be like learning to use a pencil all over again – except that, this time, I'm not five years old. Are you hungry? There's some pizza keeping warm in the oven.'

'Famished,' I said, raking my eyes over his face. His

disappointment had left him deliciously vulnerable and the idea of giving him succour appealed to me. I started to rise but he held up his hand. 'I'll get it.'

I let him wait on me and watch me eat but insisted on clearing away. He was sitting on one of the armchairs watching the news when I went back into the lounge. I perched myself on its padded arm and gently stroked his hair. 'You'll be fine,' I assured him. 'It's ideas that count.'

He leaned back and submitted to my petting. 'That feels good,' he said.

As I cradled his head against my chest and felt him nuzzling his cheek to my breast, my heart began to beat a little faster. Almost imperceptibly, I slid from the chair arm on to his lap.

His hand hovered above my thigh, the fingers clenching. 'Selina,' he uttered huskily, 'I think you'd better get off.'

'But I feel sorry for you,' I crooned.

'I don't want your pity,' he rasped. Then his hand slammed down and gripped my thigh so tightly that I winced.

I made my voice soft as silk. 'What do you really want, Matt?'

He stroked downwards. 'You might despise me if I told you.'

'Then show me,' I said.

But when his fingers hooked under the hem of my skirt and started clawing it up my leg, I felt a sudden rush of panic. This was happening too fast. We hadn't even kissed yet!

'Slow down,' I pleaded, covering his hand with mine to halt its progress. He whipped it from under my palm and grabbed a hank of my hair. Then, yanking back my head, he snarled, 'I don't like playing games.' His eyes were aflame and his breath felt hot and heavy on my face. Then, all at once, his lips were at my throat and I could feel my skin being drawn into the vacuum inside his mouth. He was sucking me, branding me. His vampire-like kiss draining all my resistance just as surely as if he was draining my blood.

I squirmed in his arms, shivering with lust as his moist lips detached from my neck and hungrily sought my mouth. But our frenzied kiss had barely begun when, suddenly, like a bomb going off, the doorbell rang.

The sound seemed to jolt him to his senses. 'Oh, my God, what am I doing?' He shoved me to the floor and jumped to his feet. 'Get up,' he commanded me.

'Surely you're not going to answer it?'

He flicked me with his foot. 'Get up, I said!'

As he strode from the room, I hurried to the kitchen, my mouth as dry as sand. I drank a glass of water, gulping it down as if I was dying of thirst.

I'd never seen Matt like this before. It was as if I'd pulled the cork from a bottle of something highly toxic and flammable and now its contents were spilling out everywhere. To be so volatile, I realised, it must have been brewing for a long time.

'Selina, would you come in here please!'

His voice carried a strange note of panic and I immediately thought that caller had brought bad news but, as I entered the lounge, Matt was smiling. 'Look who's here,' he said tightly. 'It's Gervaise.'

I swivelled to see a stranger standing by the door. 'Who?' I uttered blankly, forcing Matt to add, 'Miranda's brother.'

To disguise my dismay, I turned quickly back to Matt and it was then that I noticed the smudge of my pink lipstick on his mouth.

3

Gervaise Morgan! Never! Not in a million years! This hulking, scowling, bearded invader looked more like Blackbeard's brother than Miranda's, and bore no resemblance at all to the grinning, fresh-faced teenager in the faded photograph she'd once shown me.

I hadn't probed her too deeply about the cute-looking boy in the ageing snap because Gervaise had seemed as irrelevant to me as the rest of Miranda's relatives. I knew that he was her half-brother: the progeny of her father's remarriage to a Frenchwoman, and that Miranda had come to know him through visitational trips to her father's villa in Cannes. Apparently, they'd forged a close bond when their mutual parent had suffered a prolonged illness but, as far as I knew, their only contact, since his funeral, had been via letter or phone call.

It seemed a lousy irony that, of all the times to turn up out of the blue to surprise his sister with a visit, Gervaise should elect the very day that she'd flown out of the country. From my point of view, in light of what had just happened between Matt and me, it was shit bastard timing and the tight smile I greeted him with was as welcoming as a slap in the face.

I scrutinised him from head to toe, seeking confirmation of a genetic link to Miranda, but all the prima-facie evidence was for a genetic link to the 'missing link', and the only similarity to my stepmother was in the jet black hair they shared. Yet, whereas hers was straight as a die, his was thick and wavy.

Physically, they were opposites: Miranda petite and slender, Gervaise tall, and built like a heavyweight boxer. He appeared to resemble their father more than she did.

His tanned and weathered face was half-hidden behind a rampant bushy beard, and the only attractive thing about him was the pair of dazzling sky-blue eyes that peered out from under the dense black canopies of his lashes.

He was wearing an open-necked khaki shirt with the sleeves rolled up to the top of his biceps, loose khaki trousers, and a pair of worn and dusty hiking boots. I looked at them critically before lifting my gaze to discover myself the subject of scrutiny. He was staring specifically at my mouth and then, with clinical precision, his eyes hawked across to the tell-tale smudge on Matt's lip. He was clearly adding two and two together and making it obvious that he didn't like the maths.

Obliviously, Matt invited him brightly to sit down and make himself at home. 'Can I get you something to eat and drink?'

Gervaise nodded cordially. 'I could use a coffee and maybe a sandwich.' He had a deep voice with the merest trace of a French accent.

'Coming right up,' Matt said.

I half-lifted my hand to warn him about the lipstick, but Gervaise was watching me and I decided it would serve no purpose. The damage had already been done.

As Matt went out, I sat down on the sofa and Gervaise sat next to me, sprawling his long legs out in front of him.

'Selina.' He said my name as if tasting it. 'Miranda's told me a lot about you. But not everything, it seems. You're older than I thought you'd be; she still speaks of you as if you're a kid.'

'She hardly mentions you at all,' I said nastily. 'I thought you were supposed to be in the Middle East somewhere.'

'I was,' he agreed, 'but now I'm not.'

The intensity of his gaze was making me uncomfortable and, to avoid it, I reached for the remote control and turned off the telly.

'It's curious,' he said.

'What is?' I asked, glancing back at him.

'That you and Matt should wear the same colour lipstick.'

His directness surprised me but I didn't let it show. 'Why is that curious? Don't you kiss each other in France?'

He nodded slowly. 'I'm told that kissing is something we do very well.'

'There you are then,' I said.

'There I am then what?'

'You'll know the difference between an innocuous kiss and a meaningful one.' I spread my hands as if to signal an end to the subject. But he wasn't ready to let it drop.

'So why did Matt look so guilty when he answered the door?' It was a loaded question expressed with hands and eyebrows in a way that was typically French.

'Perhaps he'd forgotten to put the cat out,' I suggested flippantly.

'You don't have a cat.' He ran his finger along the sofa and held it up. 'No cat hairs.'

'You don't miss much, do you?' I said.

He shrugged. 'I'm a journalist. We learn to notice things.' He was looking directly at my throat where Matt had kissed me and, for a second, I thought he was psychic, but then it dawned on me dismally that Matt must have branded me with a fresh, rosy lovebite.

I could feel myself shrinking into the sofa as I said in a feeble voice, 'I suppose journalists have to be careful about jumping to conclusions?'

'Indeed,' he said. 'But it's surprising how often things turn out to be exactly how they look. Are you sleeping with him?'

'How dare you!' I exclaimed, leaping to my feet. 'Who the hell do you think you are, coming in here with your dusty boots, making all kinds of accusations?'

My anger seemed to amuse him. 'I believe I'm your step-uncle,' he said. 'Doesn't that merit a kiss in this country? Or does that only apply to non-relatives like Matt?'

I slumped into an armchair. 'Well now, I would have kissed you, Uncle Gervaise, but the thing of it is – I'm allergic to beards.' It was almost true – I hated beards and I certainly didn't trust the men who wore them.

When Matt came in, carrying a tray, I was relieved to see that all traces of lipstick had gone. But he must have removed it inadvertently, for he showed no sign of nerves as he handed Gervaise a plateful of sandwiches.

'Miranda will be devastated that she missed you,' he remarked.

'It was a stupid idea,' Gervaise acknowledged. 'I should have telephoned.'

'But I hope you'll stay a few days,' Matt urged him.

I shot him a blistering look. Was he out of his mind? Let the gorilla spend the night, but first thing in the morning put the bastard on a plane and send him back to the planet of the apes!

'If you're sure it's not too much trouble,' Gervaise said, subjecting me once again to the piercing blue challenge of his eyes.

'Oh, it's no trouble at all,' I said sweetly.

Matt went outside and, a moment later, returned

dragging behind him what looked like a huge black body bag. It was a massive holdall with probably enough clothes for several months. 'Shall I take this upstairs?' he enquired.

'No, leave it,' said Gervaise. 'I'll take it up later.'

Matt looked relieved. 'It's heavy,' he said.

'It's come straight from the Middle East,' Gervaise explained. 'There's probably a hundredweight of sand in there after eighteen months on the road.'

'Were you reporting on the war?' Matt asked.

Gervaise nodded. He was munching on his third sandwich. 'It's a pleasure to eat something that doesn't taste of camel shit,' he said.

While he and Matt fell in to discussing the war, I covertly observed our intruder. He seemed to be taking up a lot of space in the room and it wasn't just down to his size. There was a powerful presence about him that commanded the attention; an imposing self-assuredness that bordered on arrogance. I saw intelligence and astuteness in his eyes, but noticed also their propensity to sparkle with sudden humour. Such a man, I realised, would make a formidable adversary, and the sooner he was gone the better.

Aware of my antagonism, he changed tactic and launched a charm offensive: tilting his head when he spoke to me, softening his gaze, exaggerating the movements of his eyebrows. But I was having none of it and kept my responses formal and clipped.

Presently, he said, 'If you don't mind, I think I'll turn in. I'm feeling a bit jet-lagged.'

'I'll show you to your room,' Matt offered.

Gervaise stood up. 'Just tell me where it is.'

'First door on the left at the top of the stairs,' I informed him.

He flicked me a wink and then stooped to pick up his

bag. Curiosity drew my eyes to his arse: it was lean-hipped and firm. Apparently, all his bulk was in his back and in his chest.

I was grudgingly impressed when he hoisted his bag as if it held only feathers and hefted it over his shoulder. 'Goodnight,' he said.

As soon as the sound of his clomping boots on the stairs had receded, I looked at Matt. 'We need to talk.'

'Not now,' he cautioned, picking up the tray.

I followed him out to the kitchen. 'We need to discuss what happened.'

'What happened was wrong,' he declared. 'I lost my head for a moment; I wasn't thinking straight.'

'Don't give me that shit. You knew exactly what you were doing and so did I.' Annoyingly, he was putting cups into the sink. Grabbing his arm, I spun him to face me. 'Will you forget the fucking cups! We *need* to talk!'

'Do you want him to hear us?' he rasped. 'Is that what you want?'

I lowered my voice. 'Just don't try and tell me that you didn't know what you were doing.'

He went back to filling the sink. 'Selina, you need to understand that when a man's cock starts acting on its own initiative, it doesn't stop to rationalise. It just waves itself like a magic wand and his ability to reason disappears. All he can think about is what his cock wants because, right at that moment, it's the centre of his universe and the only thing worth breathing for. How can any man be sure of what he wants when, half the time, it's his prick that's calling the shots?'

'Oh, I see,' I said sarcastically. 'That clears it up then – you were venting off testosterone and I just happened to be there. Well, wasn't that convenient?'

He didn't answer but started washing up the cups.

'Matt,' I said, sighing, 'this isn't about hyperactive

hormones or random erections; this is about two people being turned on by each other.'

'But it wouldn't have happened if Miranda was here,' he insisted, 'and now that Gervaise is, it isn't going to happen again.'

'He's a bloody nuisance,' I agreed, 'but his being here doesn't change anything.'

'Oh, yes it does, it changes everything,' he said. 'I'm glad he's here, it's brought me to my senses. I'm not going to piss up my life with Miranda just because of a kiss.'

'How can you say that?' I whispered, sliding my arms around his waist and hugging my pubis to his rear. 'Look at my neck; look at what you did to me. If Gervaise hadn't turned up when he did, where do you suppose my ankles would be right now?' He dropped the cup he was holding and as it crashed into the sink, I brought my lips to his ear. 'We can't go back to the way it was, you know we can't.'

He raked his fingers through his hair. 'We have to go back. It'll be hard but ...'

'It'll be too hard,' I interjected, letting my hand slip down to his crotch, 'and what's more –' I started rubbing him '– it'll only get harder.'

His hands grasped the edge of the sink. 'Oh, stop,' he gasped. But his cock was beginning to swell and judders of arousal were twitching through his body.

'You see, Matt,' I purred, 'I know your little secret. You've been wanting this for a long time, haven't you – haven't you?' His head lolled and his chest began to heave as I teased his trapped erection. 'You've been wanting me to touch you like this.' I nipped at his earlobe. 'It's been gnawing away at you, hasn't it?'

He spun round and grasped my shoulders. 'Yes,' he hissed fiercely. 'Yes!'

But just as he was about to kiss me again, we both heard the sound of Gervaise's bastard boots clumping down the stairs.

Matt thrust me from him. 'Stay away from me,' he growled.

Gervaise almost knocked him flying as they collided in the doorway. 'I need to piss,' muttered Matt, clutching his crotch to conceal his erection. Gervaise stepped aside and let him pass.

'What do you want?' I demanded coldly. 'I thought you'd gone to bed.'

He thrust his thumbs into the waistband of his trousers and wandered around the kitchen. 'I fancied a nightcap,' he said. 'Sometimes I don't sleep too well. It comes of never knowing if a bomb's going to drop on your head in the night. Do you have some brandy?'

'There's some cognac somewhere,' I mumbled irritably. I found it in the cleaning cupboard beside a bottle of bleach and was half-tempted to mix him a cocktail of the two.

'Will you join me?' he asked, as I poured out a glass for him.

'No, I won't,' I declined. 'I'm going to bed.' I handed him his brandy.

'Not so fast,' he said, grabbing my wrist with his free hand. But instead of speaking, he lifted his glass and drained it, still clutching me. 'So, are you going to tell me what's going on here?' he demanded, slamming the empty glass down.

I tugged against his vice-like grip. 'Nothing's going on.'

He sat down in a chair and swung me in front of him. 'Can you see the word "sucker" tattooed on my forehead?'

'No,' I answered sullenly.

'Good,' he said, 'because I was beginning to think that I must look like some kind of arse-picking idiot.'

I eased my hand from his grasp. 'What makes you so suspicious?'

He cast a thumb over his shoulder. 'Because Matt's looking guilty again and you –' he raked his eyes over me '– well, you're just looking hot.'

I fanned my face with my hand. 'It *is* hot, don't you think?'

'I don't mean that kind of hot. But if that isn't enough for you, then perhaps you can explain to me why Matt was cuddling a hard-on just now?'

'We were horsing around,' I said. 'You know what men are like – they get excited.'

'Oh, so that's all it was,' he snorted sarcastically. 'Well, let me tell you something, Selina. I don't like the idea of you horsing around with my sister's boyfriend. And I don't think she'd like it either. In fact, if she was here right now, I'm pretty sure she'd be telling you, in no uncertain terms, that it's time you fucked off and got a place of your own.'

'This is my home!' I snapped. 'She can't throw me out. I own half of it!'

He saw something in my eyes that made his own widen. 'You don't like her at all, do you?' he realised.

'Now you're being ridiculous,' I said. 'I'm not having this conversation. I'm going to bed.'

'No, wait,' he commanded. 'I think I'm on to something. Are you trying to steal Matt to get back at Miranda for some wrong that you think she's done you?'

I threw up my hands in exasperation. 'Are you sure it isn't novels you write, Gervaise? Because you've one hell of an imagination.'

'What I have is a nose for a story,' he told me, 'and I'm sensing one here. It's a pathetic little tale about an ungrateful spoilt brat with a fucking great chip on her shoulder.'

'Go ahead, make it all up,' I goaded him. 'It's what reporters do, isn't it, when they can't be bothered to find out the facts?'

'Not this one,' he said. 'I just keep digging till I get to the truth.'

'Then you'd better keep digging,' I advised him. 'And when you come out in Australia, do me a favour – go find yourself a didgeridoo, shove it up your arse and let your mouth do the talking for a change.'

He pretended to flinch as if I'd struck him. 'That's quite a temper,' he said, blinking his thick black eyelashes. 'Are you aware that when you're angry the colour of your eyes changes from aquamarine to turquoise?'

His observation inflamed me. 'Are you attempting to flirt with me?'

He smiled. 'Are you kidding? I wouldn't dream of it; you'd probably go straight for my jugular.' His eyes moved deliberately to the stain of Matt's kiss on my neck. 'Is that recent?'

'As a matter of fact, it is,' I declared. 'And, before you ask, my boyfriend isn't a vampire, he just got carried away.'

'You have a boyfriend?'

'Well, naturally,' I lied. 'You don't think that Matt did this, do you? Trust me, we're not that close.'

I must have looked too pleased with my defence because a single black eyebrow rose sceptically as he said, 'Actually, I don't trust you at all. Call it instinct.'

'Suit yourself,' I huffed and, with a dramatic toss of my hair, flounced from the room.

'I saw that exit in *Gone with the Wind*,' he shouted after me.

Once in my bedroom, I flung myself on my bed and

punched the pillow. *Take that you bearded baboon!* I was furious with him for a whole list of things: for being Miranda's brother, for arriving unannounced, for interrupting my plans, for being much too astute and for having the audacity to confront me!

How dare he accuse me of trying to steal Matt just to get back at Miranda? It was a ludicrous idea. I wanted Matt because I wanted him. This had nothing to do with revenge. But, as I lay there thinking, a little voice niggled at the back of my mind – *Are you sure about that?* Oh that's peachy, I thought, now he's got me doubting my own motives.

He was mounting the stairs now and I could hear them creaking under the weight of his clomping boots. How I hated the sound of those boots!

Holly was eager for news the next day. 'Did you make any progress last night?'

'It was all going splendidly,' I told her, 'until this great bearded fly wearing dusty old boots landed smack in the middle of the ointment.' I explained about Gervaise.

'Phew,' she whistled. 'Miranda's brother? Flies don't come much bigger than that! Is he like her?'

'That's difficult to say,' I replied. 'She doesn't have a beard.'

Holly didn't share my aversion to facial hair. 'The trouble with you, Selina, is you've no imagination.'

I looked at my fingernails distractedly. 'I don't care to imagine what he's hiding beneath that beard: a weak chin, a harelip, who knows? The whole thing is a disfigurement as far as I'm concerned.'

'I disagree,' she said. 'The great thing about beards is that they come right off, whereas a dick-nose tends to be permanent. Does he have a dick-nose?'

'I didn't notice a bell-end,' I said.

'So, that's a plus,' she asserted. 'Is his hair as dark as Miranda's?'

'I suppose so.'

'Then it's black. He's beginning to sound tall, dark and handsome, Selina.'

'So is King Kong – to a monkey,' I said.

'Eyes?' she persisted.

I put my finger to my forehead and pretended to consider. 'I believe he has a matching pair.'

'Colour?' she huffed.

'Blue.'

'Aha!' she exclaimed.

'What the hell is "aha" supposed to mean?' I flicked a paperclip at her.

She caught it and nodded sagely. 'You had to be looking closely at him to notice the colour of his eyes.'

'Not these eyes,' I said. 'They come at you like lasers.'

'Hmm,' she murmured, 'I love him already. He sounds the kind of man who wouldn't have any trouble at all in finding a girl's knickers in the dark. So, when do I meet Mr Laser-blue Eyes?'

'Hey, your knickers are overcrowded as it is,' I reminded her. 'Have you forgotten Paul?' I was referring to her current boyfriend.

'Paul who?' she responded blithely.

'Oh, it's like that, is it?' I wasn't surprised. Holly's relationships with men were like mayflies – sexy but short-lived. Yet I'd been hoping for her sake that Paul might be different. 'What's the matter with you, Holly? Paul's nice, I thought you liked him.'

'It isn't enough though, is it, just liking someone?' she reasoned. 'I like chicken tikka but I wouldn't want to have its babies. The trouble with Paul is that he's the kind of man who packs his slippers in his overnight bag and keeps turning off my lights to save on electricity. It's like he's fifty before he's even forty.' She gave a small shudder. 'I think he's trying to move in with me, a sock at a time. I found a whole bunch of them under my bed the other day and was forced to confront the dilemma of whether to wash them or throw them in the bin. It was the acid test of commitment, I suppose. So, I did what you'd expect and tossed the woolly fuckers into the garbage. If Paul had been wearing them, he'd have gone too. I'd say that's evidence of a dead man walking, wouldn't you?'

'I think you're being too hasty,' I said. 'Paul's got a lot going for him. He's sweet natured, charming . . .'

'Are you talking about me again?' queried Harry, strolling in through the open door, swinging a carrier bag in his hand.

'We certainly were,' confirmed Holly. 'But, if you'd waited half a second, you'd have heard my friend say that as well as being charming and sweet natured, you're a dickhead with lop-sided bollocks.'

Harry pulled a hangdog face. 'They're only lop-sided because the pair of you keep taking pot shots at them. Who were you really talking about?'

'Paul,' I supplied.

'Ah, now you're talking dickhead,' he said.

'Holly's thinking of dumping him.'

He lifted his eyebrows. 'Another one bites the dust? Who's next on the conveyor belt?'

'Funny you should say that,' Holly answered with a grin. 'Selina's just been telling me that Miranda's brother has turned up at her house. His name is Gervaise. He's French and he's unattached.'

'If he has a pulse and a prick then he's your type,' Harry said. He turned to me. 'But is he man enough for the job?'

'He's certainly big enough,' I said. 'Do you remember Bluto?'

Harry nodded. 'You mean the big lunk who fought Popeye over that skinny bitch Olive? Hey, you could be in with a chance, Holly, if this Gervaise goes for the lanky, boat-footed type.'

'I do not have big feet,' she protested.

'So do you wear those size nines for a joke?'

Scowling, she muttered, 'You'll be checking out my shoe size with your teeth in a minute. Who asked for your input anyway? This is girl talk.'

He plonked the carrier bag on to the desk in front of me. 'What's this?' I asked. 'Have you been doing my shopping?'

'It's your school uniform for tonight,' he said, rubbing his hands together gleefully. 'I can't wait to see you in it.'

'Ooh, let me see,' squealed Holly, snatching up the bag. She thrust her head inside. 'He's thought of everything,' she reported. 'There's even stockings and suspenders in here and ... Oh, I don't believe this!' She dug her hand into the bag and withdrew on the end of her finger a tiny white G-string. The minuscule crotch piece bore the company name, Masquerade, together with its mask-on-a-stick logo.

'Harry!' I barked, looking at him sternly. 'What's the idea of giving me these?'

He widened his eyes. 'It's good publicity?'

'Only if someone happens to have their head up my skirt!'

'You could flash them now and again,' he suggested.

'And you can go fuck yourself,' I suggested right back. I snatched the briefs from Holly. 'There isn't enough material in these to make an eye-patch for a mouse!'

'I think they're cute,' she said. 'Have you got any more, Harry? I'll wear a pair tonight.'

I gaped at her. 'You can't seriously think that this is the kind of thing that Madonna wears?'

Harry meanwhile was staring at me. 'Is that a hickey?' he asked, hooking his finger into the roll-neck of my sweater and tugging it down. 'Now, that's what I call getting into the part,' he declared. 'I haven't seen one of these since I was a schoolboy. Who did it, Bluto?' For some reason he looked at Holly.

'I didn't do it!' she cried.

'I didn't say you did,' Harry murmured huskily. 'But, now you've given me the image, let me hold it for a minute.' He closed his eyes and heaved a wistful sigh.

Holly and I exchanged weary looks and made simultaneous wanking gestures. 'I get the message,' Harry said. 'I'm outa here.' But he paused at the door to wink at me. 'Don't forget, I want to see you in that outfit!'

As soon as he was gone, Holly jumped up to inspect the lovebite. 'Did Matt do this? The man's an animal! Is this your punishment for ignoring his warning not to fuck with him?'

I was about to answer her when the telephone rang. I picked it up. 'Masquerade, Selina King.'

'Good morning, Selina. How are you?' The speaker's Italian accent pronounced him as Luca Verdici.

'Luca,' I answered brightly. 'I've been meaning to call you.' I pulled a face at Holly as she drew a finger across her throat.

'You know it upsets me when you don't return my calls,' he said.

'I'm not avoiding you,' I lied. 'Holly's only just given me your message.' Holly glared at me. 'Look, there's not much point in you coming in on Friday. I don't have your money yet. I need more time.' There was sinister silence on the other end of the phone. 'Luca, are you there?' I asked anxiously.

'I'll be coming in anyway,' he said. 'It's time you and I had a little chat.'

'Very well, if you insist, I'll see you Friday.' I put down the phone.

'Now, there's a man not to fuck with,' Holly cautioned. 'I take it he wouldn't be put off?'

'I can handle him,' I stressed. 'I'll let him blow off a head of steam and then I'll bat my eyelashes and show him some leg.'

She looked worried. 'Do you want me to come in?'

'No, it's your day off. I'll be fine.'

'Well, if you're sure,' she said reluctantly.

'I'm sure,' I said. 'Now, let me tell you about Matt.' But, once again, I was interrupted by a phone call.

It turned out to be one of those days where the phone kept ringing and a million things needed sorting out. The hours flew past and, before I knew it, it was half past five and Holly had gone. I was due at the school for the dinner–dance at seven and I hadn't tried on my outfit yet to see if it fitted.

When Harry saw me walking past his office on my way to the ladies with the carrier bag under my arm, a broad grin spread across his features and his eyebrows gave a little shrug of anticipation. I saluted him with my middle finger: to show him that I had no intention of letting him see me in it.

The blouse was too tight and strained across my breasts, and the skirt was so short that instead of showing a saucy glimpse of stocking-top, I was exposing a full three inches of milky white thigh. But it was too late to do much about it.

I tied the necktie in a slovenly manner and put my hair into bunches. But as I bent down to put on my shoes, the blouse popped a button that tiddlywinked into the sink and was swallowed by the plughole. Rising, I saw that my breasts in their white lace bra were now brazenly on display, like two dough balls in a doily. Titillated by their sauciness, I threw caution to the wind and daringly put on the G-string.

My reflection in the mirror looked wantonly sexy, especially with the livid brand of lust still on my neck. I could feel myself being turned on by my appearance and by the memory of Matt's savage passion. I began to stroke my thighs, imagining his hands.

Despite what I'd told Gervaise, it had been a while since I'd had a boyfriend. My body was hungering for sex and the longer I stood there thinking about it, the more famished I became.

The idea of masturbating crossed my mind. But then I thought of Harry, sitting alone in his office, waiting patiently, getting excited, and quite probably playing with himself.

Dear horny Harry – I couldn't possibly disappoint him!

4

Starting with my ankle-strap shoes, Harry's salacious hooded eyes took in everything, and the slow trawling of his prurient gaze had a sizzling effect on me. He knew what I was thinking from my flushed and eager face and, dropping the pen he was holding, leaned back in his chair and rotated his finger.

I pirouetted obediently and as I faced him again, he blew hot breath from his lips in a soundless whistle and beckoned me forward. 'Come here, little girl, I have some sweeties for you.'

I linked my hands behind my back and skipped non-chalantly over to his side of the desk. 'What kind, mister?'

He stood up. 'They're right here in my pocket. Why don't you help yourself?'

Pouting cutely and with my eyes wide and innocent, I dug my hand into the pocket of his trousers. 'You're lying, mister, there's only a big fat cock in here.'

'That's right,' murmured Harry. 'What do you suppose you have to do to earn a piece of my candy, little girl?'

I put my thumb in my mouth and pretended to think. 'Something naughty?' I guessed.

'I'll tell you,' he said, sitting down and drawing me into the space between his legs. 'You just stand there and let Uncle Harry run his hands up the backs of your legs – like this. Then you let him grope your peachy little arse because that's what he likes to do.' I shivered as his lewdly gliding hands caressed and moulded the pliant globes of flesh laid bare by the G-string. 'And while he's stroking your soft, silky skin,' Harry continued, 'you unbutton your blouse.'

With a little shrug of mock puzzlement, I did as I was told. 'What now, Uncle Harry, shall I take out my titty?'

'Yeah,' he croaked, nuzzling his face into my cleavage and tugging at my bra with his teeth. When I scooped out a breast, his tongue trailed languidly to my nipple.

'Oh, God,' I moaned, clasping his head as he suckled me. He always knew exactly how to rouse me: his skilful hands sliding smoothly over my flesh, his mouth wet and lascivious.

'This reminds me of our first time,' he uttered huskily. 'You were so lush and sweet at seventeen; a succulent plum just waiting for someone to take a big juicy bite out of you. Do you remember?'

I nodded. He'd been the first 'real man' to show an interest in me and I'd been utterly infatuated with him. 'You told me over and over how much you wanted me,' I whispered. 'You flooded your eyes with longing and made your hands shake like you'd never touched a woman before.'

'You lapped it up,' he said. 'You couldn't wait for me to slide my finger under the edge of your panties, just like this.' I squirmed as he did it. 'Your hot little pussy was fidgeting and twitching. You were panting like a bitch on heat.'

'I was so wet,' I groaned. 'I'd never been so wet before.'

'I could feel how wet you were when I was fingering your steamy little bud.'

'Do it, Harry,' I urged him. 'Do it now.'

I felt an instant rush of pleasure as he applied gentle pressure to my clit, teasing and tugging its fleshy hood with exquisite sensitivity until I was quivering inside and out. Gasping, and greedy for more of his hand than the constraint of my panties would allow, I stripped them off and parted my legs.

He foraged into my pussy lips, drenching the balls of his fingers with my oily wetness. Then, slicking my nub, he circled and rubbed it until a fierce imperative seized my body and I clutched at his shoulders, gulping for breath.

Locking his arm around my waist, he ground his palm into my pubis, rubbing harder and faster to harry me towards my climax. Then, as I began to quake, he grabbed my two bunches of hair and kissed me passionately on the lips.

Desperate for his cock, I tore down his zipper and, thrusting my hand into his pants, grasped his turgid prick. He eased me back on to the desk, panting and shaking as I pumped him.

'I'm going to fuck you, little girl,' he grunted hoarsely. 'But first we have to play with Uncle Harry's pink balloon.' He snatched a condom out of his drawer and pressed it into my hand.

At seventeen, I'd made a mess of putting it on, but now I slipped it easily over his cock. 'Come on then, mister, shove it in.'

The impetus of his initial thrust threw me backwards and made me grunt as he pushed through the muscled ring of my sex, filling me to the brim. I lifted my legs and, twining them round him, galloped him on by slapping my heels on his butt. He gripped my stocking-topped thighs and, with his thumbs beneath the suspenders, shunted his cock in and out.

This was Harry at his most magnificent: rippling with lust, yet firmly in control and beating a rhythm that matched my heartbeat. I threshed ecstatically, accelerating swiftly to a bucking climax that jerked him off and swept him into his. For a brief pulsing moment, we clung together as one, then, 'Phew!' he whistled, flopping back on to his seat. 'That was a fuck and a half.'

I levered myself upright. 'I can't believe I did it again! What is it about you, Harry?'

'You're still a long way from being over me,' he said, carefully removing his condom. 'We could be fucking like this every day if you weren't so stubborn.' He handed me my panties and, as I put them on, he urged, 'Baby, let's start up again. You know you want to.'

'Put your dick away,' I advised, 'you're letting it do all the talking.'

Sighing, he fastened his trousers. 'I don't understand you. Why can't you see that what we had is worth reviving? There's still life in it.' He watched wistfully as I covered my breasts.

'Forget it, Harry, it's history,' I said.

He pulled me gently on to his lap. 'What we did just now wasn't history.'

'It will be tomorrow.'

His green eyes clouded. 'Why must you be so stubborn?'

I stroked his craggy cheek. 'You broke my heart once, you bastard. Do you think I'd let you do it again?'

'It wasn't fair of you to give me that ultimatum,' he insisted. 'How could I leave Alison when she was carrying my child?'

I shrugged. 'It seemed a reasonable request at the time – bearing in mind how much I loved you.'

He tugged on my tie. 'You were just a kid, you didn't know what you were asking. Besides, I thought I owed it to you to let you live a little.'

'You turned me down for my own sake?' I gave a mirthless chuckle. 'Oddly enough, it never occurred to me that you were being altruistic.'

'For your sake, for the baby's – what difference does it make? The timing was all wrong.'

'You said you loved me.'

He shook his head. 'I've never said that to any woman. The truth is I don't think I'm capable of it. I adored you, Selina – I still do – and I didn't want to end our affair. That was your choice and I went along with it because I thought you'd come back to me when you'd grown up a little. I just don't know what's taking you so fucking long about it.'

I pulled out of his arms and stood up. 'Let's not do this, Harry, it's over with.'

He clasped my wrist. 'It isn't over till it's over,' he stressed. 'How many times must I screw you to prove it?'

Extracting my hand from his grip, I checked my watch. 'Look at the time!' I exclaimed. 'I'm running late and I haven't called a taxi yet.'

'I'll run you,' he said, rising to his feet. 'But this conversation isn't finished. There's something I've been meaning to tell you – but it'll keep.'

Sitting next to him in the car, I kept stealing glances at him. I felt confused because, despite my current obsession with Matt, my feelings for Harry ran so deep that they continued to bother me whenever I examined them. I'd admitted to myself in the past that his rejection of my ultimatum had shattered me, and that our subsequent parting had left a massive, yawning chasm in my life that no man since had come anywhere close to filling. Perhaps even this rekindling of my schoolgirl crush on Matt was yet another attempt to make myself whole again. Would I still want him if I hadn't lost Harry?

I wondered why I was even asking myself this question and then realised that it was Harry's knack of making the years in between seem insignificant, like the whole thing happened yesterday.

As we pulled up outside the school, he said, 'Thanks for helping me out with this. I really appreciate it.'

'What else are friends for?' I asked.

He cupped my face in his hands and kissed me. Finding my lips soft and responsive, he kissed me again more deeply, igniting the embers of desire once more.

'Jesus,' he groaned, 'if you don't get out of here, I'm going to end up fucking you again. Go on, get out, you horny bitch.' He practically pushed me from the car. Once outside, I opened my coat and flashed my Masquerade panties at him. He pulled an agonised face and, as he drove off, I found myself wondering if I'd only loved him because he was such a terrific fuck. It would have been a natural mistake for a teenager to make.

The school hall was bustling with as much noise and mayhem as if there were pupils inside instead of a bunch of thirty-something adults. Peeping through the door, I saw that three long rows of tables had been set up, boys on one side, girls on the other. There was a trio of waiters dressed as schoolboys serving the women, but I could only spot one female serving the men. I was relieved to see that her school uniform was just as revealing as mine.

I found another waitress in the kitchen and a fourth waiter, dressed only in shorts and a school cap. He was having a crafty smoke. The girl was in her late twenties with henna-ed hair caught up in a swinging ponytail and huge brown freckles painted all over her face like measles. She grinned hugely when she saw me. 'Are you the cavalry?'

'I'm Selina,' I said, taking off my coat. 'I'm not a proper waitress so I don't know if I'll be much good to you, but I'm here to help.'

'Thank fuck for that,' declared the young man, drawing

on his cigarette. 'We're two girls short and they're doing their nuts in there. I was beginning to think I'd have to dress up in drag.'

'I'm Jenny,' the girl said. 'This is Rick. He's right about that – the natives are turning nasty. They think Harry's shortchanged them. But you'll more than make up for it – you're gorgeous.'

I thanked her. 'What do you want me to do?'

'Here,' she handed me a notepad and pen. 'You're on the third row serving men only. Take their orders for drinks and find out what they want for dinner: fish and chips or bangers and mash. If they're veggie they get chips and mash. Watch out for the ginger wanker at the head of the table. His name's Gary and he arranged the whole thing, so he thinks he can do what he likes with the waitresses. Put him in his place by all means but try not to laugh at the hamster on his head.'

'What?' I giggled.

'He's wearing a hairpiece.'

A big cheer went up as I entered the hall but it was followed by boos from rows one and two when they realised that I wouldn't be serving them.

The 'ginger wanker' was delighted. 'Well, lookee here!' he exclaimed. 'Where did you come from, beautiful?' I tried not to look at the top of his head.

'Good evening everyone, I hope you're having a nice time.' I made sure that my smile took in everyone.

'We are now,' enthused Gary. 'Isn't that right, lads?'

Heads nodded: some of them a little unsteadily. I checked out the empty beer bottles on the table and concluded that they must have been drinking heavily since they'd arrived.

'Can I take your order for dinner please?'

Gary beckoned me over. 'I have the numbers here, my lovely.' As soon as I approached him, he threw his arm around my hips and cuddled me up to him. 'How about a kiss, wench?'

'Your order?' I prompted him sharply.

'Fourteen fish and chips, seven bangers and mash, and we'll have sixteen more bottles of beer.' The last part of his order prompted a rousing chorus of:

Sixteen more bottles of beer, sixteen more bottles of beer
Mademoiselle is a bike; Mrs Bull is a dyke
'Rubber' Cox is a fucking great queer!

'Is that your Alma Mater song?' I asked.

'They're teachers,' Gary explained. 'Rubber Cox taught music using his prick as a baton – fucking arse-bandit.' He thrust a ten pound note into my cleavage. 'Plenty more where that came from if you play your cards right.' His hand dropped down to check the cheeks of my buttocks. 'Nice botty, sweetheart.'

When I returned to the kitchen, I saw Jenny unloading empty bottles from her tray into a bin bag. She noticed the ten pound note peeking out my blouse.

'All tips go into the jar on the counter to be divvied up at the end of the evening,' she advised me. 'The more you let them grope you, the more they'll give you.'

'I didn't come here to be groped,' I said. 'I'm just doing Harry a favour.'

She gave me an old-fashioned look. 'They expect it,' she said. 'Look, love, I'm struggling to bring up two kids on income support – so how about doing me a favour? Harry's paying us in peanuts so the tips are crucial. I'm not asking you to sleep with anyone.'

Feeling chastened and prudish, I put the tenner into the jar and gave my order to the chef. 'Help yourself to beer,' he told me, nodding towards a crate. 'They're all paid for so the punters can have as much as they like.'

I loaded up a tray, teetering on my high heels under

the weight of it. When Gary saw me staggering in, he jumped up and for a second I thought he meant to help me but, instead, he lifted my skirt. 'Look at this, lads!'

'Fuck off,' I growled at him.

'Don't be like that,' he said, slipping another tenner into my stocking-top. He squeezed my bum as I plonked down the tray and then leered at my breasts as I unloaded the bottles. 'You're fucking lovely, you are.'

'Take no notice of the Ginger-nut biscuit,' the man sitting next to him said. 'It's so long since he shagged anyone, his knob packed a suitcase and left the country.'

'Up your arse,' rumbled Gary. 'You're only jealous, Stalker, because my wanger's bigger than your shrivelled pisser. I never bothered taking a cricket bat on to the pitch because my knob was so fucking big and fucking hard.'

'So how come you played like a girl?' jeered Stalker.

'Oi, Stalker!' someone shouted as a bread roll came hurtling towards him and bounced off the back of his head. 'Howzat?' enquired the voice.

'It's a six!' cried someone else and five of the group stood up for a Mexican wave. I was relieved when the women intervened to stop a bread fight.

'They're worse than children,' I complained to Rick as I passed him with my tray of empty bottles.

'It'll get worse,' he forecast. 'I've just seen one of them filling a condom with water.'

By the time I'd finished serving the dinner, I'd been pinched black and blue and had chips, bits of fag packet, and even a sausage shoved into my stocking-tops, but I soldiered on, smiling through gritted teeth.

When it was time to take the order for dessert, Gary wrestled me on to his lap and thrust a folded twenty pound note so deep into my panties that it slid between my pussy lips. Clambering to my feet, I withdrew it, only to have it snatched back and sniffed. 'I'm keeping this one,' he said, thrusting another into my hand.

'Spotted dick?' I snarled.

He snickered like a chimp. 'You've been talking to my doctor.'

I bent down to whisper a prediction into his ear: 'You'll be talking to your doctor very shortly, twat-head, trying to explain how you came to have a stiletto heel wedged so high up your arse that it'll take surgery to remove it.'

But he was too drunk to heed my caution and kept making grabs for me as I served the dessert. When I'd had just about enough, I sidled up to him as he was trying to light a cigarette. 'Let me do that for you,' I offered sweetly, taking the box of matches from his hand. 'Oops, sorry, butterfingers,' I apologised, dropping a lighted match on to his hairpiece. It combusted like a firework.

'Hey, Ginger-nut, you're on fire!' shouted Stalker. Then several things happened at once. Shouts of 'Fire! Fire!' went up around the table; Gary tore off his flaming hairpiece; then a water-filled condom, lobbed across from another table, smashed into his face like a pig's bladder and, bursting open, drenched him.

A laughing Stalker pointed a finger. 'Ginger-nut's a secret spamhead!' he yelled. 'We'll have to call him Gary Baldy from now on!' His friends agreed and officially re-christened the former redhead by emptying a bottle of beer and a Bacardi Breezer on his head.

Shortly after the incident, the tables were cleared away and the dancing began. We carried on serving until the booze ran out, and then divided up the tips and went home. It was quarter past eleven when I got in. Matt was sitting in the lounge alone.

'Where's Big Foot?' I asked him.

He raised his eyes to the ceiling. 'In bed: he turned in early. Where have you been, Selina? I was worried about you.'

'Didn't I say I'd be late?' I shrugged out of my coat and dropped it on to the sofa.

'What the fuck are you wearing?'

I was so weary that I'd forgotten I was still wearing the school uniform. Matt sprang from his seat and paced around me like a tiger, his eyes glowing amber. He seemed furious but I could tell that he was turned on.

'It's just a costume,' I said. 'You've seen me wear them before.'

'Not like that,' he growled. 'You look like a slut.'

'I believe that's the general idea,' I asserted, vaguely resentful of his implication. 'What are you being so stuffy about?'

'You're supposed to be management,' he fumed. 'Was it Harry's idea to dress you up as a hooker?'

Now I was getting peevish. 'I was helping him out, he needed a waitress.'

'Oh really?' he enquired, circling me again. 'What were you serving – your tits on a plate?'

'It was a school reunion thing, if you must know,' I answered balefully. 'I served bangers and mash and spotted dick. It was all very unappetising and, actually, I'm quite hungry.'

I strode out to the kitchen and poured myself a bowl of cereal. Matt's outrage intrigued me for I sensed that his anger stemmed from arousal. He may even have thought that I was being deliberately provocative. *Perhaps I should be?*

Sitting down at the kitchen table, I made sure that my skirt was hiked up at the back so that the first thing he'd see, should he follow me, would be my impertinent buttocks mooning at him through the ladder back of the chair. I hoped it looked accidental.

I was barely into my third spoonful of cereal when I grew conscious of his presence. I pretended to be unaware of him standing silent and watchful by the doorway, his breath purring softly. It excited me to think of him ravishing my flesh with his eyes.

'You look so young,' he uttered at last, his voice no more than croak. 'It reminds me of when I first met you.'

I lowered my spoon as a sudden shocking thought entered my head. 'Were you attracted to me then?'

He came up behind me and placed his hands on my shoulders. 'It was lucky for me that you weren't the Lolita type,' he murmured. 'Who knows what might have happened?'

'Did you know I had a crush on you?'

He twined his fingers into my hair. 'Yes I did.'

'Then why didn't you do something about it?'

'Do something about a kid with a crush? What do you take me for?'

I leaned my head back, stretching my throat so that he could see his mark on me. 'I used to lay in bed at night listening to you making love to Miranda,' I told him. 'I'd pray for you to come into my room and do to me what you were doing to her. Sometimes I'd mas . . .'

He clamped his hand over my mouth. 'Stop it! I don't want to hear any more.' But I tugged his palm from my lips.

'I wanted you to be the first,' I continued, 'but you were so wrapped up in Miranda that you never even looked at me.'

'Oh, I looked,' he admitted. 'I saw you blossom and grow more beautiful each day but, just as you were ripening, that bastard Harry plucked and deflowered you. He took your innocence and made you his whore.'

'Let's leave Harry out of this,' I snapped. 'I had to grow up sometime and somebody had to make a woman out of me – it just happened to be him.'

'So, is it finally over between the two of you?'

I sighed. 'It's been over a long time.'

'That's not what Miranda says,' he rasped. 'She says you still fuck him.'

I twisted my head to face him. 'So what if I do? It's only sex and Harry's good at it.' I stroked a hand over my breasts. 'I like good sex.'

'I'll bet you do,' he said.

I stood up and perched on the edge of the kitchen table. 'We could have good sex right now . . . right here on this table.' I licked my lips invitingly. 'Wouldn't you like that?'

His fiery eyes raked over me. 'Have you forgotten our visitor? Gervaise could walk in at any minute.'

I dropped my voice to a breathless whisper. 'That makes it so much more exciting.'

The desire in his eyes was now a raging inferno and I could see his willpower melting away. He didn't try to stop me as I extended my leg and massaged his crotch with the sole of my shoe. 'What are you waiting for, Matt?' I asked urgently.

He shook his head slowly. 'You're a bad girl, Selina.'

'You're right,' I agreed, turning around and spreading myself across the table like a sacrifice. 'I should be punished.' I hitched my skirt up over my butt. 'Why don't you spank me?' I didn't really know what to expect, but I was certain that he'd find the offering of my arse irresistible.

However, the vicious wallop I received took me completely by surprise, thwacking down on my cheeks with a force that cannoned me into the edge of the table, winding me so badly that I couldn't even yelp.

'That's what comes of being a naughty girl.' His voice was chillingly soft. 'I hope you've learnt your lesson.'

He marched out and, as I stood up, rubbing my wincing flesh, I heard him mounting the stairs. 'Ouch,' I uttered belatedly.

It had hardly been the erotic little spank that I'd anticipated, but a brutal assault intended to degrade me and put me in my place. I couldn't decide if this was his way of trying to control me or whether he'd simply lost control of himself. Either way, once the pain had subsided, I found myself flushed with excitement. The wilder he became, the more I wanted him it seemed. I knew that I was playing with fire but I couldn't help myself. I was tantalised by him. I wanted to release his pent-up passion and submit myself completely to the feeding frenzy of his lust. I wanted him to ravish and brutalise me until there was nothing left but tenderness and, ultimately, love.

The presence of Gervaise didn't matter at all. The only thing that mattered was achieving my objective and I knew that I had to pursue it while Matt was still inflamed. If I let him cool down, I'd be missing the best chance I'd ever get.

With my mind made up, I climbed the stairs determined to throw everything into a final act of seduction that no man could possibly resist.

After stripping myself naked in my room, I tiptoed down the hall to pause outside the guestroom where I heard Gervaise snoring like a prodded pig. *Excellent!*

I then crept along to the main bedroom and quietly opened the door. For a moment the light from the hall illuminated the room but, as I closed the door behind me, it was plunged back into darkness. Matt was breathing as if in a light sleep.

I fumbled my way to the foot of the bed and then, lifting the duvet, crawled underneath. Matt jolted as I insinuated myself between his legs, but he didn't utter a sound. Encouraged, I felt for his cock and found it semi-erect. 'Just lie still, Matt,' I whispered. 'You're going to enjoy this.' As I lifted his cock, it grew in my hand with a life of its own: thickening, swelling, stretching, and still he said nothing.

Under my practised fingers, the marbled veins of his shaft began to pulse with blood until it was glowing with heat like a plutonium rod. It was much bigger than I'd thought it would be and I needed two hands to support it as I slipped its bulbous head into my mouth. Almost at once, my sliding lips induced a rumbling groan and his back arched upwards as my tongue licked and flicked at the sensitive ridge around the base of his helmet. I took as much of him into my mouth as I could and sucked in my cheeks to squeeze on his shaft as I began to bob my head.

When I felt his body begin to twitch and quiver and heard his ragged breaths, I was convinced that I'd taken him to a point beyond reason, and lifted my head from his cock, intending to journey upwards. But his hands clamped down on my skull, forcing me to continue, and each time I tried to detach my mouth, he increased their pressure. I tried to protest but I was gagged by his prick, and could only submit as he pumped my head harder and faster, his bucking hips now forcing a rhythm of their own.

When I tasted the salty come bubbling from his dick, I realised that he had no intention of releasing me. So, with a mighty yank, I tore my head from the prison of his hands and scrambled up his body, searching for his mouth.

When I couldn't find it, I was confused. Why had he turned his face from me? And who, for crying out loud, had put a hedgehog in his bed!

Then suddenly and sickeningly the awful truth dawned on me. 'Gervaise!' I shrieked. My hands fluttered over his face: eyes, nose – beard! Oh my God!

His deep voice confirmed my worst fear. 'Don't worry,' he said calmly, 'I'm not about to scream.'.

But he was more than ready to laugh and was busting his sides with it as, in my frenzy to escape, I tripped, stumbled and staggered over everything. I even managed to plant my stupid foot into one of his shitty boots and, when the damn thing wouldn't release me, I had to clump down the hall still wearing it.

Roaring with laughter, Gervaise called out, 'Sweet dreams, Sugarlips!'

I tore off the boot and hurled it at his door.

5

I slept fitfully, every so often jolting awake from the same hideous nightmare about a shadowy ape-like or sub-human creature that, after coshing me over the head with a giant salami, would try to force it into my mouth and make me swallow it whole. At 6 a.m., I finally eluded the sausage-wielding phantom by falling out of bed and waking up properly.

Dragging myself to the bathroom, I decided to make an early exit from the house before either of the men woke up, for I was in no mood to face Matt and positively paranoid about bumping into Gervaise.

I couldn't even allow myself to think of him until I'd washed, dressed and drained a cup of coffee. But even the comforts of daily ritual couldn't diminish the awfulness of my predicament or reduce the enormity of what I'd done.

I felt utterly mortified. How could I have made such a ludicrous mistake? It was like something out of a pantomime where the only thing missing had been the audience shouting: 'Look out, he's underneath you!'

Of all the cocks in the world that I could have put in my mouth, I'd picked the prick of the man that I most wanted rid of. It hardly seemed the most appropriate means of persuading him to leave. I smacked my hand against my forehead. *You stupid, stupid idiot!*

But there was no sense in beating myself up. I'd done what I'd done, and all I could hope to do now was minimise the humiliation that Gervaise would undoubtedly heap on my head. To limit the damage, I'd have to lie through my teeth.

I was still thinking about what I would say to him when, suddenly, his dread voice cracked into my thoughts like a starting pistol. 'Good morning ... Sugarlips.'

As he came into the kitchen, I couldn't bring myself to look at him. 'You're an early bird,' he commented. 'Couldn't you sleep?' I tried to respond but my tongue had turned to rubber and the only sound I could make was like the grunting of a deaf mute.

He moved deliberately into my field of vision and I saw that he was wearing a black towelling robe with, possibly, nothing underneath. It was pulled together loosely and I half-expected the salami cosh that had haunted my dream to rise up from its folds and wag itself accusingly. He seemed unnaturally calm as he poured himself a coffee. 'Curiously enough, I slept like a baby.' The tone of his voice suggested that somewhere within his vast, black beard he was grinning like a self-contented Buddha.

I gave him what I hoped was a woozy look and, clasping my head, whimpered, 'Please don't shout, Gervaise, I have a hangover like a Kalashnikov going off in my head.'

Annoyingly, he chuckled. 'Nice try, Selina, but you'll have to do better than that.'

Since my plan was to convince him that I'd been outrageously drunk, I persisted with it. 'I'm not kidding,' I stressed. 'My skull feels like a tumble dryer that's spinning my brain at maximum speed. You see, I went to this dinner-dance last night and got absolutely hammered.' *Did that sound plausible? I think it sounded plausible.*

'Uh-huh.' Gervaise nodded. 'So, this is your excuse, is

it? Now let me guess: are you claiming alcohol-induced amnesia or is it "I was too pissed to know what I was doing"?' He sat down opposite me and his blue eyes drilled into mine.

Damn the grinning gibbon, he always seemed to be a pole vault ahead of me! 'Neither actually,' I reported haughtily. 'I remember getting into bed with you but I thought I was somewhere else. I knew what I was doing but I thought I was doing it to someone else.'

It took him a minute to figure out if what I'd said made any sense. 'So, who did you think you were with?' he asked eventually.

'I don't believe that's any of your business.'

His eyebrows furrowed and he rubbed his bearded jaw. 'Since when is what happens to a man's cock in his sleep none of his fucking business?'

'Your damn cock had no business being in Matt's bed!' I stormed.

'Ah, so you knew it was Matt's bed then?'

Oh, shit in shit sauce! 'No . . . yes . . . what I mean is . . .' I floundered '. . . I do *now*. But, at the time, I thought it was my boyfriend's.'

He drummed his fingers on the table. 'That's curious,' he said.

Oh, bugger, he was using that word 'curious' again, just as he had when he'd challenged the presence of my lipstick on Matt's mouth. 'What's curious?' I asked bleakly.

'That your boyfriend's name should be Matt as well.' I stared at him blankly. 'Lie still, Matt,' he quoted.

I could feel a flush creeping into my cheeks. 'I was drunk,' I reiterated lamely.

'I think you thought I was Matt,' he stated decisively, 'and that beggars a number of questions.'

Leaping on to my high horse, I snarled, 'What gives you the right to question me?'

He took a sip of his coffee. 'Miranda.'

I fell off my high horse into a steaming pile of figurative manure. 'Yes, well, I realise what it must look like. But, honestly, Gervaise, you've got it all wrong. I admit to flirting with Matt but it's nothing serious and I certainly wouldn't do ... what I did ... that thing.'

'Give him a blow job?' he articulated helpfully.

'For Chrissake, I know what I did!' I exclaimed, launching into another offensive. 'Why didn't you stop me? Why did you let me carry on? You must have known I was making a mistake.'

He lowered his eyelashes and again I suspected that, behind the furry mask of his beard, he was biting his cheek to stop himself from laughing. 'I only did what any other red-blooded male would do in the circumstances. I was a little shocked at first but then I simply resigned myself to the ordeal and lay back and thought of France.' His teeth flashed whitely as he chuckled. 'Listen, Sugarlips, even without your luscious mouth around my cock, I'd have to be crazy or queer to kick a body like yours out of bed.'

I shuddered and flapped my hands. 'Must you keep going on and on about it? And please, *please* don't call me Sugarlips.' I got up and started taking food from the fridge. 'Can't we just forget about it? Why don't I cook you a nice English breakfast?'

He neither agreed nor disagreed but sat silently watching me as I lay out the food. But even his quiet scrutiny seemed like mockery; my fingers turned to butter and I began to fumble everything. To breach the void of silence, I said, 'You still haven't told me what you were doing in Matt's room.'

'That's still *my* question and you still haven't answered it,' he said.

I gave a weary shrug. 'I've given you the only answer that I have. I'm sorry if it doesn't satisfy you. Would you mind answering *my* question now?'

'Matt insisted on swapping rooms,' he replied. 'He thought I might find the double bed useful should I wish to entertain a ladyfriend while I'm here. Funny, isn't it? He must have known I'd get lucky.'

I spun round to gape at him. 'But you're only here for a short stay. What makes him think that you can't exist without sex for a couple of days?'

He folded his arms and returned my stare with another of his penetrating gazes. 'Actually, I've decided to stay until Miranda gets back. I told Matt yesterday.'

I was horrified. 'But you can't!' I wailed.

He pulled an obstinate face. 'Matt's OK about it; why shouldn't you be?'

I had a million reasons but I chose the most obvious. 'There's tension between us already, do you honestly think that we could share a house for three weeks?'

'I don't see why not, so long as we stick to our own bedrooms,' he answered with a smirk. 'That's assuming you're not planning to jump my bones again.'

I swept a critical gaze over his hulking shoulders. 'You mean there are bones inside all that beef? How do you like your eggs, by the way: fried, boiled or by the bucket-load?'

'Hard-boiled and tough to crack,' he answered grimly.

'That figures,' I said.

His watchful eyes were still making me nervous and I was glad of having something to do. Presently, he asked, 'How does a cucumber fit into an English breakfast?'

'Huh?' I checked the food that I'd removed from the

fridge and, oddly enough, beside a pack of bacon lay the interloping cucumber. 'I can't think what made me get that out,' I declared.

'Can't you?' He cocked an eyebrow. 'I reckon Sigmund Freud might have a pretty good idea.'

I picked up the cucumber and jabbed him in the chest with it. 'Some might say that Sigmund Freud was a sad old sick-dick who saw phalluses in food because his own floppy wiener couldn't cut the mustard. As far as I'm concerned, this is merely a cucumber – it is *not* your cock.'

'No it isn't,' he agreed. 'For one thing, my cock isn't green – but you know that now, don't you?' He gave me a conspiratory wink.

Embarrassed again, I slammed the saucepan containing the eggs down on to the hob, wincing as their shells cracked together. 'I'd prefer it if we didn't discuss your penis, if you don't mind.'

'OK,' he agreed, 'I'll stop talking about it if you stop thinking about it.'

'I'm not thinking about it!' I exclaimed, taking a rolling pin from a drawer.

Gervaise scratched his head. 'Are you planning on making pastry with that?'

'What?' I stared at the object in my hand. What the fuck did I want with a rolling pin? I shoved it quickly back into the drawer and started frying sausages. 'You men are all the same – you're obsessed with your pricks. If you're not playing with them, you're thinking about playing with them. Whereas a woman isn't the least bit interested in a man's prick unless it happens to belong to the man that she's interested in.'

But Gervaise, transfixed by the raw sausage I'd been wagging during my lecture, wasn't listening. Looking down at it, I realised that, fatigued by the wagging, it looked exactly like a limp dick. Goddamn it! Did everything in the bloody kitchen have to be cock-shaped?

When he burst out laughing, I became furious. 'Shut up!' I exploded. 'Do you know what I'd have done if I'd known it was you last night?' I lifted the raw sausage and viciously bit off one end. Then, with a heinous glare in his direction, I spat the piece into the sink and turned on the waste disposal.

He stopped laughing and rubbed his cheek ruefully. 'You know ... I think I'll pass on those sausages.'

I turned away, not only to smother a giggle, but also to remove the remnants of raw sausage from my mouth. I'd made my point, but it had tasted horrible.

The meal was a disaster. I'd managed to burn everything, including the boiled eggs. Gingerly sifting through the cremated bits of food on his plate, I heard Gervaise mutter, 'You sure are better at some things than others.'

Enraged, I grabbed the frying pan and took a swing at his head. He ducked in the nick of time and the pan whistled across his scalp. Half rising, he snatched it from my hand. '*Merde!*' he exclaimed. 'You flaming fuck-wit, I've only just got back from dodging missiles at the frontline! And shall I tell you something – the food was better and even the bloody hostiles were friendlier.'

'No one asked you to come here,' I hissed. 'And if you were any kind of gentleman you'd let the matter drop instead of persisting with your childish innuendoes. Have you any idea how embarrassing this is for me?'

He slammed down his knife and fork. 'I'm not sure what's sticking in my craw,' he said, 'your rotten food or your rotten attitude. You should be apologising to me for what you did. It was a goddamn sexual assault and just because I'm a man doesn't mean I wasn't offended by it.'

His words struck me like a slap. He was right. Of

course he was right. Technically, I'd abused him and it hadn't even entered my mind to apologise. 'I *am* sorry,' I uttered contritely. 'I'm terribly sorry. I should have said so at once.'

I saw the laughter twinkling in his eyes a split second before it bellowed from his mouth. He shook his head in mirthful disbelief, his shoulders rocking as he spluttered, 'I'm pulling your leg, Sugarlips. You can't honestly think I was serious, can you? Listen, sweetheart, if you want to gobble my cock, you just go right ahead. You know where it is.'

'You bastard!' I screeched and, sweeping my hand across the table, tipped the remains of his breakfast on to his lap.

He looked down at the mess and then up at my face with an expression of impish impertinence. 'Do I take it this means that a follow-up fuck is out of the question?'

'Oh!' I huffed, furious with myself for wanting to laugh. I stormed out of the kitchen just as Matt was coming in. 'What's the hurry?' he asked, barring my exit.

'I'm late for work,' I said irritably.

'But it's early.'

I tried pushing past him. 'I have a breakfast meeting with a client.'

'Give me fifteen minutes and I'll run you,' he offered.

'No, it's OK, I'll catch the bus.'

He dug his fingers into my arm. 'I'll run you.'

I glanced back at Gervaise who was still picking food from his lap. 'Thanks,' I said tightly. I wasn't happy about being waylaid, but the steely look in Matt's eyes demanded my compliance. As I sat waiting for him in the lounge, I wondered whether the slap he'd given me last night had been administered as a punishment or as a foretaste of things to come. Could he be demonstrating a sadistic streak? Was dominance his thing? For my part, assuming a submissive role would mean a radical rethink of my sexuality and, although I didn't see myself as being remotely masochistic, I was not averse to exploring the idea for its novelty value alone.

The moment we were in his car, he wasted no time asserting himself. 'If we're going to do this, we're going to do it my way,' he dictated.

My heart skipped a beat but I wanted to be sure that I'd understood him. 'Are you talking about an affair?'

He flicked a glance at me, his brown eyes inscrutable. 'You've made it clear that's what you want. But I warn you, Selina, there's a price to pay for getting what you want. The question is – are you willing to pay it?'

'What do you mean?'

'I'll only risk what I have with Miranda if there's a reasonable chance of getting more from you than I'm getting from her,' he answered firmly.

'More what? More sex?'

Even in profile, his handsome face looked stern and uncompromising. 'More obedience.'

So there it was. 'I don't know if I can do that,' I confessed.

'Then keep your arse covered up and stay out of my way.'

'I don't know if I can do that either,' I confessed. 'I can't help the way I feel, Matt. I want you so much.'

'I know,' he said, curling his hand around my knee. 'But the question is: "How much?"'

I looked at his hand with an almost childlike sense of awe, hardly daring to believe that this was Matt's hand touching my knee and that, for once, I wasn't dreaming. Whatever I said next would either keep it there or drive it away. 'What do you want me to do?' I murmured softly.

'Nothing,' he said, sliding his hand higher. 'You do nothing.'

The traffic ahead had slowed to a crawl but, since the car was an automatic, he continued steering with one hand while the other slid under my skirt. Because he wasn't watching what he was doing, the hand seemed strangely detached from him and, although I could see the bulges of his knuckles under the fabric, moving up and down as he massaged my thigh, it still seemed more like an alien invader than a hand.

The traffic had come to a standstill. 'Matt,' I said uncomfortably, 'people will see.'

'I want them to see,' he uttered eagerly. 'Take your panties and tights off.'

'But it's broad daylight and we're in the middle of a traffic jam,' I protested.

'I know,' he grunted hoarsely, his fingers biting into me. 'Are you going to do what I tell you or not?'

Suddenly, I knew what he wanted. It was flaring in his eyes, grating in his voice, blanching the colour from his knuckles. Meekly and obediently, I took off my underwear.

A long sigh issued from his lips. 'Good girl.'

Some way up ahead, I saw a blue light flashing. An accident had stopped the traffic in our lane and now the lane to our left was grinding to a halt. Matt put on the handbrake and, twisting to face me, drove his right hand between my legs while his left wrenched my skirt all the way up to my hips.

'For God's sake, Matt,' I mumbled nervously as a minibus full of workmen pulled up alongside us. From their weathered faces and donkey jackets I assumed them to be builders.

Ignoring them, Matt stared straight ahead through

the windscreen while his fingers burrowed into the tight curls of my pussy.

'Matt,' I pleaded again, shielding my face with my hand when I noticed that the workmen were leering through the windows of their van. They were trying to see what he was doing to me.

'Shut up,' he growled, slapping my hand away as I attempted to cover myself.

I felt horrendously exposed. The workmen were climbing over each other to get a glimpse of my naked sex and I could hear them shouting and catcalling, and drumming their hands on the window to draw my attention.

But I didn't look at them. Instead, I watched Matt's hand lewdly caressing the dark triangle of my pubic hair, his middle finger buried inside my crack, exploring the soft tissues of my inner lips but teasingly avoiding my clit. Growing horny and hot and with my body now twitching with lust, I closed my eyes and, sighing submissively, surrendered to his touch.

He spread my legs and with his palm bearing down on my pubic mound, rubbed his hand back and forth. I lifted my haunches and gyrated my hips, straining upwards to meet the pressure.

'Look at them,' he grunted hotly. 'Look at them watching you.'

But I had entered the abandoned state of arousal and no longer cared about the onlookers. On the contrary, their voyeuristic presence was adding to my pleasure. 'Fuck them,' I gasped as his fingers sheared between my pussy lips and started teasing my swollen nub.

'I said "Look at them",' he commanded.

I opened my eyes and, when I saw the grotesque flattened faces of the workmen pressed against the steamy windows of the bus, I felt a thrill so intense that my whole body shuddered. They were raping me with their eyes, molesting and violating my pussy with their leering hungry gazes.

'Give them more,' Matt urged me, spreading my legs even wider.

I tilted my body towards them, writhing ecstatically as Matt increased the friction between my legs. I bucked and threshed and, caressing my breasts, let them see my rapturous face contorting in exultation. For in nourishing their desire, I was feeding my own: imagining all their hands upon me, all their hot hungry mouths and their hard, pulsing cocks. Tongues licking, pricks prodding, fingers probing, spunk spraying: buried under bodies like a queen bee covered in drones, all fighting each other to fuck me. Taking it in turns, one after the other: fat cock, small cock, never ending cock. Then abruptly, a palsy of pleasure overtook my body and I jerked as if the car seat had suddenly become an electric chair shooting sizzling volts of ecstasy through my veins.

But as soon as my climax subsided, I felt horribly self-conscious and, when I heard a tumultuous cheer rising up from the minibus, I shrank down in my seat, sick with embarrassment. I wanted to cover myself but Matt kept beating back my hands.

'Oh, please, Matt, no,' I begged. 'They've seen enough.'

He looked half-crazed with glee. 'They haven't seen your arse. Show them your arse. Go on, moon the dirty bastards.'

'No, I won't do that, it's childish.'

'Yes, you fucking will.' Grabbing me, he yanked me on to his lap and started pulling at the back of my skirt. I fought him off frantically. 'Stop it, I've said I won't do it!'

Just at that moment, the minibus began moving off down a slip road and, with a disappointed grunt, Matt released me.

I couldn't make out the faces of the workmen through the steamed-up back window but I could see some of their flattened noses pressed against it like swatted flies. Sagging with relief to see them go, I turned to look at him. 'You're kinky,' I said. 'What the hell is someone like you doing with someone as straight-laced as Miranda? I can't see her mooning a busload of builders, not in a million years!'

He snorted resentfully. 'She's so precious about her damn privacy that she won't even fuck with the light on. She'd never let me do anything like that to her.' He shifted the gear lever into drive and the car crept forwards. The traffic had begun to move again. 'Did you like it?' he asked, glancing sidewise at me as I wriggled back into my underwear.

I didn't know what to say. It had been my first experience of exhibitionism and, although I'd enjoyed being watched, the thrill had been attained through my degradation and, on the whole, I didn't feel that an exuberant climax was worth the humiliation. The honest answer to his question would be to admit that I was probably too inhibited to make a habit of it. Yet I didn't want him to think me a prude.

'I'm not sure,' I answered evasively. 'I wasn't expecting anything like that.'

His fingers tightened on the steering wheel. 'So now you know what to expect, do we understand each other? Do we have a deal?'

'You make it sound like a business arrangement,' I commented critically.

'What's wrong with that?' he replied. 'We're both seeking to gain something out of this.'

I stared gloomily out of the window. His assessment depressed me and fell a long way short of what I wanted.

'What you're offering me is what I'm already getting from Harry,' I said.

He shrugged indifferently. 'Then get it from Harry.'

I felt confused and wrong-footed by him. Did he want me or not? I didn't like his vagueness and I was damned if I'd let him keep testing me while he was figuring himself out. 'I guess I'd better think it over,' I said.

Neither of us spoke for a while but as he pulled up outside Masquerade, he asked, 'What is there to think about?'

I detected a note of anxiety in his voice. Was he wondering if he'd imposed too many ground rules? I decided to nourish his doubt. 'To tell you the truth, Matt, I'm tired of being someone's "bit on the side". I want a man who's willing to put more into a relationship than his dick and if that isn't you then maybe we should quit before we start.' I got out of the car and strode into the building without looking back.

But I was nowhere near as calm as I appeared and went immediately in search of Holly to canvas her opinion. Harry's office was empty but as I approached my own, I heard her voice from within, 'Go on, Harry, do it,' she was urging. 'You know you want to.'

I opened the door to an intimate scene. Holly was reclining across my desk but all I could see of Harry was his hand resting on her hip.

I let the door bang behind me. 'Good morning, people.'

Harry peeped out from behind Holly's shoulder, his expression so guilty that, for a moment, I thought they'd been up to something, but then he coughed out a huge puff of smoke. Holly slid off the desk and winked at me slyly.

'Harry!' I barked. 'Is that what I think it is?'

He looked at the cigarette in his hand as if he couldn't

make out where it had come from. 'It was rape,' he insisted. 'She thrust her stiff lighted fag into my mouth and the next thing I knew I was bucking my lips and smoking.'

'Shame on you, Holly,' I scolded her. 'Are you trying to seduce him into an early grave?'

'It's for his own good,' she answered charitably. 'He'd never cope with old age. How could he ever use a Zimmer frame? This is a man who can't even do a hand jive without tripping himself up. I know, I've been dancing with him.'

'The only thing that used to trip me up was your bloody great canoe feet,' Harry protested. 'Sure, I used to tread on them, but so did everyone else on the dancefloor.'

'You lying toe-rag!' Holly wailed.

'I'm not kidding,' he said. 'It was like dancing with Coco the clown.'

I was smiling but only superficially because I'd always imagined their 'fling' to be just that: a brief sexual relationship, which hadn't worked out. The idea of Holly dancing with him was making me feel jealous, because I never had.

Something of what I was thinking must have shown on my face because Harry changed the subject. 'How did it go last night?' he asked me.

'OK . . . I think,' I said.

'What do you mean "think"? Did you have any trouble?'

'Well, it got a bit rowdy,' I replied. 'But it was mostly good clean fun, apart from the persistent groper with the ginger syrup whom I dealt with in a reasonable manner.'

'How?' Holly asked.

'I set fire to him.'

'Sounds reasonable,' she said.

'Oh, shit,' Harry groaned, slapping his hands to his cheeks. 'The guy with the rug made the booking. What was his name . . . Gary –'

'Baldy,' I submitted, without thinking.

He stubbed out his cigarette. 'And you set fire to him?'

I grinned sheepishly. 'Only to his hair but, don't worry, he took it off.'

Harry screwed up one of his eyes and the other boggled at me. 'You realise he'll sue me?'

'Then we'll sue him right back,' I declared. 'Let's see what the courts make of a man who shoves his sausage into a woman's stocking top.'

Harry scratched his head. 'I don't think I know what to make of that myself.'

'Your telephone's ringing,' I alerted him, hearing the sound through the door.

'That'll be Gary's solicitor,' he forecast glumly. Then, slumping his shoulders, he shuffled off to answer it like a condemned convict, dragging an imaginary ball and chain behind him.

I noticed Holly watching him with an adoring look on her face. 'He's so cute,' she confided.

'He's too damn cute,' I said.

The smile slipped from her face as she deciphered the look on mine. 'You've been screwing him again,' she deduced.

I nodded helplessly. 'Don't ask me how it happened. I swear his cock has developed a sixth sense. It's always in the right place at the right time.'

'I think he trains it like a sniffer dog,' she said.

'It was my own fault,' I admitted. 'I paraded myself in that stupid school uniform and that sexy look of his must have sheared right through my knicker elastic because they were down around my ankles before I could say knife.'

'What is it about men and school uniform?' she wondered. 'Do they all have a latent paedophile in them? It wouldn't surprise me since most of them stopped evolving at Neanderthal.'

'That's man-hating talk,' I pointed out.

'Rubbish,' she said. 'Just because I don't rate them as a species doesn't mean I don't find them useful when it comes to opening jars and such. Plus any creature that owns a dildo-shaped object that doesn't need batteries is totally worth preserving.'

'The trouble with those objects is that they don't declare their identity,' I complained. 'Only last night, I encountered an impostor.' Her eyes grew wide as I explained about the cuckoo in Matt's nest. '... and the bastard would have come in my mouth if I hadn't jerked my head away,' I concluded angrily.

Holly thought it was hilarious. 'You gave head to a man that you want to get rid of?' she exclaimed. 'This is too bizarre even for you, Selina. He must have thought it was his birthday. What the devil do you do when you want a man to stay?'

I shielded my ears from her laughter. 'Oh, don't,' I pleaded. 'How do you think I felt when I realised I'd been polishing the knob of a man with more face fur than Fagin?' She couldn't speak for laughing so I poked her. 'It isn't funny!' I insisted, plonking down in my chair.

She pulled herself together and attempted to be serious. 'So, what's his cock like? Are we talking regular here or quarter-pounder? What's the matter?' she cried as I shot her a look. 'Can't a girl be curious?'

I rolled my eyes despairingly. 'I hardly think that his cock size is relevant considering it was the wrong bloody cock.'

'It could be relevant to me,' she said, 'seeing as I

packed up Paul's slippers last night and threw him and his army of socks out the door.'

'Oh, Holly,' I sighed, 'you didn't.'

She nodded complacently. 'Things came to a head when he decided to fix my dripping tap – right in the middle of muffing me. Can you believe it? This guy is wearing my bush for a beard and he's thinking about DIY! But I was calm and let him fix the tap – one drip deserves another after all. Then I washed my hands of him. So now that I'm free again, any information regarding a single man's credentials is highly pertinent, which leads me neatly to enquire . . . did you have to open your mouth wide, or what?'

'Oh, for heaven's sake – the damn thing could fill a baguette,' I stated grudgingly.

'And did he talk about plumbing at any stage?'

I laughed. 'No, he didn't.'

'Then I definitely want to meet him,' she trilled.

I looked at her doubtfully. 'That could complicate things, Holly.'

'Can they get any more complicated?' she reasoned. 'It seems to me that you and Matt will never make any headway while Gervaise is in the picture; what you need is a diversion.'

It was an interesting point. If Gervaise's attention was drawn elsewhere, he might relax his vigilance. 'I'll introduce you to him on Saturday,' I decided. 'But don't you dare mention what I did to him last night. It's the most embarrassing thing I've done since I had to wear that "Oinky Pig" outfit for the book launch of *Oinky goes to Belgium*.'

Holly cracked out laughing. 'I remember,' she chuckled. 'I still feel guilty that we let you go to that launch without telling you about Oinky's little problem.'

'You were rotten,' I grizzled. 'I had no idea why every-one was looking so horrified. With his fat belly sticking out in front of me, I didn't notice that they'd sewn his curly tail on to the front of the costume by mistake and that everyone thought the dirty little porker was flashing his corkscrew cock at all the kiddies. If that enraged mother hadn't lunged at me with a pair of nail scissors while I was doing the "Oinky Dance", I might never have known.'

Holly, who was laughing hysterically, ran to the door and bumped into Harry. 'Get out of my way,' she squealed. 'I'm pissing myself.'

He stared after her as she bolted to the loo. 'What's got into her?'

'Oinky Pig,' I muttered flatly.

A broad grin spread across his features. 'Who raked that little pervert up?'

I waved my hands. 'Don't ask.'

He came round to perch on the edge of my desk. 'I'm glad she's out of the way because I've something to tell you,' he said.

He sounded serious. 'Don't tell me that was really Gary's solicitor on the phone,' I pleaded anxiously. 'Look, I'm sorry I lost my temper with him.'

He gave me a tender look. 'That fiery temperament of yours is part of what makes you such a passionate woman,' he said, leaning forward to cup my cheek. 'Compared to you, Alison is a wet-fish. And that's why I've decided to leave her.'

I gaped at him. 'You what?'

'That's right,' he said, nodding, 'I'm leaving her. I want you back, Selina.'

6

It had started out as lunch and a chance to talk things over. But, inevitably, one thing had led to another and somehow I'd ended up naked in a muddy field in the middle of nowhere, with my head pressed against the dashboard of Harry's Landrover and my arse pointing up towards its sunroof. He'd picked a beautiful spot, but the scenery was lost to me because my eyes were squeezed tight shut and I couldn't hear the birdsong above my own lustful panting and the squishing sounds of Harry's fingers in my pussy.

The burgers he'd bought at the drive-thru lay abandoned on the back seat where he'd tossed the bag after snatching it from me in order to kiss me possessively.

His kiss had taken me by surprise but what had turned me on so quickly was the way he'd launched himself at me, ripping down my panties and heatedly ravishing my sex. I'd never seen him this ravenous before and, roused by his enthusiasm as much as his hands, I'd responded passionately: my body eager for his, my senses craving intimate contact, skin upon skin, breast against chest. Kissing hungrily, we'd removed each other's clothes and, for a moment, had wrapped our yearning bodies together, savouring the sensual feel of our nakedness.

Then, overcome by urgency, he'd slid into the passenger seat and pulled it right back so he could stretch out underneath me and watch my bare arse jiggling like crazy in front of his face as he finger-fucked my slavering hole like it was going out of fashion.

'I could eat your peachy butt,' he groaned, smashing his lips to my buttock and pinching a mouthful of flesh with his teeth. 'Come on, baby, slide yourself on to my cock.'

I was more than ready to receive him, but the angle was awkward and when I lowered myself to meet his straining erection, its swollen helmet skimmed inside my pussy lips, slithering and slipping on my wetness. Ignoring my pleas to guide it in, he parted my sex with his thumbs and let his cock rub over the dewy membranes of my sensitised inner lips. 'Oh, God, shove it in,' I begged him. However, the desperation in my voice brought out the devil in him. 'Tell me how much you want me,' he bargained huskily.

'A fucking lot,' I whimpered. 'Don't tease me, you bastard.'

He rubbed his hot bell-end over my clit. 'Is that the best you can do?'

'Damn it,' I gasped as he badgered my swollen bud. 'I want you ... I want you to fuck me.'

'I want you to fuck me *please*,' he suggested, nudging the tip of his prick into me.

'You ... *oh, oh, oh*, ... yes ... please ... whatever,' I muttered helplessly.

'Pretty please,' he insisted, pushing the thickest part of his glans into my opening.

'*Ahh ... ooh* ... pretty please.'

'Now tell me how gorgeous I am.'

By now his cock was in deep enough for me to push myself down to its base, so I knew that I had his balls in my court when my sex clamped around him. Sucking breath in through his teeth, he clutched my hips with sudden urgency. 'Oh, baby, that feels good.'

'You're so hard,' I murmured, rotating myself upon the solid fleshy rod now trapped deep inside me. He grasped my breasts, gently pinching my nipples as I writhed like a snake, swivelling around his prick like a pole-dancer.

'My beautiful baby,' he croaked, burying his face into my long hair to kiss along my shoulder blades in a way that made me quiver and break out in goosebumps. He was back in control of events and taking his time like he always did, caressing and relishing the feel of my flesh. Running his warm lips over my body and trailing his fingers over my tingling skin. Then, slowly, his cock began pumping; its rhythmic prodding slick and insistent. He directed my hips, pushing and pulling, and gradually increased his tempo as he sensed the quickening within me and responded to my downward thrusts with powerful upward jabs until he was bouncing me on his lap, stabbing me on to his cock. Then, gasping and grunting in unison, we accelerated feverishly into a torrid, yowling climax.

When it was over, he clasped me tightly while his twitching prick ebbed back to life. 'Now do you see?' he uttered softly. 'This is why we belong together.'

I lifted myself up so that he could shunt back into the driver's seat. 'It's a pity you didn't say that a couple of years ago,' I reproached him.

'I had the baby to think about,' he said, flicking his loaded condom out of the window.

'And now you have a toddler.'

'I've been thinking about Katy,' he replied, 'and it isn't right for her to grow up in a loveless home with two parents who are constantly bickering.'

I was about to tell him that Katy still needed him, but decided that it wasn't a fit subject to discuss without any clothes on. 'Let's get dressed,' I suggested.

When we were decent, he leaned back and sighed. 'Fucking hell, I could use a cigarette.'

'We ought to get back,' I pointed out. 'Holly'll be wondering where we are.'

'But we haven't talked about us yet,' he objected.

'There is no "us",' I told him, 'except in the business sense.'

He gave me an incredulous look. 'You call that "business" what we just did? I call it "unfinished business".'

'We still fancy each other, that's all,' I said. 'We'll grow out of it eventually.'

'Don't you want me back?' he asked. 'I meant it when I said I'd leave Alison for you.'

'There was a time when I'd have jumped through hoops to hear you say that,' I admitted. 'But things have changed. For one thing, I'm in love with someone else.'

'Oh.' His mouth dropped open. My admission had taken him by surprise. 'I didn't even know you were seeing anyone. Who is it?'

I decided to confide in him. 'It's Matt.'

'Miranda's Matt?' When he saw me nod, he rubbed his thumb between his eyebrows. 'Is it a two-way thing?'

I shrugged and looked out of the window. 'I don't know yet.'

He touched the fading stain on my neck. 'This would be his, I suppose. Are you sleeping with him?'

'I would be if it wasn't for Gervaise,' I replied.

'Ah, yes.' He bobbed his head in comprehension. 'So I've Miranda's brother to thank for your complicity today. I didn't realise you were fucking me out of sexual frustration.'

He looked so dejected that I squeezed his arm. 'You know damn well that isn't true; I screw you because I can't help myself. It's like you and those cigarettes – I gave up loving you a long time ago but the addiction is still there and in my weaker moments I give in to the craving. But I genuinely want to give up. You're bad for me, Harry.'

'You think I'm bad for you?' He looked at me archly. 'I really fucked things up for us, didn't I?'

'You had your reasons.'

'They weren't good enough reasons,' he acknowledged. 'I should have left Alison when you asked me to. I never loved her. Our marriage was a sham right from the start.'

'Then why *did* you marry her?' It was something I'd never understood.

'Does it matter?'

'Yes,' I realised quite suddenly. 'Whenever I've asked you about it, you've always avoided answering.'

'I suppose I didn't think it was important.'

'You're doing it now!'

He heaved a deep sigh. 'OK then, I married her for her money.'

'I'm not buying that,' I said. 'You're a shit but you're not a shyster. Just tell me the truth, Harry.'

He gave a hollow chuckle. 'You won't like the truth – it's too absurd.'

'Tell me anyway.'

He lifted his hand to his face, shielding his eyes from me. 'I married her on the rebound.'

A shocked breath of laughter leapt from my mouth. It was the last thing I'd expected him to say.

'I told you it was absurd,' he said.

And it was. Getting married on the rebound was something the heartbroken did, whereas heartless bastards like Harry didn't even fall in love!

'On the rebound from whom?' I uttered numbly. When he didn't answer, I snatched his hand from his eyes and looked into them. Then, suddenly, the penny dropped.

'Was it Holly?' I grasped his shoulder and shook him. 'For God's sake tell me. Was it Holly?'

'Yes, it was Holly,' he answered tersely. 'So what?'

So what? Was he joking? 'What the hell happened?' I asked him.

He turned on the ignition. 'I don't want to talk about it.'

'Did she hurt you that much?'

'We hurt each other,' he grunted, jabbing the gearstick into reverse and backing out of the field. 'But we've kissed and made up and we're friends again, and that's how I want to keep it. Don't rake up the past, Selina; she won't thank you for it and neither will I.'

'But there's something I need to know, Harry ... did you love her?'

'Look, I didn't bring you out here to talk about Holly,' he reminded me. 'I have a question of my own – if this thing with Matt turns out to be a dud, do you think there's a chance for you and me?'

My feelings were all over the place. 'I don't know,' I said. 'But don't make me a part of whatever decision you reach about Alison.'

'That answer makes it harder for me to leave little Katy,' he said, 'but it doesn't change my mind about her mother. I've had it with Alison. So go ahead and do your thing with Matt and let's see if he can cure your addiction to my prick – if that's all it is.'

We drove back to Masquerade in silence, both of us deep in thought. When we entered the office, Holly looked at us suspiciously. 'What have you two been up to?'

'Nothing,' Harry barked at her. 'Where's the schedule for next week?'

'On your desk,' she said, casting a questioning glance at me. I waved her into my office.

'He's come back in a lousy mood,' she grumbled as we sat. 'What did you have for lunch – sour grapes?'

'We had a long chat,' I told her. 'Apparently, he's decided to leave his wife.'

Holly's hands flew to her cheeks. 'What?'

'Don't looked so shocked,' I said. 'It's not like they have a happy marriage.'

But she seemed stricken by the news. 'Why didn't he tell me?'

'I expect he will,' I said awkwardly. 'It's just that he told me first.'

'But why?' she demanded angrily. 'I've known him longer than you; I knew him before he was married.'

'That doesn't mean you own him, Holly.'

'No.' She slumped in her seat. 'You can't own someone like Harry. That would be like trying to cage air.'

I peered at her closely. 'You seem upset about it. I thought you hated Alison.'

'I do,' she confirmed. 'She's the most obnoxious woman I've ever met.'

I nodded: I'd met the stuck-up bitch myself a few times and disliked her immensely. I had never had any qualms about screwing her husband. 'Why do you suppose he married her in the first place?' I posed the question as casually as I could.

'Because he's a bloody fool.' She got up and pretended to look inside the filing cabinet.

I chose my next words carefully so that she wouldn't suspect that I was fishing. 'He told me she'd caught him on the rebound.'

She walked to the window and stared out. 'That proves he's a bloody fool. Only a blithering idiot would marry a cow like Alison just to get back at someone.'

'He didn't say he was trying to get back at someone,'

79

I pointed out. 'I got the impression that she snared the poor sod while he was nursing a broken heart.'

She laughed ironically. 'Harry doesn't have a heart.'

I decided to confront her. 'What did you do to him, Holly?'

'Shit!' she exclaimed.

'Holly, look at me.'

When she turned, I saw that her eyes were sparkling with tears. 'How much has he told you?'

'Not much,' I said. 'He didn't want to talk about it.'

'Neither do I,' she asserted.

'Goddamn - it! Why won't either of you talk?' I exclaimed. 'You've both deceived me about your relationship. Don't I deserve an explanation? I thought the three of us were friends.'

She sat down and her soft grey eyes beseeched me. 'I'm asking you as a friend,' she pleaded, 'don't dig up the past. Leave it buried and let it rot.'

'But you don't understand –' I let my voice trail away. How could I tell her that the reason I needed to know was because Harry wanted me back? She might still be secretly in love with him and I couldn't risk hurting her. Lightening the mood, I laughingly said, 'He must have been crazy to marry Alison. This is a woman so anally-retentive that she walks with her calves pressed together.'

Holly grinned gratefully. 'A woman who shits through a hosepipe, gets in touch with her Yin, and attends vaginal relaxation classes. If you ask me, it was only a matter of time before Harry got fucked off with her seaweed stews and the stench of pot-pourri.'

Happy to have cheered her, I switched the subject to Matt. I didn't tell her what we'd done in his car, but I told her the terms he'd laid out. When I'd finished, she commented contemptuously, 'If he wants obedience he should get himself a dog. I hope you told him where to get off.'

'It isn't that simple,' I said. 'He knows I want him and that gives him all the aces.'

'Not all of them,' she said, pointing to my crotch. 'What about the ace in your hole? If I were you, I'd make him sit up and beg for it. I find it's always best to let the man do the rolling over.'

'It honestly isn't that simple,' I repeated. 'You don't know what he's like. He's not the rolling over type and I'm not even sure that he wants me that much.'

'Then you need to increase his appetite,' she advised. 'Make him jealous – that always works.'

'How can I make him jealous?' I asked forlornly. 'I don't even have a boyfriend at the moment.'

'Then fake one,' she said. 'Masquerade's books are full of wannabe actors who'd do anything for a buck. Buy yourself a boyfriend. It's a lot less complicated than trying to pick one up and you'd be totally in control of what he says and what he does.'

'It's an interesting idea,' I speculated. 'A rival could shake Matt up. And if Gervaise thinks I really do have a boyfriend, it could throw him off the scent and convince him that I'm not serious about Matt. But I couldn't use one of my own people; it would have to be one of Harry's.'

'Some of his strippers are "resting" actors too,' Holly told me. She clapped her hands excitedly. 'Leave it to me, Selina; I'll arrange a little party at my flat on Sunday, just you and me and a few of the boys. You can take your pick of them. It'll be fun!'

'I'll bring plenty of wine with me,' I said. 'I don't think I could do this stone cold sober.' I tapped my wristwatch. 'Look at the bloody time! I haven't done a lick of work today. Buzz off, Holly, I have canvassing to do.'

'I'd offer to help you with it,' she said, 'but Harry wants me to make a start on the VAT return. If you're still on the phone when I leave, good luck with Luca Verdici tomorrow and I'll see you on Saturday at your place – assuming that you're still alive and not sleeping with the fishes.' She met my scowl with a laugh. 'Only joking!'

After she'd gone, I threw myself into my work, determined to gain at least one new customer before the day was out. I completely lost track of time and it didn't really register when Holly and then Harry popped in to say goodnight.

It only struck me that I was alone in the building when I heard footsteps approaching my office and glanced up to see an unnaturally tall silhouette of a man through the frosted glass of my door. 'Who's there?' I called out in a panicky voice.

The door burst open, making my heart leap into my mouth. But it was only Matt, wearing, of all things, a policeman's helmet! 'You frightened me,' I gasped. 'What are you doing here?'

He seemed pleased by my nervousness, as if he'd intended to fluster me. 'I came to pick you up. It was Gervaise's idea. He's cooking dinner for us tonight. Isn't that nice of him?'

'He cooks?' It vaguely surprised me that the lumbering ox would know his way around a kitchen.

'He's French – they all do,' Matt said. 'I picked up a bottle of wine on the way.'

'Where did you pick up the helmet?'

Matt tilted it over one eye. 'I saw it on Harry's desk. I assume it belongs to one of his strippers.'

'It kind of suits you,' I said.

'Maybe I should consider a career change,' he mused.

'You're thinking of becoming a policeman?'

'No – a stripper. What do you think?'

I tapped my finger on my chin. 'That's hard to say. I haven't seen you move.'

He turned his back to me and, humming 'The Stripper', began bumping and grinding his hips. 'How about this?' he asked. But I was so transfixed by the movement of his pert, sexy arse that I could only mumble my approval.

He rotated towards me, unbuckling his belt. 'Is this how they do it?' He whipped the belt from its moorings and cracked it across my desk. As I nodded enthusiastically, he moved his hands to his waist, unfastened the button of his fly and drew his zip slowly down. 'Is this what turns them on at those ladies' nights?'

I licked my dry lips, enthralled as I watched his hand creep into his underpants. It excited me to see him fondling himself with such a dirty, lascivious look on his face.

When his cock was hard, he pulled it out and moved his hand up and down its length. It looked smooth and robust and I wanted to touch it. But he kept his distance and I could only watch, gulping, as his hand clamped around his swollen shaft and started pumping.

His eyes looked almost evil as he moved around the table, lewdly jerking himself off and getting more and more excited. His roughness amazed me. I couldn't believe that he could yank and pull so spitefully on his cock without hurting himself.

But he kept pumping harder and faster, growing oblivious of me as his rapture consumed him. I could feel my pussy wincing as I imagined the frenzied friction burning and rasping inside me. I couldn't take my eyes from his cock. I yearned to grab it and claim it, but I could see that it was throbbing and pulsing, ready to explode. There were pearls of come dripping from its end.

'Matt!' I warned. 'You're coming, for God's sake!'

In the nick of time, he snatched the helmet from his head and let his cock belch into it, bucking and groaning until every last drop had drained out of him. I felt a surge of frustration and annoyance that he'd wasted himself in front of me.

'I've always wanted to do that,' he sneered, peering into the spunk-soiled helmet. 'I hate the fucking police.' He handed it to me. 'You'd better clean this up.'

'That was a disgusting thing to do,' I seethed.

'Wasn't it though?' he answered smugly.

I pushed past him and, holding the helmet out in front of me like a chamber pot, took it to the toilet where I sluiced it with disinfectant. After scrubbing it out, I returned it to Harry's office, hoping that the pungent smell of pine would disperse overnight.

Matt met me in the hall with my coat and smiled darkly as I snatched it from him. 'Don't pretend you didn't like it,' he said.

I didn't speak until I was in the car, then I rounded on him. 'Why did you do that? What was the point?'

'Do what?' he asked, glancing slyly at me.

'What you just did.'

'What would that be then?'

I huffed in exasperation. 'You know what I mean.'

'Say it,' he urged me.

Although I sensed that, once again, he was trying to control me, something compelled me to utter the word that he wanted to hear: 'Wank.'

As soon as I'd said it, my sex clenched lustfully. What the hell was he doing to me? Was it some kind of weirdly erotic mind-fuck?

'Have you thought about what I said this morning?' he hinted softly.

I attempted to play him at his own game. 'What would that be then?' I asked.

He shook his head slowly and the clicking of his tongue seemed to mock me. '*Tut, tut, tut*, – wrong answer.'

I felt hopelessly out my depth, as if floundering in a murky swamp of degenerate sexual desire with Matt's foot on my head, trying to push me under. Although I was resisting instinctively, somewhere deep inside I was tantalised by the prospect of the thrilling and dangerous alliance he proposed.

I closed my eyes, trying to rescue my thoughts from the mire. All I could see in my mind's eye was the image of him wanking and suddenly I realised that his sordid self-abuse had been a deliberate act intended to arouse and appal me. He was testing me again.

'I'm still waiting for an answer,' he pressed me.

'I still don't have one,' I said.

'Do I take that as a "no" then?'

'Take it any way you like.' I was determined not to be bullied.

My attitude seemed to rile him. He stabbed his foot on the accelerator and the car lurched forward. He broke the speed limit all the way home.

As we entered the house, he thrust the bottle of wine that he'd bought into my hands and stomped upstairs; I carried it through to the kitchen.

Gervaise was standing by the hob, stirring something in a pot that smelled of garlic. We greeted each other cordially and then I asked him what he was making.

'Coq au vin,' he replied. 'And what a coincidence,' he added, looking at the bottle in my hand. 'You have the wine and I have the . . .'

'Cock?' I suggested. 'Honestly, Gervaise, if you're going to start up with those smutty innuendoes again –'

He pouted in a way that was typically French. 'I was going to say that I have the meal all ready to dish up.'

'Oh.' I blushed.

'It was meant to be a peace offering after the way I rubbished your breakfast this morning.'

'It was a rubbishy breakfast,' I conceded.

'I won't argue with that,' he said. 'Hand me those plates, will you?'

The food looked divine and tasted delicious. However, when I generously offered my compliments to the chef, Gervaise spoilt everything by replying with a grin that he was pleased I'd enjoyed his coq and then he'd point-edly invited me to help myself to seconds.

Fortunately, Matt had been too self-absorbed to notice my embarrassment. He'd eaten in silence and, after the meal, had gone straight to bed, leaving Gervaise and me to glower at one other.

'What's troubling Matt?' he asked as we did the wash-ing up.

I lifted my shoulders. 'Search me.'

He turned his head to consider me and I was struck once again by the vivid blueness of his eyes. They were decidedly the most beautiful eyes I'd ever seen on a man. 'That's an interesting proposition,' he said. 'I wonder what I'd find.'

I gave him a wry smile. 'What would you expect to find – crotchless knickers?'

'Perhaps not,' he replied, 'but I doubt if I'd find a chastity belt.' We both laughed. 'You know, you're really very pretty when you smile,' he observed.

'That's a back-handed compliment,' I objected ungratefully. 'A lot of men find me attractive whether I'm smiling or not.'

'Undoubtedly,' he said, 'but I suspect that a lot of men don't realise there's an ugly side to you. They're probably beguiled by those aquamarine eyes and that glossy mane of hair. What colour do you call it?'

I wasn't about to tell him that my copper and bronze hi-lights were artificial. 'What colour is bullshit?' I retorted. 'Not even a Frenchman can get away with wrapping up an insult in a compliment. What did you mean by ugly?'

He handed me a dripping plate. 'Your hatred of Miranda is ugly. What have you got against her?'

'You mean apart from the way she got over my father before his body was cold in its grave?' I asked sullenly.

He frowned. 'You're wrong about that.'

'What would *you* know about it?'

'I know what she told me,' he said. 'But there's something else, isn't there?'

'She gave me some bad advice,' I revealed. 'And it cost me dearly.'

'Everyone gives bad advice from time to time,' he noted philosophically.

'Deliberately?'

'Perhaps you'd better explain.' He pulled out the plug then, taking a half-dried plate from my hand, steered me into a seat. 'Go on,' he prompted me.

I heaved a sigh. 'I was seeing a man – a married man. I was deeply in love with him, but it was the old, old story – he wouldn't leave his wife. Miranda suggested, no *insisted*, that I should give him an ultimatum and I was stupid enough to listen to her.'

'That doesn't sound like bad advice,' he commented.

'I was just a teenager,' I continued. 'My father had died and I needed guidance. I believed her when she said it would work. But it didn't. Some time later, I heard her telling Matt that she'd guessed this man would collapse under pressure and knew it would end the affair.'

'It still doesn't sound like bad advice,' he reasoned. 'This man, if he'd loved you, would have left his wife without being forced to. Perhaps Miranda believed he was stringing you along, taking advantage of your youthfulness.'

'The affair would have run its course if she hadn't interfered,' I uttered sourly. 'But, as it is, I'm still involved with him and I can't seem to close that chapter of my life.'

'You will when you find the right man,' he stated confidently.

I gave my head a mournful shake. 'Perhaps he *was* the right man.'

He patted my hand and then covered it with his own. 'I don't think so.'

I found myself staring at his strong, brown hand. It was so big that it made mine look tiny and I could feel its warmth and electricity. Curiously, long after he'd removed it, I could still feel the pressure of the gentle squeeze he'd given me.

7

'Where the bleedin' hell is he?' moaned Daisy. 'I haven't got all day.'

'He'll be here any minute,' I assured her. 'Why don't I fetch you another cup of tea while we're waiting?'

She gave a curt nod of her blue-rinsed head. 'Go on then, girl. But show it the bleedin' milk bottle this time.'

I smiled at her tolerantly. She was grumpy, rude and eccentric – but an absolute treasure. Well into her seventies, Daisy was a retired seamstress who ran-up simple costumes for me on an ancient old sewing machine that she affectionately referred to as 'Horse'.

Anxious to keep her sweet, I hurried out to the firm's tiny kitchenette, which comprised a sink, a fridge and a kettle and, by the time I returned with her second cup of tea, Jack had arrived and they were eyeing each other warily.

'Who's this bleedin' sod?' she enquired.

'This is Jack,' I announced. 'He'll be wearing the costume.'

'Do what?' she cried, running her rheumy blue eyes over his tall, skinny frame. 'This ain't the bleedin' bloke I measured up. Jack, you say? Jack the bleedin' beanstalk, more like.'

'Oh, I say,' complained Jack who, by contrast, was 'awfully' posh. 'I *am* in the room you know.'

'Ooh, hark at him!' Daisy cackled. 'He sounds like the lord of lah-di-dah land.'

He politely ignored her. 'You weren't terribly precise over the telephone,' he told me. 'What role am I to play?'

I had to brace myself to tell him for, as an amateur Shakespearean actor, he had lofty aspirations and a Micawber-like tendency to expect too much. 'A pea,' I blurted out.

'I beg your pardon?'

'A Pingles frozen pea to be precise,' I clarified feebly.

His thin lips formed an inverted 'V'. 'Oh God,' he whined. 'Is this what my life has become?'

'Cheer up, son, it could have been worse,' Daisy clucked consolingly.

'In what possible way?' he cried.

She took a sip of her tea. 'Well, it's better than being a turnip.'

I held up his file on which I had written 'willing to do anything, except spiders'. 'This is what you told me,' I reminded him.

'I know, I know.' He fluttered his hands. 'Don't misunderstand me, I wasn't expecting to play Oberon or Caesar, but ... a *pea* for goodness sake?'

He was starting to annoy me. 'Do you want the job or not? Don't jerk me around, Jack. I only called you in because someone else has let me down after landing a part in a stage play.'

'Lucky basket whoever it was,' he sniffed. 'Is that my costume?' He looked mournfully at a huge green sphere squatting like an enormous pumpkin on the floor.

'And this,' said Daisy, handing him a pea-green leotard. 'But it won't bleedin' fit. The other geezer was a good four inches shorter than you.'

'It'll stretch,' I said. 'Take it to the loo and try it on, Jack.'

After he'd gone, Daisy muttered disdainfully, 'Bleedin' toffee-nosed twit. Where does he think he is – Shaftsbury

Avenue? I bet the silly sod changes his mind and refuses to do it.'

'Of course he'll do it,' I said, 'he needs the money.' However, after fifteen minutes, I wasn't so sure. He hadn't come back and I was about to go in search of him when Harry's voice crackled over the intercom. 'Selina, what the fuck's going on? There's a bloody great pea the size of Mars careening around in my office!'

'That'll be Jack,' I said. 'What's he doing in there with you?'

'He seems to have lost his way,' Harry laughed. 'Apparently, he can't see where he's going. You'd better come in here.'

Daisy and I jumped up and hurried into his office where we found Jack blundering about inside the pea costume with his arms outstretched. 'The eyeholes are too high,' he complained. 'I can't see a wretched thing.'

'Blimey,' cried Daisy, 'he must have a tall head!'

'You were right,' I admitted to her, 'the costume's too small.'

'No, dear, the costume's just right – it's *him* that's too big. Gawd love us!' she cried. 'Look at his meat and two veg! His balls are sticking out like Brussels sprouts!'

Indecently enhanced by the tautness of the leotard, Jack's prominent pea-green testicles were standing out like billiard balls. 'Can you do something, Daisy?' I begged her. 'I can't send him out like *that*.'

She rearranged her heavy bosom and guided the bloated pea into a chair. 'Sit down, luvvy, while I put on my thinking cap.'

'Would anyone mind if I rehearse?' Jack enquired. 'We're doing the Scottish play at the Oldsbury Theatre next week.'

Rubbing his forehead, Harry muttered grimly, 'Am I

seriously expected to sit here and listen to a pea reciting Shakespeare?'

'I'm sorry,' I uttered plaintively. 'We'll be as quick as we can.'

Just then, one of Harry's strippers walked in: a good-looking young black man whom I'd spotted in his office earlier that day. 'What have you come back for, Mark?' Harry asked. 'I gave you your outfit this morning.'

'I know,' replied the young man, stealing a glance at me and smiling flirtatiously. 'But I've something to tell you: my helmet's all sticky and stinks of disinfectant.'

Daisy leaned towards me and whispered confidentially, 'Sounds like a dose of the clap.' She raised her voice. 'Try bathing it in TCP, son.'

He gave her a puzzled look. 'Bathing what?'

'Your helmet, you berk.'

Mark dipped inside the carrier bag he was holding and withdrew a policeman's helmet.

'I think my telephone's ringing,' I babbled, scurrying out before anyone spotted the Belisha beacons flashing in my cheeks.

I waited ten minutes before venturing back. Mark had gone but Harry was scratching his head bewilderedly while Daisy, with her nose in the policeman's helmet, was trying to decide if she could smell cat's piss or pine. Aloofly detached from them both, the oblivious pea was holding Harry's stapler at arm's length, reciting, 'Is this a dagger which I see before me, the handle toward my hand? Come, let me clutch thee . . .'

'That's *Hamlet*, isn't it?' Daisy proclaimed. 'I wonder if he's playing the pied piper.'

'It's *Macbeth* actually,' Harry corrected her.

'Buggeration!' wailed the pea, leaping up to perform a series of hurried rotations. 'Are you all philistines? It's dreadfully bad luck to name the Scottish play!'

Daisy looked blankly at me. 'What the bleedin' hell is he on about and why is he doing the hokey-cokey?'

'It's some sort of superstitious ritual,' I explained. 'He has to do it if anyone says *Macbeth*. Ooh, sorry, Jack,' I apologised, as the pea jumped up and started spinning again.

Jack staggered back into his seat, clutching his huge green head. 'I'm feeling quite dizzy now,' he whined. 'Could we get on with this, please?'

Directing him to stand, Daisy scratched her chin. 'The best I can do is cut out a new set of eyeholes and sew a fig leaf or something over his family jewels.'

I glanced at my watch. 'You've an hour to make the alterations.' I told her. Then I ordered Jack to go with her and wait at her house for the costume. 'You've to be at Iceworld for three o'clock,' I stressed.

'Do I have any lines?' he asked, rising.

'Oh, yes,' I remembered. 'You're to repeat their slogan as often as you can – "Pingles Peas are the pea's knees." Have you got that?'

'I believe so,' he sighed. 'It's hardly a soliloquy.'

'Perhaps they ought to change it to "Pingles Peas are knock-kneed",' Daisy tittered, drawing our attention to Jack's bony legs. Her laughter infected first me, and then Harry, with a fit of the giggles, made worse when the unamused pea attempted a dignified exit but smacked straight into a wall instead. Taking pity on him, Daisy led him out by his hand, leaving the two of us chuckling hysterically.

'I love this job,' spluttered Harry, wiping his eyes, 'and it's about to get even sillier. In ten minutes I'm off to an appointment with Mr Chin at the Lotus Leaf restaurant. He wants to discuss a Bavarian evening!'

I started giggling again. 'Why would a Chinese restaurant want to hold a Bavarian evening?'

'I know it sounds like a joke,' chortled Harry,' but it doesn't have a punch line; Mr Chin is totally serious.'

'Good luck to you,' I said. 'I don't think I could keep a straight face.'

'I'd advise you to keep a straight face when you meet up with Scarface this afternoon,' he warned.

'What makes you think that Luca Verdici doesn't have a sense of humour?' I asked.

'Watch his mouth when he smiles,' he suggested. 'Only one side ever lifts up. It's like he's ready to stab you even when you're telling him a joke.'

'You're just lousy at telling jokes,' I replied. 'And you deserve to be stabbed after that one about the vicar and the penguin this morning!'

'Oh, yeah? And who's the joker who hired a thespian to play a pea?' he retorted. 'Anyway, you can tell Luca from me that I'll be in touch with him if I can pull this Bavarian thing off.'

I felt guilty about promising that I would, for what Harry didn't know yet was that his credit account with Luca had been frozen along with mine.

Luca's unfairness in penalising both sides of the business, which he knew to be separately managed, was the first thing I set out to discuss with him when he entered my office later that day.

I had dressed provocatively for the meeting, in a short skirt and low-cut top, and was greeted with a leer of approval, which incorporated the lop-sided smile that Harry had so accurately described.

There was something about him that made my skin crawl and yet I didn't know why he repelled me. For, despite the scar on his cheek, he was strikingly handsome: dark-eyed and olive-skinned with immaculate blue-black hair, and, although slightly shorter than I was and with a frame far too slender for my taste, I ought still to have found him attractive. But instead he repulsed me. Perhaps he used too much hair gel or perhaps I simply didn't like men who had fingernails more beautifully manicured than mine.

'You look ravishing today,' he commented in a thickly accented voice that should have been charming – but it wasn't.

I, nonetheless, fluttered my eyelashes and lavishly complimented him on the stylish Italian suit he was wearing, which had probably cost more than I owed him.

He made a flamboyant gesture. 'Enough of the pleasantries,' he said. 'You know why I'm here. Do you have my money?'

I flirtatiously flicked my hair behind my shoulder. 'Like I said on the phone, I need more time.'

His dark brown eyes had a soft liquidity that seemed strangely at odds with the hardness of his tone. 'You've had long enough.'

I stood up and walked to the window, hoping to soften him up by drawing his attention to my legs. 'Look, I know I've mismanaged the account,' I admitted. 'But Masquerade has been a good customer in the past and all I'm asking for is an extension. It's not like you need the money, Luca.' I turned to face him. 'You're a rich man.'

He flicked imaginary fluff from his trousers. 'I didn't get rich by being soft on debtors and allowing other people to use my money. I'm a businessman, Selina, not a bank manager.'

I clasped my hands pleadingly. 'I can understand you being harsh with me, but it makes no sense to cut off supplies to Masquerade Unmasked. It's a separate account and Harry doesn't owe you a penny.'

'That's true,' he agreed. 'But as far as I'm concerned, he's your partner and that makes him equally liable for your debt.' He ran his eyes over my legs. 'However, I shan't lean on him until I've exhausted all my other options.'

The idea of Luca 'leaning' on Harry appalled me. 'Just give me a couple of weeks,' I pleaded. 'You'll get your money, I promise. I'll even pay you interest.'

He pursed his thin lips. 'Now you're mistaking me for a loan shark. Don't you get it, Selina? It isn't about the money – it's the principle of the thing. I spelt out the rules when I agreed to supply you: you pay Luca Verdici before you pay anyone else.'

I made my eyes wide and appealing. 'Can't you break your own rules? Surely you can make an exception in my case?'

'I never make exceptions,' he said.

I returned to my chair and, sitting down, leaned towards him. 'Never?'

His gaze wandered into my cleavage. 'I'll be frank with you, Selina. It's widely known that patience is not a virtue of mine and, much as I like you, I've no intention of debunking that myth.'

'It sounds like you've already made up your mind to sue me,' I concluded.

His eyes narrowed menacingly. 'If I were to sue my customers for every pound of flesh they ever owed me, I'd be up to my neck in paperwork. There are more effective ways of dealing with debtors.'

'What do you mean?' I uttered nervously.

'Precisely what you think I mean,' he said.

His veiled Mafioso-style threat had me cowering inside. He let it sink in before lowering his voice to whisper coercively, 'But it needn't come to that. There's another way of settling this.'

Hesitantly, I asked, 'What's that?'

He smoothed his gelled hair. 'I could ask a small favour of you.'

'A favour?' I choked back a laugh. 'You sound like Don Corleone. Who do you want me to shoot?'

Ignoring my facetiousness, he stood up and moved to the back of my chair. 'You know I desire you,' he murmured into my ear. 'I don't think you realise how much it upset me when you refused to go out with me.'

'I didn't mean to offend you,' I said, trying not to flinch as he rested his hand on my shoulder. 'I just thought it best to keep our relationship on a business footing.'

The hand slid down my arm. 'That's where we differ. Personally, I enjoy mixing business with pleasure.'

I seized his wandering hand. 'What do you want from me, Luca?'

'I should have thought that was obvious.'

I jumped up and spun round to face him. 'I'm not for sale, if that's what you're thinking.'

He blatantly shifted his gaze to my breasts, making me acutely conscious of their nakedness beneath the thin material of my top. 'Five hundred pounds,' he stated.

'I beg your pardon?'

He gestured benevolently. 'It would mean a substantial reduction in your debt, as well as buying you an extra week to come up with rest of the money.'

Angered, I exclaimed, 'Do you seriously think that I'd sleep with you for five hundred pounds?'

He tilted his head as if calculating the extent of my outrage. 'Probably not,' he judged. 'For so little a sum, I would expect no more than a piece of you.'

'I think we'd better end this conversation before I smack your face,' I warned.

He turned his cheek towards me. 'Go ahead,' he urged.

'But before you strike, consider what I'm saying. Distasteful as it sounds, it's a way out for you, Selina.'

I let the hand that I'd raised drop to my side. Much as I wanted to hit him, we both knew that I couldn't afford to indulge my pride. 'What do you mean by a piece of me?' I demanded.

His soulless dark eyes peered deeply into mine. 'Your breasts.'

'My . . .?' I looked down at myself.

'Breasts,' he repeated huskily. 'Those plump luscious tits that you've been trying to make me notice ever since I arrived. Well, *cara mia*, I've noticed.'

I felt my cheeks glowing hotly. 'I wasn't flaunting myself to tempt you. I was trying to distract you,' I admitted, 'but I didn't mean to . . .'

'I don't care what you meant,' he interjected, flaring his nostrils. 'I want to fondle your breasts – right now. And I'm willing to pay for it.'

I gulped. 'You'd pay five hundred pounds just for that?'

'Just for that,' he confirmed. 'Are you flattered? You should be. They're not a virgin's breasts, after all. How many men have touched them – ten . . . twenty? That's a lot of sweaty palms and groping fingers.'

'They didn't *all* have sweaty palms,' I said sardonically. 'You can't be serious, Luca. Why would a successful businessman with looks, money and brains pay for something that he can get free, with bows and bells on, just by whistling for it?'

'I don't want the kind of woman that comes when I whistle,' he answered sharply. 'I want what I can't have – and that's you. Do you think I don't know that you despise me, Selina? Don't bother trying to deny it. I can see it in your eyes and in your body language. You smile when I touch you but I know that you're cringing inside and that's what excites me. I want to conquer your revulsion, caress and arouse you until every cell in your body is screaming with lust. I want to see you on your knees begging me to fuck you.' His voice cracked and grew hoarse. 'The first time we shook hands, you wiped your palm on your skirt when you thought I wasn't looking. That gesture showed me exactly what you thought of me and gave me such a hard-on that I had to excuse myself and go to the toilet for a wank. And do you know what I did? I put a little of my spunk on my fingers and wiped it on your skirt.' He laughed. 'It amused me to think of you puzzling over that stain.'

Stunned by his outburst, I could only mutter, 'I'd no idea that you felt like this.'

He gave a sinister cackle. 'Why do you think I let you run up this debt? All those times you smiled and flirted, I knew what you were thinking. But you never guessed what I was thinking.' He tossed his head triumphantly. 'You thought you could handle me, didn't you? But instead you walked into my trap.'

'I'm not trapped,' I said defiantly. 'I'll just have to borrow what I owe you.'

He shook his head. 'It's too late for that. The wolf is at your door and his jaws are open wide. If you don't give me what I want – I'll bite.' I recoiled as he reached out his hand. 'Don't be a fool,' he murmured, moving closer.

I felt the edge of the desk digging into my thighs as I tried to back away and then his hands gripped the wood on either side of me, making a cage of his body and his arms. Imprisoned, I whispered fearfully, 'What are you going to do?'

He didn't answer but suddenly his hand jumped on my throat like a rat. I squealed in terror, thinking he was going to strangle me, but then his fingers splayed out across my collarbone.

'Your skin is like velvet,' he murmured, tracing an arc above the scooped neckline of my top.

I shuddered. His touch felt like slime, trickling over my skin and oozing into the valley of my cleavage as he stroked between my breasts.

'How do you feel?' he rasped. 'Nauseous? Disgusted? Is it horrible being touched against your will?'

'All of the above,' I snarled. 'If you really want to know, you make me sick.'

'And you make me horny,' he said, pressing his groin to my leg so that I could feel the swollen bulge of his manhood. His creeping fingers began to skim beneath my neckline. 'Any moment now, I shall plunge my hand inside. What do you think of that?'

I took a deep breath. 'Why don't you just get on with it?'

He moved his fingers down another inch. 'I'm in no particular hurry. Tell me what you're thinking.'

'I'm thinking about the money,' I lied. 'It's like you said, I've had plenty of sweaty palms touching me before. I can pretend that I'm doing this for charity.'

He gave a sneering laugh. 'That's not what you're thinking at all.'

'Then what am I thinking?'

'You're thinking you might like it.'

He was horribly right. My nipples were tingling and the aureoles around them had started to pucker in antici-pation of his hateful touch. I cursed my sensitive breasts, but I couldn't contain their instinctive response when at last his hand thrust down.

'You see?' hissed Luca, smirking as he rubbed a rigid nipple. 'You can't help yourself.'

I bit my lip, trying not to gasp as he skilfully caressed my breasts, his clever fingers making them swell and heave as he fondled and kneaded my flesh. My lungs began snatching for air as my heart beat faster and my clit began to throb.

'You love it, don't you?' he said, pushing between my legs to rub himself against me. 'Your nipples are so hard and hot; wouldn't you like me to cool them down with my tongue? Just ask me to and I will.'

If he'd gone ahead and done it, I wouldn't have stopped him or even wanted to, but there was no way I'd ask him. *Not in a million years, you fucking creep!*

'I think you've had your money's worth,' I snapped, pushing him from me.

Too late, he realised his mistake. 'I guess you're not quite ready to beg yet. But I think I've proved my point: your body seems to like me well enough.'

'If I paid any attention to what my body likes, I'd spend all my time in bed with a vibrating plastic dick,' I commented dryly. 'And as for my nipples getting hard – you should see them when it snows! Don't mistake reaction for attraction, Luca; I still find you repulsive.'

He nodded. 'Even more so, I should hope,' he surmised. 'If I've gained your utter contempt through this abuse, it will have been worth every penny. I'm not after your love, Selina; I want your hate.'

I looked at him searchingly. 'Why?'

'Because sex is infinitely more exciting that way. A woman is never more passionate than when she hates.'

'You're twisted,' I told him. 'I don't want anything more to do with you. I'll get your money one way or another and then I want you out of my life.'

'You have until next Friday,' he said. 'I want all of it or none at all. There's only one way you can pay by instalment and I think you know what that is.'

I nodded to let him know that I'd understood. 'I'd like

you to leave now,' I said, walking over to stand by the doorway. I tried to look dignified, but he'd made me feel cheap.

He came over and lifted my chin. 'Oh yes,' he purred. 'There is pure malevolence in your eyes. You've no idea how sexy it is.' Then he pressed his lips to mine before I could stop him. '*Ciao*, Selina.'

Glaring at him hatefully, I drew my hand across my mouth and then ostentatiously wiped his revolting kiss on my skirt as I watched him walk away.

I was feeling pleased with the gesture until a voice said dryly, 'Do you know you've just smeared lipstick on your skirt?'

'What? Oh shit!' I was too annoyed even to be startled by the voice, which was coming from Harry's office. I assumed it was he but when I glanced through the doorway, I was astonished to see Gervaise swivelling in his chair and grinning like a hairy hyena. I strode in to confront him. 'What are you doing here?'

'I've been waiting for you,' he replied.

'Waiting?' I repeated.

'Matt loaned me his car, so I thought I'd drop by and take a look at your operation. When I saw you had company, I came in here to wait.' He nodded towards the door. 'Is that the guy with the Transylvanian neck fetish?'

I screwed up my face. 'What are you talking about?'

He jabbed his finger at my fading lovebite. 'Your boyfriend, Nosferatu?'

'Oh, I see. No, that was Luca; he's a business associate,' I explained.

He thrust out his jaw. 'Then you've a funny way of doing business. Do you always shake hands with your tits?'

I gulped. 'You saw that?'

'It looked to me like he was groping you,' he said. 'But, hey, what do I know? Maybe he'd just dropped his mobile phone down your top and was trying to find it.'

I grinned awkwardly. 'We were ... er ...'

'Horsing around?' he suggested cynically. 'Like you've been doing with Matt? I believe that's what you called it. Tell me, do you have a whole stable of stallions for these equine adventures of yours?'

'Why don't you mind your own fucking business?' I snarled. 'I don't need to explain myself to you.'

He spread his hands expansively. 'Listen, Sugarlips, I don't give a fuck who you fuck, so long as the guy in question isn't living with my sister.' He stood up. 'Are you going to show me around? Where do you keep the costumes?'

I pointed to the wall-to-wall wardrobe that Harry had built himself. 'In there mostly.'

He strolled over and slid back a door. 'Wow!' he declared. 'This is quite a collection.' He reached in and pulled out a French poodle outfit. 'I bet you look cute in this.'

'Those costumes are for strippers,' I said.

He looked at me blandly. 'And your point is?'

I gave my head a haughty flick. 'My point is I'm not a stripper.'

He looked wistfully at the costume. 'That's a pity.' Continuing to rummage through the clothes, he suddenly spotted something that made him crack out laughing. 'I don't believe this!' he exclaimed. 'You have a strippergram courgette? Who in God's name wants a giant zucchini sitting on their lap at a stag do?'

'That shouldn't be in there,' I said. 'It's one of my promotion costumes. And it's not a courgette, it's a ...' I let my voice trail away – a giant gherkin would have sounded even more ridiculous. 'Never mind what it is; it doesn't belong in that wardrobe. It should have been put in my stock room.'

His eyes lit up. 'You have a room for giant vegetables? This I'd like to see.'

'Actually there isn't much in there,' I said. 'Unwanted costumes are either sold to fancy dress shops or cannibalised and recycled.'

'How do you recycle a courgette?' he wondered.

'Ah,' I said cannily, 'I have a genius called Daisy, who's amazing with needle and thread. She'd probably sew on some tentacles and turn it into an alien.'

'Hmm,' he murmured, 'the Courgette from Outer Space: it terrorised the Earth until captured by an elite squad of mercenary vegetarians who grilled it for 24 hours and then ate it.'

I giggled. 'If that's an idea for a novel, you'd better stick to journalism. Can we go now?'

He grunted a negative. 'Not until I take a peek at that stock room.'

I gave a shrug of resignation. 'Very well, if you must.' I led him into my office and nodded towards the stock room door. 'In there.'

'You're not coming in with me?' He twitched his eyebrows cheekily.

'I'll be putting my coat on.'

I was doing just that when I saw Harry bounding down the corridor, his face wreathed in smiles. He launched through the door and swept me into his arms. 'I got the deal,' he announced, steering me backward on to my desk. 'Fancy a celebratory fuck?' Then, before I could stop him, he had his hands up my skirt and was kissing my neck. 'Pack it up, Harry,' I squealed. 'Stop –'

'Horsing around,' supplied Gervaise, coming out of the stock room with a withering look on his face.

'Hi,' said Harry, smiling. 'I guess you must be Bluto.'

8

Although it was still light enough to see his face, his beard concealed his expression as effectively as a balaclava helmet. Inside it, I was sure that he was scowling and, listening to his hands tapping on the steering wheel, I became convinced that he was drumming out his disapproval in subliminal Morse code.

Since leaving Masquerade, we had driven in silence for a whole ten minutes, and I was just about ready to explode after waiting impatiently for him to say something – anything – that would give me a chance to defend myself. Why wouldn't he speak? What was going on inside his head? Desperate to know, I mentally lifted an enormous sledgehammer and braced myself to smash the silence. I gave him one more minute and then I let him have it:

'I know what you're thinking and I don't give a fuck. But I won't let you sit there, silently reproaching me. So, why don't you just come out with it and call me a slapper? Do you know what your problem is, Gervaise? You've been out in the Middle East too long and you've forgotten how liberated Western women are. Just because I fool around with men doesn't make me a slut. But that's what you're thinking, isn't it?'

'I wasn't thinking that at all,' he refuted.

'Oh,' I uttered deflatedly. 'Then what *were* you thinking?'

He glanced at me narrowly. 'Bluto?'

'Jesus Christ, is that all?'

'Is that *all*?' he bellowed. 'Fucking Bluto? What would *you* think if someone called you that?'

'I'd think it was time to see a doctor for an oestrogen top-up,' I said. 'It's just the beard, for goodness sake.'

He glanced at himself in the rear view mirror. 'What's wrong with the beard? A lot of women say that it makes me look sexy.'

'They're lying,' I said. 'It makes you look like –'

'No need to say it again,' he intercepted. 'I'm wounded enough as it is.'

'Then shave the bloody thing off,' I suggested. 'Are you such an ugly fuck underneath that you're frightened to show your face?'

'As a matter of fact, I'm incredibly handsome,' he bragged.

'That's what Quasimodo said when *he* wore a beard,' I retorted.

'Well, I wouldn't give a peanut for your opinion if I had a whole bag of them,' he told me. 'A woman who lets herself be groped by a man with enough oil on his head to baste half a dozen chickens has no taste in men at all. How can you even fancy a man whose hair contains more cholesterol than a tub of margarine?'

'I don't fancy Luca,' I said. 'Whatever you thought you saw wasn't what it looked like.' To avoid explaining myself, I swiftly changed the subject. 'What did you think of Harry?'

He considered a moment. 'I liked him,' he decided. 'He's the one you had the affair with, isn't he?'

'How do you know that?'

'Because I'm astute, incisive and perceptive,' he said. 'Plus Miranda mentioned his name in a letter.'

'She wrote to you about my affair!' I exclaimed.

'She was worried about you.'

'She had no right to do that,' I stormed. 'You're a bloody outsider.'

His fingers tightened on the steering wheel. 'I'm her brother,' he affirmed, 'and, believe it or not, she was having a hard time knowing how to deal with her spoilt, selfish, pain-in-the-arse – and yes – *slapper* of a teenage stepdaughter after the dumb little bitch stupidly got herself involved with a married man who...' he broke off unexpectedly.

'Who *what*?' I prompted him.

He hesitated. 'She wouldn't want me tell you this ... but I think you ought to know. She knew he was a philanderer.'

'That's just an old-fashioned name for a flirt,' I said.

'Look it up in the dictionary,' he advised me. 'It's a man who can't keep his hands off women: a man who can charm the knickers from a nun. Doesn't that sound like Harry? I can see how you fell for him. I can't help liking him myself. But it seems that Miranda wasn't quite so impressed.'

'What do you mean? She hardly knew him.'

He took his eyes from the road to flick a glance at me. 'That didn't stop him from making a pass at her.'

'What!' I couldn't believe my ears.

He nodded grimly. 'He tried it on.'

'When?' I demanded. 'I don't believe you.'

'What do I stand to gain from lying?' he asked. 'I don't know when or where it happened. You'd better ask Harry if you really want to know. I can't imagine he'll deny it. Why should he? She didn't mean anything to him; she was just another woman, just another piece of arse.'

'She was my stepmother,' I lamented. 'How could he do that to me?'

He heaved a deep sigh. 'Don't you get it? She had a pussy he hadn't fucked yet.'

I fell silent, thinking about what Holly had said: *Harry doesn't have a heart*. Had he cheated on her too?

Gervaise interrupted my thoughts. 'Now do you see why Miranda tried to split you up?'

'She could have told me,' I muttered ungratefully.

'How could she? You were crazy about him; you'd never have believed her. Persuading you to give him that ultimatum was the kindest thing she ever did for you. It opened your eyes to how he really felt.'

'No.' I shook my head. 'She was wrong to interfere. Harry *did* love me enough to leave his wife, but he couldn't because she was pregnant. I didn't tell Miranda about it because I knew she'd despise me.'

'Then you've only yourself to blame,' he concluded. 'You should have known that you were asking too much of him. You can't pin your selfishness on Miranda and pretend it was all her fault. She was just trying to be a good mother.'

His words inflamed me. 'She's not my mother. My mother died when I was three years old. And you're not my uncle. So back off and keep your nose out of my affairs.'

'You viperous little bitch,' he snarled. 'Do you honestly think that I'm going to sit back and let you sink your poisonous fangs into Matt? If what I saw today is your idea of "horsing around", then the poor fuck is in deeper trouble than I thought. I'll be watching you every minute of the day and if you so much as sniff him, I'll cut off your nose.'

Realising that I'd just shot myself in the foot, I tried to placate him. 'Look, Gervaise, the only man I'm interested in is my boyfriend. So you've nothing to worry about.'

'Ah yes, the elusive boyfriend,' he said. 'So where is he and what's his name?'

'I told you to mind your own business,' I snapped, deliberately shooting myself in my other foot because I couldn't answer his question. Having run out of feet, I was relieved when the car pulled up outside the house.

'By the way,' I said as we were walking up the path, 'I hope you're in tomorrow evening. My friend, Holly, is coming round and she'd like to meet you.'

He looked at me sceptically. 'Why would your friend want to meet me?' he wondered. 'You can't possibly have told her anything nice.'

'Oh, I didn't,' I agreed. 'It's just that when she was a kid she had a monstrous crush on Bluto. I'm sure you'll get on famously.'

Despite what I'd said, I didn't really expect them to click. So when Saturday evening arrived, I was surprised to get the thumbs-up from Holly within half an hour of them being introduced. Having decided that she fancied him, she flirted outrageously.

'I hear you've just come back from the Middle East,' she said, reaching out to ruffle his beard. 'Is this a souvenir or have you always had one?'

Gervaise smiled as he poured out some wine for her. 'You know how it is, *when in Rome*; I grew it to blend in with the Arabs.'

'I never saw an Arab as big as you,' she commented. 'Do you plan to shave it off now that you're back?'

Moving the bottle to my glass, he flicked a surly look at me. 'I haven't decided,' he said. He filled me up and then turned back to Holly, all smiles. 'What do *you* think?'

She fluttered her eyelashes. 'Oh, I wouldn't be too hasty,' she told him. 'A girl can have a lot of fun with a beard.' I couldn't believe she'd said that: it was the equivalent of throwing her knickers over his head!

His grin grew broader. 'You're going to have to elaborate,' he said.

'I was thinking in particular of when a man has a beard and a woman ... doesn't, if you see what I mean.'

Oh, for fuck's sake, Holly! I was actually annoyed with her for being so blatant. Especially when I caught Matt looking at me and rubbing his chin speculatively. I shot him a glance that warned him not even to think about it: one gorilla in the house was quite enough.

Matt stood up. 'It's a pity I have to leave at such an interesting point in the conversation,' he said, 'but I always go bowling on Saturday night with Alan next door. Perhaps you ought to come with me, Selina, and leave these two people to get better acquainted.'

I gazed wistfully at his bum as he stooped to pick up his bowling bag, but had to drag my eyes away when I sensed Gervaise watching me like a rottweiler. 'Good luck with your game,' I muttered innocuously.

After he'd gone, Gervaise entertained us with some hilarious anecdotes of his adventures abroad and, as I watched his animated features, I began to grow aware of his charisma and could see why Holly seemed captivated by him. He was laying on the charm with a trowel, making his eyebrows dance and using his expressive hands to emphasise his words. He'd even thickened his accent to make his voice sound sexier and was flirting so effectively with his eyes that Holly, as if on cue, commented on them.

'Where did you get those beautiful blue eyes?' she enquired, peering into them.

'From my grandmother, according to Miranda,' he replied.

'Ooh, say that again,' she urged him.

'Say what?' he queried.

'Miranda,' she sighed. 'I just love the way that your

tongue makes love to the letter "R" in the middle. I bet you could give a girl an orgasm just by *saying* the word "clitoris".'

'That's an interesting theory,' he said, cupping a hand over her ear and whispering into it; she feigned an erotic shudder.

'That makes me wish I had a name like Rosemary.'

'Rosemary,' he indulged her, rolling both of the Rs on his tongue.

'Mmm.' She licked her lips. 'When you were learning English did they ever teach you to say *"around the rugged rock the ragged rascal ran"* by any chance?'

'Actually, I learnt quite a few different tongue-twisters when I was practising my oral,' he submitted with a smile.

Her eyes widened. 'Oh, really? Could you say something else with a lot of Rs in it, please?'

'How about "drooling tart"?' I suggested caustically; their flirtation was making me prickly.

Gervaise looked taken aback, but Holly just giggled. 'It's OK,' she said, 'Selina gets uncomfortable when she thinks I'm being too obvious. One of the things I like about her is that she doesn't pull her punches. What do you think, Gervaise, am I being too obvious?'

He flicked his eyebrows and grinned. 'A little perhaps. But I prefer it to ambiguity. It's hard enough to guess what a woman wants when you know her, never mind when you don't. Take Selina for example. Her smile is like a crocodile's. I can't tell if she wants to kiss me or bite off my head.'

I grimaced at the idea of kissing him. 'I'd be only too happy to demonstrate which of those two options appeals to me,' I retorted, baring my teeth.

'No need,' he chuckled. 'The look of horror on your face says it all.'

'You seem able to read women better than you think,' I told him.

He turned back to Holly. 'What's her boyfriend like?' he enquired. 'She won't talk about him.'

I looked sharply at her but she handled the question deftly. 'He's gorgeous, fit and sexy. What more is there to know? How about you, Gervaise, do you have a girlfriend back home?' I mentally applauded her nimble deflection.

'Her name is Veronique,' he said, 'but it's a long time since I've seen her.'

'You don't seem in any hurry to get back to her,' I observed.

He pulled a sour face. 'Believe me, I'd like nothing better than to be at home right now, shagging the arse off my girlfriend. But fate has a strange way of buggering up one's life.'

It almost tripped off my tongue to remind him that fate had buggered up my life also, for I'd be shagging Matt now if it weren't for him. Luckily, the words stayed in my head.

Holly tactfully pretended not to know what he was talking about. 'Shagging?' she queried disappointedly. 'I thought the French made love.'

He refilled her glass. 'You forget I'm half-English. I only make love when I'm *in* love; everything else is a fuck.'

She looked at him coyly over the rim of her glass. 'Do you fall in love often?' she asked hopefully.

'Only when he looks in the mirror,' I cut in. 'Gervaise is convinced that he's handsome under that beard.'

Holly stared at me as if I'd gone blind. 'He *is*,' she stressed.

* * *

Two hours later, in the privacy of her flat where I was spending the night, I cross-examined her over her comment: 'What did you say that for?'

'I meant it,' she said. 'I think he's gorgeous.'

'But he's a bloody fur-ball with eyes,' I protested. 'I've seen sexier looking muppets.'

'Believe me, Selina, he's hiding his light under a bushel; or should I say bushy? If you can't see that for yourself then you'll just have to take my word for it. There's a whole lot of man in there.'

'You mean a whole lot of ape,' I insisted. 'Considering our different tastes in men, I'm surprised that we both fell for Harry.'

'Oh, that's easy to explain,' she said. 'Harry's irresistible.'

I stirred the cup of coffee she'd given me and, without looking up, muttered grimly, 'Miranda didn't think so.'

After I'd told her what Gervaise had said, I was surprised by her calm reaction. 'How typically Harry,' she murmured bitterly.

'Did he cheat on you, Holly? Is that why you split up?'

'Did he cheat on me?' She laughed. 'You bet he did!'

'Won't you tell me about it?'

To my astonishment, she started crying. 'I did something awful,' she sobbed. 'I wish I could tell you, but it hurts too much to talk about it.'

'Then don't,' I said, putting my arm around her shoulder. 'But, if you want my advice, it won't stop hurting until you do. Why don't you try talking to Harry?'

She raised a knuckle to her quivering lip. 'Because I don't know what's under the scar. If I open it up, he might hate me again, and I couldn't bear that.'

My curiosity was dying to know what she'd done that

could be so dreadful, but I could see how upset she was and didn't want to press her any more. While she dried off her tears, I plugged the gap of awkward silence with a graphic account of my meeting with Luca Verdici.

She listened in horror and, after I'd finished, she scolded me. 'How could you let him do that, Selina?'

I looked at her in surprise. 'I thought you'd be the last person to criticise me.'

'Why – because I've slept with guys for money? I did that to keep a roof over my head at a time when I was desperate and broke. And I only had sex with attractive men that I would have shagged anyway. That doesn't make me any less of a tart, but at least I had standards. I'm ashamed of you, Selina. Luca Verdici is a slime-ball.'

'I didn't exactly have any choice,' I said. 'He made me an offer I couldn't refuse.'

'He threatened you?'

I nodded. 'It looks like you were right about him.'

Holly drew her knees up to her chest and wrapped her arms around them. 'He scares the living daylights out of me. But at least a tit squeeze is better than being garrotted in your sleep – or was it?'

I made myself think back. 'To begin with it was horrible ... but then – and I don't know how – the bastard turned me on.'

'You're kidding!' she exclaimed.

'I swear to God. It was the weirdest thing that's ever happened to me.'

'It's like Matt; it's the power thing,' she said. 'It seems to be a bit of an aphrodisiac for you. Well, we can't let the creep get his hands inside your knickers – heaven knows what might happen! We'd better start twisting a few arms to get some money in. I'll hit the phones on Monday and you get the begging bowl out. If push comes to shove you're going to have to ask Matt for a loan.'

'Matt can't help me; he's out of work and, anyway, their savings are in Miranda's name,' I informed her.

'Then what about Gervaise?' she suggested.

I pulled an 'absolutely not' face. 'I'd sooner fuck Luca,' I said.

She frowned. 'I don't know why you're being so stubborn. I'm sure he'd help you out if he knew about Luca.'

'I don't want him knowing,' I snapped. 'I don't want his fat French nose anywhere near my affairs.'

'He doesn't have a fat nose,' she disputed, 'and as for those eyes –!'

'Yes I know,' I said sharply. 'You liked his eyes, his arse, and everything else. You couldn't have made it clearer if you'd sent him a text message.'

'You should be pleased that I found him attractive,' she said. 'It makes my task of diverting his attention a whole lot easier. In fact, I plan to be so distracting over dinner on Monday night that he might even forget to come home.'

'You have a dinner date?'

She whisked a hand through her fluffy blonde hair. 'You know me, I don't piss about. Phase one of our operation is now firmly under way and tomorrow we'll fix you up with your bogus boyfriend. I've invited three gorgeous, fit, and sexy men over – so I wasn't exactly lying to Gervaise – and they'll do anything for money.'

'Anything?' I queried.

'Trust me,' she said, nodding gleefully. 'We're going to have a *lot* of fun.'

9

By seven o'clock on Sunday evening, after a bottle of wine and three double vodkas apiece, Holly and I were ready for just about anything. The boys were due any minute but whatever nerves I might have felt had been anaesthetised and I'd begun to grow recklessly excited at the prospect of having three young men at my disposal.

We'd spent the whole day giving each other make-overs. 'You look fabulous,' she said, making a final adjustment to the position of my hair on my shoulders. She'd spent ages crimping it to make me look like Cleopatra and, with my eyes made-up like an Egyptian's, I felt sultry and exotic. I was wearing a slinky black dress, strappy silver sandals, and absolutely nothing underneath.

To complete the picture, Holly made me recline on her sofa with my long legs outstretched, and put a champagne glass in my hand which, although it contained only vodka, added to the illusion that I was a pampered rich bitch. The cameo was set and, satisfied at last, Holly sat down to look at me.

'Fantastic,' she said. 'You make me wish I was a lesbian.' She, herself, was wearing a sexy French maid's outfit that she'd borrowed from Masquerade.

When at last the doorbell rang, she scooted out and I giggled as I heard her say, 'Good evening, gentlemen. May I please take your coats and shirts.'

Still in the regal pose she'd put me in, when she reappeared I gave my hand a dainty twirl to summon her into the room. 'Your guests, my lady,' she announced, sweeping back her arm to usher in the troupe of bare-chested men who'd lined up behind her. 'Allow me to introduce: Huey, Dewey and Louie.'

Cut off their heads and they could have been clones. They were the same height, give or take a whisker, and they all had six-pack torsos and bulging biceps. But they weren't naturally big like Gervaise, who'd probably had muscles as a foetus, and their bodies seemed overly large for their frames. These were pumped-up men who'd spent hours in the gym working out: the type who roasted themselves on sunbeds and used bikini-line wax on their chest hair for that smooth-as-a-baby's-bum look. They were typical strippers.

When I finally got round to examining their faces, it didn't surprise me to discover that the trio shared good looks, fastidious grooming and toothpaste-commercial teeth in common; thus compounding the impression that they'd all been sired by the same magnificent stallion.

As Holly introduced them by name, flashy smiles appeared in triplicate. There was Kyle, whom she assured me wasn't gay despite his floor-sweeping eyelashes and cutely pretty face; then George, who was pale-skinned but had Caribbean features; and lastly Dane, who had bleached blond hair and, though he looked Scandinavian, spoke with a Birmingham accent. I couldn't decide which of the three would look better on my arm.

After telling the boys to sit down and have a drink, Holly dragged me into the kitchen for a girlie consultation.

'So – who do you prefer: Huey, Dewey or Louie?' she asked.

I shrugged indecisively. 'Well, they're all nice-looking,' I said, 'but I doubt if they've a brain cell between them. That's fine for a one-night stand, but they're not the kind of men I'd normally date.'

'I didn't choose them for their intelligence quotient,' she pointed out. 'They're wannabe actors with empty wallets who look good and don't ask questions. All you have to do is tow one around for a couple of days and, before you know it, you'll have Matt on his knees and Gervaise off your back.'

It sounded good in theory, but I wasn't convinced that Gervaise wouldn't see right through it; he was one of the sharpest men I'd ever met.

But when I voiced my concern, Holly merely winked. 'Don't worry about Mr Laser-blue Eyes. I intend to make sure that he has something much more interesting to look at. With any luck, he won't even notice if your boyfriend's black, white or polka-dotted.'

'Well then, what about Matt? Do you honestly think that I can transform him from a control freak into a pussycat simply by making him jealous?'

'Matt thinks you're ready to walk on hot coals to get into his pants,' she answered scornfully. 'But when he sees that you've decided to pass and move on, I think he'll jettison his rule book and start chasing you. I saw the way he looked at you when you were talking to Gervaise. He's even jealous of him.'

'I don't think I'd like it if he started eating out of my hand,' I said.

'How do you know?' she challenged me. 'Having power over a man is a buzz. If you haven't tried it yet then tonight's the night, my friend.'

I looked at her curiously. 'What do you mean?'

Her wide grey eyes sparkled mischievously. 'Haven't you ever paid for cock?'

'Of course not!' I exclaimed.

She giggled. 'Don't look so shocked; a lot of women do it. Do you remember that conversation we had about men and those convenient dildo-shaped objects that they keep between their legs that don't need batteries?' I nodded. 'That's how you need to imagine these guys,' she continued. 'Not as human beings but as providers of the best damn sex toys in the world. You simply hire them by the hour. Come on.' She beckoned me. 'Let's go and do some window shopping before you decide which one you want to buy.'

The men, in our absence, had stripped to their underpants and were doing one-handed press-ups on the carpet. Pretty-boy Kyle was the first to keel over, which prompted the others to jeer and call him a faggot.

'Don't knock yourselves out, boys,' Holly advised them. 'One of you may need to conserve his energy.'

Dane looked disappointed. 'Only one? I was hoping for an orgy.'

Holly wagged a finger at him. 'Listen, sweetie, you should have abandoned all hope before entering here. You're at Selina's mercy now and you'll do whatever she tells you.'

Beginning to grasp the idea, I boldly instructed the three men to stand in a line and exhibit their arses.

'Let's have your pants off,' Holly commanded them. 'This isn't a bathing beauty contest.' To my amazement, they obeyed her like poodles.

'Bloody hell,' I exclaimed, greedily running my eyes along the row of tight bronzed buttocks. 'It's like trying to choose from a box of Belgian chocolates. How do you pick just one when they all look so scrumptious?'

Kyle tittered. 'That sounds like a line from the blue movie version of *Forrest Gump*.'

'Keep quiet,' yapped Holly, giving his buttock a slap.

'Hey, go easy on the merchandise,' he moaned.

Ignoring his plea, I marched down the line squeezing each of their luscious butts as if testing the ripeness of peaches, which felt so satisfying that I reversed course and did it again. If Holly hadn't grabbed hold of my pinching fingers, I would have kept it up all night. 'Enough already,' she chided, pushing me back into my seat. While the men were rubbing their rears, she clapped her hands to bring them to order.

'Arse number one,' she said. 'You're out on a date with Selina and a woman starts giving you the eye. What do you do?'

'All depends what she's looking at,' George answered smoothly. 'If it's my love hump, I'd give her Masquerade's number and advise her to book a private session.'

'That's commendably businesslike,' I said, 'but you'd be giving the game away. Arse number two, we're at an expensive West End restaurant – what wine would you order with fish?'

'I'm allergic to fish,' Dane sniffed, 'and I only drink Perrier.'

Unimpressed by his answer, I moved on. 'Arse number three, what would you do if a hulking bearded Frenchman accused you of faking a relationship with me?'

'I'd tell the furry frog-munching git to fuck off,' Kyle grunted sternly.

Holly and I looked at one other. 'That's a bloody good answer,' I said.

George glanced over his shoulder. 'If you've finished the personality check, can we move things on to the physical? I've got a love lizard going to waste here.'

'No kidding,' said Holly, jumping up. Cuddling up to his bum, she slid her hand around to his crotch. 'It's true,' she confirmed. 'Make a note, Selina, number one gets points for initiative.'

Watching her caressing him, I decided to do a hands-on examination of all three contestants. 'Simon says put your hands on your heads,' I instructed them.

As they lifted their arms, Holly proposed that we

turned them round to face us, but I disagreed. 'I rather like the view from this side,' I said.

Stepping back from George, she shrugged. 'I keep forgetting that this is your party. Perhaps I'd better just sit down and watch.'

I began with Kyle, trailing my fingers lightly up the backs of his thighs and then splaying them out across his flanks, marvelling at the firmness of his flesh. Then my hands toured over his back, exploring the taut muscles holding his arms up. 'Very impressive,' I commented, finally curling my fingers around his biceps to administer a squeeze.

It excited me that I could touch any part of him without fear of being molested myself. He just stood there like a statue, letting my hands flow over his body.

Moving on to Dane, I grew a little more daring and, noting his pendulous ball sack, pushed my hand between his legs to stroke his plums. Then, cupping my palm around his heavy scrotum, I bobbed down and ran the full flat of my tongue across its warm creped surface. There was a whoosh of in-drawn breath, but Dane held himself steady and kept his hands on his head.

George, however, was a lot more vocal and ground his arse into my crotch as I put my arms around him to explore his powerful chest. I teased him by rubbing my hand across his belly, for although I couldn't see his erection, I could feel it flapping against my knuckles. 'Take hold of my love stick, baby, and let's fuck until we're yodelling,' he suggested.

But I didn't touch his cock. Instead, I stepped back. 'You can lower your hands now, boys.'

Holly folded her arms and looked at me impatiently. 'Have you made up your mind yet?'

I made a gesture of helplessness. 'There's just nothing to choose between them.'

'You're not looking in the right place!' she exclaimed. 'Try turning them round.'

'You can't judge a man by the size of his cock,' I protested.

'What!' she cried. 'Selina, you've just tongued a man's bollocks like a dog. It's a little late for scruples, don't you think?'

She was right of course; I was being a twat. 'Let's do eeny, meeny, miney, mo,' I proposed.

'No dice,' said the mixed-race George. 'I object to the bit about catching niggers by their toes. What fucking sick whitey thought that up?'

'You're a whitey yourself, you bigoted bozo,' Kyle pointed out. 'Your skin's not as dark as my suntan.'

'Don't you go insulting me, batty boy,' George warned. 'I may be white on the outside, but I'm a brother underneath, and a Caribbean love god at that.'

'Oh, for Chrissake,' wailed Holly. 'Let's all get off our moral high grounds, shall we? Do I need to remind you what we're here for? It isn't to clap hands and sing songs about Jehovah.' She turned to me. 'What exactly is your problem?'

I levelled with her. 'It's like when they bring you a couple of live lobsters in a restaurant. I just can't bear to look at their faces when I choose which one's for the pot.'

'In that case,' she said, 'I have the perfect solution.' She thrust her hand into the pocket of her frilly white apron and withdrew three small silver packages.

'Condoms?' I queried. 'Is this your answer to life, the universe and everything?'

'Not entirely,' she replied, dashing out into the hall. She was back in a trice with a headscarf. 'Condoms and a blindfold,' she supplemented. 'Put them together and the meaning of life becomes clear: it's all about who you shag and how.'

Intrigued, I allowed her to tie the scarf around my eyes. 'What happens now?'

'It's wanking time,' she said. 'Hold out your hands and two of the boys will slip you a little present. I'll take care of the other one.'

I spread my palms and was instantly presented with two soft sausagey lengths of flaccid cock. 'It's lucky for you that I'm ambidextrous,' I said, stroking the dicks with my thumbs. As they stirred into life, the one in my left hand doubled its size almost instantly, whereas the one in my right took its time but came in twice as thick. When both pricks were hard enough to grasp, I started pumping them gently.

At first, it felt like a peculiar form of bust exercise because of the way my breasts were jiggling. But, as the men started moaning, I began to warm to the task. On the sofa beside me, Holly was rocking back and forth, giving the impression that the cock she was wanking was a monster.

'You're not to speak,' she cautioned the men as their grunting grew louder. 'The whole idea is for these cocks to remain anonymous. If you're hard enough for a condom, put one on.'

The two dicks I was holding seemed reluctant to leave the warm, cosy burrows of my clenched hands. 'Let them go,' Holly urged me. 'They look about ready to fly.' She was right. As I uncurled my fingers, the two cocks sprang away from my palms.

There were some scuffling sounds and then I heard George say, 'Aw, man, you've gotta be kidding.' And then laughter broke out among the three of them.

'What's going on?' I demanded.

'Just one second,' Holly told me. Then suddenly the darkness inside the blindfold became pitch black. She'd turned the light off! The men started laughing raucously and I could sense them dancing about.

'Holly, what the hell is happening? Can I take this bloody scarf off?'

'One more second,' she giggled. 'I'm just getting them lined up. OK now, boys, not a sound. Don't give yourselves away. I'm going to count to three, Selina, and then you can take the blindfold off. One ... two ... three!'

I snatched it from my eyes. 'Oh, my God!' I burst out laughing. The room was cloaked in darkness and all I could see, bobbing around in the inky blackness, were three luminous cocks. She'd put all three men into glow-in-the-dark condoms!

'It's time to pick your boyfriend,' she told me.

Once I'd recovered from the initial shock, I looked at each of the glowing dicks in turn. I had no idea whose they were, but recognised the two that I'd held from their shapes. The third was massive and I dismissed it out of hand.

'Daddy Bear's is way too big,' I said, 'and Mummy Bear's looks a bit droopy. But the one in the middle is *juuust* right.'

'Good choice,' said Holly, 'I've got a dildo shaped just like it. Do you want to give it a road test, Selina?'

'You mean without even knowing whose it is?'

'Look at it,' she said. 'What do you see?'

'I see a phallus disguised as a giant glow worm,' I said.

'Look again. It's a state-of-the-art sex toy with a voice recognition chip. It'll do exactly what you tell it to.'

Put that way, the idea of masturbating with such an exquisite piece of technological engineering was so horny a prospect that my pussy scrunched in on itself. 'OK, I'll do it,' I said.

Holly told me to close my eyes while she took the rejected candidates out. Then, as the door closed behind them, I found myself alone with a single luminous cock.

'Whoever you are, I don't want you to speak,' I said, 'but do exactly as I say.' The cock nodded. 'I want you to come over here and straddle me.'

While the cock made its tentative way towards me, I pulled my dress up to my waist and kicked off my sandals. Then, as fumbling hands discovered my nakedness, I heard a croak of surprise followed by lustful breathing.

Spreading my legs to make room for the heavy body, I let it settle into a position that enabled the glowing appendage to hover above my crack. But before I could grab it, a plundering hand snatched at my pussy, its fingers drilling for my hole. I slapped the hand away. 'I don't want you to touch me,' I hissed. The hand retracted and I heard a submissive grunt. 'That's better,' I said, closing my fingers around the fluorescent shaft. 'Now cut me some slack.'

Guiding the bell-end to my clit, I rubbed it against my sensitive nub, pulling gently back and forth so that its knobbled shaft chafed my inner lips. It felt gloriously decadent to be using a hot living cock as a sex toy and my shivering arousal prompted a flood of liquid joy. I smothered the dildo-dick in my juices and lustfully steered it around my sex, lavishly spreading my creamy liquid over my sensitive folds of skin. By now, my clit was throbbing furiously and demanding to be stimulated, so I rubbed it rapidly with the swollen cock-head and brought myself, panting, to the edge of a climax. Teetering above the chasm, I grasped the shaft in both hands and plunged my penile plaything inside me.

The cock spurred into life and with quick ramming thrusts tipped me over the edge. But as I swooped into my orgasm, rough hands pulled my body down and pushed my knees to my waist. Suddenly I was jumping like I was being defibrillated. The cock had found my G-spot and was adding high voltage electricity to my orgasmic spasms, making me scream in excruciating ecstasy. I could hardly bear it and gave a heartfelt sigh when my mystery lover finally ejaculated.

'Jesus, Mary and Joseph,' I whimpered, clasping him gratefully as he slumped on top of me. 'That was fantastic. Where did you learn how to do that?'

The mystery man's laughter exposed his identity. 'Call it a trick of the trade,' Kyle said.

We disentangled ourselves and then he turned on the light. 'Well? Do I get the job or not?'

'You'll do,' I said. 'But I want to get one thing straight: what we did just now was a one-off, an experiment. There won't be any more sex.'

'Perhaps I'd better make my own terms clear,' he stated. 'That was a free sample. And no, there won't be any more sex unless you pay for it. The kind of service I gave you just now doesn't come cheap.'

'No, right, OK,' I muttered awkwardly.

I was relieved when Holly put her head around the door. 'All done?' she queried. I nodded and she entered. 'He gave you the *zinger*, didn't he? I heard you screaming your head off.'

'You might have warned me,' I complained. 'I thought I was dying. Can they all do the zinger?'

She shrugged. 'I wish I could afford to find out.' She turned to Kyle. 'You can go now,' she told him. 'Take all the clothes to my bedroom down the hall. You'll find the others playing with my dumb-bells.'

Not long after they'd left, I called a taxi and went home myself. I found Matt on his own, watching television.

'Where's the yeti,' I asked, 'the abominable Frenchman?'

'Upstairs in his room,' Matt replied. 'He bought a laptop today and he's shut himself away to do some writing.'

'I wonder what he's writing,' I mused. 'The Apeman Cometh? Gorillas in our Midst?'

'Who cares?' said Matt, patting the arm of his chair. 'Come over here and tell me about your day.'

I went over and perched on the arm. 'I've been with my boyfriend,' I said, pushing his blond hair out of his eyes.

Furrows appeared on his forehead. 'What boyfriend?'

'His name's Kyle,' I said airily. 'Haven't I mentioned him before?'

'No, you haven't,' he answered gruffly. 'How long has this been going on?'

'A few weeks.'

His mouth tightened. 'You were seeing this guy when you started coming on to me?'

I looked away distractedly. 'He's just someone I date now and then. You're not jealous, are you?'

His hand flicked out and batted my face towards him. 'Are you fucking him?'

I pouted as if I resented the question. 'Maybe.'

'Did you fuck him tonight?'

I smoothed my hair in a nonchalant manner. 'Is that any concern of yours?'

'I think it is,' he said tightly. 'If you've been leading me on, Selina, if you've been dicking me around – what's this?' he demanded, suddenly snatching up the hem of my dress. 'It looks like a spunk stain.'

He glared at me so angrily that I stood up, alarmed. 'Let go of my dress, Matt.' But he hung on to it tightly.

'What happened? Did his gun go off before you'd even undressed? He must have been excited. What were you doing to make him so excited, huh? Were you sucking him off?'

I tried to pull away but he grabbed even more of the fabric and, although I struggled to keep the dress from riding up my thighs, he kept yanking on it until most of the material was in his hands and hardly anything was covering my pussy. I tried in vain to conceal myself. But it was too late. He'd seen that I wasn't wearing underwear.

'You dirty little bitch,' he growled, raking up the last of the fabric to expose my naked bush. Then his tongue lolled over his lip and his breath snorted through his nostrils. 'Did you let him do this?' he hawked, slamming his hand over my sex and grinding the heel of his palm into my pubic mound. 'Come on, tell me, is this what he did?'

Staring into the boiling cauldrons of his eyes, I felt a rush of exhilaration. His wildness was exciting me and the rough rasping of his hand was igniting a feverish response. With my breath sputtering in my throat, I could only gasp and moan as he grabbed my arse and pressed me tight against his grinding hand. His teeth snapped at my nipples through the fabric of my dress. It was sheer savagery, but it was rousing the animal in me and I clawed my nails into his arm.

Livid with passion, he pounced on me like a tiger, ripping down his fly as he grappled me to the floor. But then we both heard a door slam upstairs. 'Gervaise,' I gasped.

In the heat of the moment, we'd forgotten all about him. Matt groaned and rolled off me. 'I can't take much more of this.'

I crawled over to him and steered my hand inside his pants. 'Then let's just do it,' I urged him. 'I don't care about him and neither do you.'

For a moment he closed his eyes and let me fondle his turgid cock. Then, suddenly and without warning, he struck me a blow with the back of his hand that propelled me across the floor.

'Do you think I'd give up Miranda for the sake of a five-minute fuck?' he snarled. 'I told you before – I want more from you.'

I clasped my smarting cheek. 'You hit me, you brute!'

'You didn't mind me being brutish a couple of minutes ago,' he said. 'As a matter of fact, you seemed to like it a lot.' He zipped up his fly and slammed himself down in the armchair.

Getting to my knees, I glared at him furiously. 'You're an animal,' I seethed, 'a fucked-up son-of-a-bitch!' Then I jumped like a rabbit as the door swung open and Gervaise strolled in. I had to swallow my heart before I could speak.

'Goddamn it, you made me jump out of my skin,' I accused him. 'Is it absolutely necessary to sneak around the house like Creeping Jesus?'

'It was you that threw my boots into the dustbin and insisted I wear loafers,' he reminded me. 'When did you get back? I didn't hear you come in.' His laser gaze scanned my reddened cheek and then flicked to the scratches on Matt's arm. 'Did I miss anything?'

10

On Monday morning, while waiting for Harry to arrive at the office, I took out my compact and examined my face. Although all physical trace of Matt's slap had disappeared, I was hoping to see something in my eyes that might reveal what I was feeling beneath the numbness of my bewilderment. For Matt's assault had shaken me to the core and rocked the very foundations of every thought and fantasy that I'd ever had about him.

I'd known he was volatile, but I'd greatly misjudged his reaction to provocation and, like a reckless fool, had goaded him to anger. Yet, baited or not, there could be no justification for lashing out as he had and I was still reeling from the discovery of his latent brutality.

I had always rated violent men as a species even lower down the evolutionary scale than those who practised betrayal and infidelity – such as Harry – and to me it seemed unthinkable that someone as proper as Miranda could be attached to such a man.

Yet if she knew what Matt was really like, how could she have been so easily offended by Harry's attempted pass at her? Could it be that Matt had suppressed this side of himself until I'd brought it to the surface, goading him, just as I'd goaded Gervaise into his gloating exposé of Harry's misdemeanour?

My thoughts marched off in that direction and I grew angry with Harry again, not least for giving Gervaise a weapon to fire at me. So when he finally popped his smiling face around the door to deliver a chirpy greeting, he was met with a ballistic missile of aggression.

'Good morning, my little honeypot.'

'What's good about it?' I snarled. 'And, incidentally, I'm *not* your frigging honeypot!'

He looked at me confusedly for a second but then turned his head and called back over his shoulder in mock alarm, 'Selina, I ought to warn you – there's a grizzly bear sitting at your desk!'

'Shut up, close the door and sit down,' I commanded fiercely.

He scratched his head. 'Hey, baby, this is Harry you're growling at. Should I go out and come in again?'

'Sit!' I commanded, stabbing my finger at a chair.

'OK, I'm sitting, I'm sitting.' He sat. 'So, who put the razor blades in your coffee today – Gervaise?'

'Gervaise doesn't shave,' I reminded him. 'Actually it's *you* that I'm pissed with. A little bird told me something about you at the weekend.'

He stroked his chin. 'What kind of little bird – a robin? Or was it a little bird with big grey eyes and fluffy blonde feathers?'

'It wasn't Holly,' I said. 'But the "who" doesn't matter. I just want to know if what I've heard is true.'

'OK then, let me have it,' he said.

'Is it true that you made a pass at Miranda?'

He crinkled his nose. 'Baby, that birdie of yours is a dodo. I haven't seen Miranda since your twenty-first.'

His reply disappointed me. 'I was rather hoping you might deny it.'

'I would if I could,' he professed, 'but the truth is I can't remember. If the birdie says I did then I probably did. It sort of sounds like me, doesn't it?'

'What do you mean *you can't remember*?' I yelled. 'This is Miranda we're talking about, not some wagglearsed floozy that happened to stray too close to your itchy fingers. Damn it, Harry, I loved you! How could you even think about groping my stepmother?'

'That's not fair,' he protested, 'you might at least credit me with some subtlety – I haven't groped since I was a teenager. I think you're blowing this out of proportion, turning an arse squeeze into a torrid affair. And isn't Miranda the kind of woman who'd consider it a pass if I blew smoke in her face?' He gave me an innocent look. 'I don't know what I did, but I know I didn't fuck her.'

'But what if she hadn't blanked you?' I challenged him 'What if she hadn't said no?'

'Then I might have done,' he admitted. 'I suppose it depends how drunk I was and whether you had your period or not.'

'You unconscionable shit!' I hurled at him.

He stood up. 'Sure I'm a shit. But can we finish this later? I have an urgent phone call to make.'

'Yeah, fine,' I said. 'Fuck off.' As I watched him go, I felt a prickling of tears at the back of my eyes. For years I'd believed that, deep down, he'd really loved me, but Gervaise had shattered that illusion by exposing him as a groping octopus who hadn't even cared enough about me to put a no-go zone around my relatives.

My thoughts turned to Holly. What beastly thing had Harry done to make her retaliate with something too awful to talk about? But as my brain accused, my heart defended. He wasn't a monster. He was just a man with more testosterone than he knew what to do with.

Eventually, I reached a verdict of 'not guilty through reason of rampant sexuality' and as soon as Harry came off the phone, I went into his office to deliver it.

'You're forgiven,' I declared. 'You can't help being a shit; it's programmed into your genes. Shall we kiss and make up?'

Smiling, he opened his arms. 'I've a better idea; let's do cunny and felatio to prove that we really mean it.'

'Don't mind me,' said Holly, walking in.

'You're late,' Harry growled at her, 'and I've a bone to pick with you.'

She rolled her eyes. 'You've always got a bone, you dirty old man; shall I tell you where to shove it?'

'I'm serious, you scatter-brained helium-head,' he ranted. 'I thought I told you to pay Luca Verdici last month?'

'Eat my anus,' she told him. 'I did.'

'Then why is he refusing to take my order for the Bavarian folk dancing costumes? I've been on the phone to some stupid bimbo this morning who seems to think the account is frozen.'

'Perhaps the cheque's been mislaid,' Holly suggested.

Harry nodded, allowing for the possibility. 'Well, if that's all it is, I take back what I said and reinstate your basic human right to swallow my dick to the hilt.'

She curled her lip. 'Harry, you're a shit and, for your information, I wouldn't put your dick in my mouth if it was made out of toffee.'

He shook his head woefully. 'This from someone who used to fill her cheeks with my balls and do hamster impressions?'

'I seem to remember that you did a pretty good impression of a rodent yourself,' she reminded him.

'Yeah, well, it isn't easy to do Frank Sinatra with a mouthful of muff,' he replied.

Holly looked at me helplessly. 'What am I to do with him?'

'You can do his VAT return,' Harry suggested helpfully.

'Not this morning,' she asserted. 'I'm hitting the phones with Selina; we're chasing up debtors. So if you hear sounds of weeping and wailing – ignore them.

Has Selina told you about her new boyfriend, by the way?'

'You mean Matt?'

'No, I mean Kyle.'

'Kyle?' His eyebrows shot up. 'Pretty-boy Kyle?' When I nodded, he squinted at me. 'Doesn't he bat for the other side?'

'You think he's gay?'

He shrugged. 'I don't know if he's gay, but he's certainly in touch with his feminine side.'

'What makes you say that?'

Harry stood up and walked over to the wardrobe. 'I guess you haven't seen his act.' He slid back the door and, after rummaging inside, withdrew the French poodle costume.

My mouth plopped open in disbelief. 'That's his?'

Harry nodded. 'He calls it Fifi.'

I swung round to fire an accusatory glare at Holly. 'Did you know about this?'

She giggled. 'Honest to God, it's a new one on me. But since we both know that Kyle chases pussy, I think we can safely assume that it's not his feminine side he's in touch with – so it must be his canine side.'

'Oh, stop bloody laughing,' I stormed. 'What kind of moronic matchmaker fixes up her own best friend with Fifi the poodle?'

'The same moron who's dating Gervaise for you,' she reminded me.

Harry strolled back to his desk looking puzzled. 'So let me get this straight,' he said, turning to Holly. 'You're going out with the Frenchman –' he looked at me '– and you're going out with the French poodle?'

We sat him down and endeavoured to explain our campaign. 'So you see,' I concluded, 'the whole point of the exercise is to help me win Matt from Miranda.'

'You're a devious minx,' he told me. 'You must want this guy an awful lot.'

My mumbled affirmative didn't sound too convincing. The truth of it was that recent events had placed serious doubts in my mind and, actually, the only thing I remained certain of was that whatever I had started with Matt needed to be resolved before Miranda got back.

Later in my office, Holly asked me why I seemed so dispirited. When I revealed that Matt had struck me, she flew into a temper.

'He hit you?' she screeched. 'The lousy arse-wipe, toe-rag, bag of snot, shit-fucking, pustulating prick!' she rattled off furiously. 'What are you doing, Selina? Men who hit women are the suppurating boils on the arse-hole of humanity.'

'Cool down,' I implored her. 'He just lost it for a minute, that's all. I don't think he meant to hurt me. It was a spur of moment thing.'

'If you're going to make excuses for him, I'm switching my ears off,' she snapped. 'I've no time for bully boys. As far as I'm concerned, there's a place reserved in hell for them right next to child molesters.'

Recalling that she'd had a violent upbringing, I decided to change the subject. 'What am I to do about the costumes Harry wants? He still doesn't know that Luca's cut him off because of me, but he'll soon find out when he calls him.'

'What's the order he's trying to place?' Holly asked. 'I don't know anything about it.'

'It's for the Lotus Leaf Restaurant. They want half a dozen Bavarian folk dancing costumes; too many for Daisy to run up in a week.'

Holly was so conditioned to the madness of Masquer-ade that she didn't even flinch at the bizarreness of the order. 'What about the Hungarian costumes that we used for Quickpot's Gourmet Goulash promotion?' she suggested.

'But don't Bavarians wear lederhosen?' I asked.

'Peasants are peasants,' she insisted. 'I doubt if Mr Chin will know the difference. Besides, we can always get Daisy to doctor them up a bit. Harry will love the idea of saving money. Why don't I nip next door and suggest it before he has a chance to ring Luca?'

While she was gone, I began the task of phoning my debtors. I didn't get very far and was slamming the phone down when she came back in.

'He's gone for it,' she announced. 'I'll run the costumes over to Daisy this afternoon. What's wrong? You've a face like a broken biscuit.'

'That was Stratton Publicity,' I grumbled, glaring at the phone. 'They're still giving me the runaround.'

'What's their excuse this time?' she asked.

I smiled ironically. 'They're claiming the cheque's been mislaid.'

'They used that one three weeks ago,' she huffed. 'I've had just about enough of Peter Stratton's fancy footwork. I think it's time we took a leaf out of Luca Verdici's book and applied some unsubtle pressure.'

'What do you have in mind?' I asked warily.

She smiled a cunning smile. 'If there's one thing that Peter understands, it's publicity, and I think I know a way to throw a punch at his public image that'll have him reaching for his wallet faster than you can say "tabloid press".'

As she went on to outline her plan, I could feel a stupefied expression forming on my face like a mask. For, though ingenious, her idea was fundamentally flawed through being much too outrageous to contemplate. Yet I found myself nodding and grinning inanely when I should have been objecting and, in the end, consenting to her scheme despite the gravest of misgivings. I sensed that my tongue-tied compliance had something to do with the spectre of Luca Verdici, whose shadowy presence in the back of my mind was a constant reminder of the fate that awaited me should I fail to come up with his money.

Holly concluded her proposal by pressing home the point that the time had come for desperate measures and, as the day wore on, I became firmly convinced that she was right.

After umpteen phone calls, we had managed to secure only four hundred pounds' worth of reliable pledges, which fell a long way short of the two and a half thousand that I still owed Luca, even after selling him my breasts.

Holly laid out the remaining invoices. 'These four won't pay until the end of month; this one's gone bust, and these two are for the Small Claims Court. That confirms it, Selina, we have to do Stratton. I'll fix it up for Wednesday. But even if we pull it off, you'll still be a thousand short and then there's our other creditors.'

I heaved a weary sigh. 'They'll all have to go on ice.'

'Daisy's been on ice so long it'll take a hydrogen bomb to defrost her. You'll have to give her *something*,' Holly said.

'Get some money out of Harry for those Hungarian costumes and let her have that,' I instructed.

I spent the rest of the day ringing fancy dress shops trying to sell a pea, a courgette and a couple of Italian tomatoes. Towards the end of the afternoon, Harry wandered into my office looking for Holly.

'She's taken the costumes round to Daisy's,' I said. 'Did you give her some money for them?'

He held up a finger. 'One hundred.' He sat down and I realised that he was looking depressed.

'Hey, you look like someone who's just blown a hundred quid on a three-legged horse,' I observed. 'What's the matter?'

He rubbed his forehead. 'It's Alison. She's insisting I celebrate my birthday tomorrow. You know how much I hate those annual reminders that I'm another year closer to death.'

I nodded. 'That's why we planned a nice little meal after work, just you, me and Holly. I thought you'd told her.'

'I did,' he confirmed, 'and she was OK about it. She always plays bridge on a Tuesday so it suited her fine, but now suddenly she wants to come along and make it a proper celebration.'

'Why is that, do you think?'

He pulled a worried face. 'I think she knows.'

'That you're planning to leave her?'

He absent-mindedly searched his pockets for cigarettes that weren't there. 'I think she's seen the way that I've been looking at little Katy just lately. And I've been so restless that I haven't been able to sleep.'

'Poor Harry,' I sympathised. 'If you're feeling this miserable then maybe it's time to put your cards on the table.'

'It's just a question of picking the right moment,' he said. 'But let's get this birthday shit out of the way first. When she comes in later on, just go along with whatever she suggests.' He forced a smile. 'I don't suppose you feel like cheering up a sad old man with a hand job?'

'If the answer's yes then may I form an orderly queue?' enquired Gervaise, striding in.

Harry greeted him with a smile. 'You ain't old enough or sad enough, young fella.'

'It's Harry's birthday tomorrow,' I explained. 'He's feeling ancient. Are you here to see Holly?'

He nodded. 'My instructions are to meet her here, follow her home, dump her car, and take her for a meal.'

'Did she forget the bit about getting her pissed, taking her to bed and shagging her stupid?' Harry asked, ducking as I threw my pen at him.

'You're right, you definitely need a hand job,' Gervaise advised him good-naturedly.

Harry threw back his head and laughed. 'You're OK, Bluto. You get my vote.'

'I didn't realise I needed it.'

Harry grew serious. 'Holly's a very special lady and we love her very much. I just thought you ought to know that.' It was the first time I'd heard him speak affectionately of Holly and, for a fleeting second, I sensed feelings that ran much deeper than anything he'd ever felt for me.

Gervaise looked around him. 'Where is she, by the way?'

'She's popped out; she won't be long,' I informed him. 'Oh, maybe that's her now.' I'd heard the clatter of high heels coming down the corridor. But it wasn't Holly who appeared at the doorway, it was Alison.

She wafted in on a cloud of Joy perfume but it seemed to me that suddenly the atmosphere grew noxious. Little hairs of loathing prickled on my skin as she looked down her nipped designer nose at me like I was a piece of garbage that her dustman had dropped on her driveway.

She was as thin as an anorexic stick insect, with platinum blonde hair shaped like an elongated football helmet. Every hair was welded to its neighbour and the whole thing moved as one. Her pinched, triangular face reminded me of a praying mantis. And when it came to men, she was one.

She homed in on Gervaise, rolling the glass marbles of her eyes up and down his body. 'Well hello there, darling. You're a big boy, aren't you?' she murmured huskily.

'Mind if I take a look?' She lifted her hand to his chest and, to the astonishment of all three of us, began to unbutton his shirt. 'Someone's been eating all his greens!' she declared. 'Nice muscles and just the right amount of chest hair. But, darling, the beard will have to go.'

'So everyone keeps telling me,' he said.

'Oh, is that a French accent?' She gave her hideous pissing-in-a-tin laugh. 'You're hiring continental strippers now, Harry?'

'He isn't a stripper,' I told her. 'He's Holly's date.'

'Oh my!' She feigned mortification. 'I'm so sorry, darling,' she told Gervaise.

He waved his hand. 'I'm flattered.'

'Such a pity though,' she snickered. 'You'd look terrific in a loincloth. So, what *do* you do, darling?'

'He's a hack,' I muttered, annoyed by the way that he seemed to be lapping her up.

'Oh, really? You know, I've often thought that the seedy life of Masquerade's strippers would make an ideal story for one of the Sunday tabloids. Might that be something you'd consider?'

'It's a tempting proposal,' he said, 'but a little outside my field. The work I do isn't nearly so glamorous; I'm a war correspondent.'

Her eyes lit up as he soared in her estimation. 'Oh, I'd say that's glamorous,' she said.

'Are you interested in foreign affairs?' he asked.

'But of course.' She smiled coquettishly. 'You did say you were French, didn't you?'

'This is Alison,' I interrupted stiffly. 'She's Harry's wife.'

His white teeth glimmered like a flashlight within the inky darkness of his beard. 'Gervaise Morgan,' he supplied.

'Delighted to meet you,' she said, shrugging off her

cashmere pashmina. Underneath, she was wearing more cashmere – a white sweater that clung like snow to the pointed twin peaks of her ice cream cone breasts. 'I must say that Holly's taste in men has improved somewhat. How did the two of you meet?'

'Selina introduced us,' he replied. 'I'm Miranda's half-brother.'

'Oh, darling Miranda, how is she?' Alison fawned.

He lifted his shoulders. 'I don't know. She'd flown to America before I arrived.'

'Miranda left Matt with Selina?' She looked at me like I was a toenail clipping that she found in her couscous. 'Was that wise?' Seeing my eyebrows knit together, she tinkled with laughter. 'Only joking, my dear.' She turned back to Gervaise. 'Darling, you simply must come along to Harry's birthday bash tomorrow evening. We can make up a six. I'm sure that Selina can dredge up a man from that bottomless barrel she keeps them in.'

'I'll bring my boyfriend, Kyle,' I said tightly. Gervaise cocked an eyebrow at me and I returned his look with the smuggest of smiles.

'I hope this new one is able to communicate beyond the occasional grunt,' Alison commented. 'I seem to remember that your last boyfriend had the kind of mentality that one normally associates with timeshare salesmen, car boot traders and a significant number of traffic wardens.'

'Kyle's an artist,' I lied.

'Oh, really, what kind?'

'A piss artist,' Harry chuckled.

'Ha, ha,' Alison snorted. 'Your jokes are as old as you are, dear.'

My fingers were itching to wring her scrawny neck, but I held my temper. 'I'll have Holly book a table for six then, shall I?'

'Marvellous,' she concurred, gliding over to Harry to peck him on the cheek. 'I really must dash now, darling; I've a holistic head massage booked.' On her way out, she squeezed Gervaise's arm. 'Until tomorrow, you delightful man.'

Within minutes of her departure, Holly came back. She smiled warmly at Gervaise. 'Did I just see Alison's car?' she enquired.

'You missed her by the skin of your teeth,' I said.

She heaved a grateful sigh. 'Thank heavens for Daisy and her second cups of tea. What did she want?' Her face dropped as Harry told her. 'Oh, bugger fuck. I'd sooner spend the evening with my dentist having root canal.'

Harry raised his hands helplessly. 'It wasn't my idea. Blame Gervaise. She took one look at him and her mind was set.'

I giggled. 'She mistook him for a stripper.'

'Oh, really?' chuckled Holly. 'And what did Gervaise mistake *her* for – a human being?'

'Are you implying that my wife's a monster?' Harry chipped in.

'That would be cruel to monsters,' she said. She looked Gervaise up and down. 'So, she mistook you for a stripper, did she?'

He smiled. 'I found it quite flattering.'

'Oh, I wouldn't be too flattered,' Holly cautioned, nodding towards Harry. 'Take a look at what she married. This is not a woman of taste.'

'Hey, fuck off,' Harry moaned. 'You're not supposed to insult me this close to my birthday.'

'In that case we'd better leave,' she told Gervaise, casting me a sly wink as she hooked her arm through his. 'I wouldn't wait up for him if I were you – as they say in Antarctica: "*He may be gone some time.*"'

I noticed Harry looking troubled as he watched them

go. 'They seem good together,' he observed. 'Do you think she likes him?'

'I think she fancies him,' I said. 'Though God alone knows why. I had no idea that Holly was into primates.'

'On the contrary,' Harry said thoughtfully, 'this guy has a brain instead of an air pocket. He's in a different league to those dick-heads and goofballs she normally dates.'

'Does that bother you?' I asked.

His shrug of indifference seemed a little too quick. 'Why would I give a shit?'

'Because "we love her very much",' I quoted.

'That doesn't mean I'm willing to change her nappies.'

I dearly wanted to probe him further about his feelings for Holly, but I could sense that he was still too depressed about Alison to open up. I went over and put my arm around him. 'Hey, cheer up,' I coaxed. 'No one's making you walk the green mile. It's only a birthday party.'

'I know I'm being an arse,' he said. 'It's just that she's picked a lousy time to play the happy couple.' He made his green eyes wide and appealing. 'Do you really want to cheer me up?'

'Not if it involves my hand and your dick.'

He gave me his most irresistible smile. 'Aw, come on, baby. It'll only take a couple of minutes and it *is* my birthday tomorrow.'

What could I do? I adored him too much to deny him his early present. With a sigh of resignation, I let him lead me into the stockroom.

Once inside, he hurriedly tore down his zipper and released his stretching penis. Then, lifting my hand, he curled it around the thickening shaft and straightaway his breath groaned out of him as his face took on a rapt expression. Then, as blood surged into his veins, bringing strength and rigidity to the expanding column of flesh, he grasped my shoulders as if his whole life depended on what I did next.

I loved his cock: I loved the rudeness of its rapid response to my touch, its absolute masculinity and its urgent pulsing energy; I loved its solid smoothness, its heat, its hardness, and the sheer majesty of it. My caress adored his cock; my palm and the pads of my fingers washed and embraced it like a sacred object. I tickled his glans with my fingertips and gently trailed my nails down its length. I cupped and stroked his heavy balls. And, all the time, I watched his features contorting with ecstasy, relishing the sounds of his horny moans and his frantic gasps for breath. Slowly and deliberately, I began to slide my hand up and down.

'Oh yes,' he sighed, thrusting his hips back and forth. 'You merciful angel.'

His excitement was arousing me. I could feel cramps of hunger in my groin and my pussy contracting, squeezing moisture into my pants.

Harry read the longing in my face and reacted to it swiftly. Driving the side of his hand between my thighs, he sawed back and forth, abrading the folds of my sex with the nylon of my panties. Then he clutched my arse to steady me as my legs began to buckle.

'Oh no, Harry,' I moaned, 'not again.'

'You know you want to,' he whispered. 'Why hold this hot, throbbing cock in your hand when you can have it inside you? Come on, baby, slide your knickers down.'

But just as I was about to capitulate, I heard someone shout, 'Where is everyone?'

Alison's voice sloshed over us like a bucket of ice-cold water. We both uttered 'shit' and scrabbled to straighten our clothes.

'Harry! Where are you?' Her voice was getting nearer by the second.

As soon as he'd fastened the button of his waistband, I thrust a box into his hands to conceal the lingering bulge of his erection. 'We're in here, Alison!' I shouted, grabbing an item out of the box.

The door flew open and there she was. Her face seemed strangely frozen as if she didn't quite know what to do with it.

'Did you forget something?' I asked innocently.

'My pashmina,' she murmured, looking at Harry, at me, at the box. 'What are you doing?'

'We're trying to find some Hungarian head-dresses.' I made my voice sound matter-of-fact, as if hunting for such items was a daily occurrence.

Alison looked suspiciously at the object in my hand – a matador's hat. 'Do they fight bulls in Hungary now?'

Harry feigned wry amusement. 'I wish they did. We've found three of these so far.'

Once more, her glassy stare examined all the evidence, but she could find no fault with our story. 'By the way, darling, when I was in your office I noticed an urgent e-mail on your computer.'

'I'd better go and read it,' Harry said. When he put down the box, I didn't dare to look at his crotch in case Alison observed my furtive glance.

After he'd gone, I followed her out of the stockroom and picked up the shawl that she'd left on the chair. 'This is beautiful,' I said, handing it to her.

'I'm not usually this careless with my possessions,' she said. 'I tend to hang on tightly to the things that I own.' She draped the pashmina around her narrow shoulders. 'Do you know something, darling, for a silly little moment I thought that you and Harry – well, I'm sure that you can guess what I thought.'

'That we were screwing in the stockroom?' I gave a staccato laugh. 'That only happens in porn mags.'

'I don't read those kind of magazines,' she said, sliding her hand across my desk to pick up my dagger-shaped letter-opener. Then her lips curled into a chilly smile. 'But I'm fairly certain of what I'd do if, God forbid, I should ever find Harry in a compromising situation with another woman. Can you guess what I'd do, Selina?' She pointed the letter opener at me.

I forced myself to grin. 'Open a letter?'

Alison didn't allow herself even the semblance of a smile. 'I'd stab the bitch,' she said.

11

Bearing in mind Alison's threat, I sat down with Kyle at the opposite end of the table to Harry and focused my attention on my bogus boyfriend. To his credit, Kyle looked great; his casual slacks and Ben Sherman pullover were just right for the occasion; his dark brown hair was beautifully groomed and his pretty-boy looks were drawing admiring glances from both males and females alike. On the downside, his acting was over the top and he was hamming it up by being far too affectionate towards me.

Initially attracted by his looks, Alison's interest in him quickly waned after he fielded a couple of her questions with non-committal grunts and my heart sank when I saw her looking at Gervaise with an I-told-you-so expression.

Holly, wearing hair extensions, looked especially pretty, but she seemed uncomfortable sitting next to Harry who had angled his body away from her. She had her back turned to him and the pair of them looked like bookends. I'd heard them squabbling earlier that day but I was surprised that they hadn't made up yet.

Alison, chic in lilac trousers and purple boob tube, was poring over the menu. 'I don't suppose they've even heard of tofu in here,' she complained.

'It's a bloody steakhouse,' Harry growled.

'Isn't tofu a martial art?' queried Kyle.

'That's kung fu,' giggled Holly.

'So what's tofu?'

'Designer lard,' she said.

'It's bean curd actually,' sniffed Alison. She handed her menu to Harry. 'I can't see without my glasses. What is there for vegetarians?'

'They do cod,' I pointed out.

Alison looked at me as if I'd suggested baby seal. 'Oh absolutely not. I can't eat anything with a face.'

'Not even Mr Potato Head?' chuckled Holly.

'I don't understand veggies,' muttered Kyle. 'If God didn't want us to eat animals, he wouldn't have made them out of meat! They'd taste like cabbage and fucking cabbage would taste like bacon.'

'What about squid rings?' suggested Gervaise. 'Does a squid have a face?'

'No fish, no poultry, no meat, not even that anaemic quorn shit that pretends to be meat,' Harry reeled off sourly. 'This is a woman who'd turn down a carrot if it happened to be shaped like a penis.'

'Ah, but would she turn down a penis if it happened to be shaped like a carrot?' Kyle wondered laughing.

Gervaise glanced at me. 'Does he have a personal reason for asking?'

I giggled. 'No, he doesn't.'

Alison ordered vegetables and the rest of us ordered steaks. Kyle embarrassed me by offering to cut mine up. 'Let me do that for you, sweetheart.'

'I can manage,' I hissed, kicking him under the table.

'Oh, isn't that sweet,' Alison declared, nudging Harry. 'Why don't you attend to me like that any more?'

'Because I fuckin' hate you,' he grunted into his glass. He'd been drinking steadily since we'd arrived.

Alison stretched her lips into a grotesque imitation of a smile. 'He doesn't mean it,' she reassured us. 'He's just grouchy through lack of sleep. I don't know what's wrong with him. He was tossing and turning again last night.'

'He needs to cut out the tossing and just do the turning,' sniggered Kyle.

'This isn't Club 18–30,' Alison chided him haughtily. She popped a solitary pea into her mouth and chewed on it like a piece of steak.

'Have a bite of my rump,' Kyle offered cryptically.

She looked down her nose at the lump of red meat on the fork he was proffering. 'No thank you.'

'Kiss my arse then,' he cussed beneath his breath. Alison ate another pea.

The cross-table conversation gave way to chatting in pairs and I was forced to listen to Kyle droning on and on about his hobby of mountain biking, a subject he managed to make even duller through a total lack of animation when he talked. I realised that his good looks had quickly paled into insignificance beside the glow of Harry's charm and the sparkle of Gervaise's ebullient magnetism.

I found my eyes constantly drifting towards Holly and Gervaise and my ears straining to hear what they were saying. Evidently, something Gervaise had said was making Holly laugh like a drain and, feeling envious of her, I demanded to be let in on the joke.

'It was hilarious,' she tooted, and went on to tell us how she'd dropped a meatball on to the floor of the Italian restaurant they'd dined at last night. To spare her blushes, Gervaise had booted it under a neighbouring table where it had become kebabed upon the stiletto heel of a woman diner who'd later carried it on to the dance floor.

'Then halfway through 'Unchained Melody' it fell off and her partner trod on it,' Holly chortled. 'We were pissing ourselves.'

'That's so unhygienic,' Alison decried.

'We weren't literally pissing ourselves,' Holly said.

Alison rolled her eyes. 'I meant leaving food on the floor.' She looked sternly at Gervaise. 'You shouldn't have kicked that meatball.'

'That's right,' agreed Harry, slurring his words. 'If the poor little sod had wanted to be kicked, skewered and trodden on, you should have brought it to me and I'd have put it in my ball sac.'

'Harry, stop talking nonsense!' Alison scolded. 'You're making a monkey out of yourself.'

'I wish I *was* a monkey,' he sighed. 'If only you women hadn't nagged us down from the trees, we'd still be swinging from the branches without a care in the world.'

'If you think it was *our* idea to walk upright,' I challenged him, 'you should try giving birth sometime.'

'Of course it was a woman's idea,' Gervaise asserted. 'She made man walk on his hind legs so he could carry her bloody shopping.'

'The bitches,' moaned Kyle. 'We'd still be happily licking our dicks if they'd left us on all fours.'

'Oh, for goodness sake,' whined Alison. 'Must we drag this conversation into the gutter?' She turned to Gervaise and spoke to him in stilted schoolgirl French.

Hearing him answer in his native tongue, I was struck by how sexy his voice was and for the first time found myself wondering what he might look like without his beard. I hadn't realised how closely I was watching him until he flicked his eyes to my face and locked-on to my gaze. I pretended to be curious. 'Could we have a translation?'

'Alison was asking about Matt,' he explained. 'She wanted to know if I loved him.'

Alison tittered. 'That wretched verb *aimer*! Don't be a tease, darling, you know perfectly well what I meant.'

He smiled. 'But of course.'

'*Je t'aime,*' announced Holly, clutching his arm.

'Bloody liar,' muttered Harry.

'Maybe so,' she agreed, 'but it's the only French I know.'

'*Voulez-vous couchez avec moi?*' enquired Kyle of no one in particular.

'Only if I can be the girl,' Harry quipped.

After the waiter had cleared the table, a birthday cake with a sparkler on top was brought in and Harry shrank in his seat, cringing, as we all sang 'Happy Birthday'.

'Who's daft idea was this?' he groaned.

'Mine,' chirruped Alison. 'I'm sorry it's Thomas the Tank Engine but that's all they had left at the supermarket.' She handed him a present. 'Happy birthday, darling.'

Harry opened the box. 'It's a choke chain,' he announced.

Alison scowled at him. 'It's an identity bracelet.'

He removed the chunky silver bracelet and looked at it without enthusiasm. 'Don't we know who I am yet?'

'There's an inscription,' Alison said.

Harry turned it over and squinted at the back. 'Made in Taiwan.'

Holly snatched it from him. 'To dearest Harry with love from Alison,' she read. 'But why does it say "Harold" on the front? I thought you were christened Harry.'

'Oh, he was,' Alison confirmed. 'But Harold sounds so much more refined, don't you think?'

'Then why not find a refined bloke called Harold and give it to him?' Harry suggested. He was getting drunker by the minute and his increasing antagonism towards his wife was worrying me. In this mood, he was capable of demanding a divorce in front of everyone and, although I didn't like Alison, she didn't deserve to be ditched in public.

Perhaps sensing her danger, she rose to her feet. 'I'm going to powder my nose.'

Harry watched her retreat with a sneer on his face. 'I wish she'd use gunpowder and then take up smoking,' he growled. 'If she wasn't here, I'd be getting birthday snogs off my two best girls by now.' He swung his arm around Holly's neck and pulled her towards him. 'Give us a kiss, babe.'

Holly went to peck his cheek but he twisted his head and their mouths met. For a fleeting second, I saw the tenderest look appear on Harry's face, but Holly recoiled as if his lips had stung her.

Kyle grabbed my hand possessively. 'You're not kissing *my* girl,' he cautioned Harry, 'so don't even think about it.' *Excellent! Give the boy an Oscar.*

I noticed Gervaise looking at Kyle's hand clasping mine. Was he persuaded, I wondered. Had Kyle done enough to convince him that, with such a devoted boyfriend, I couldn't possibly be serious about Matt? I felt confident enough to meet his penetrating gaze head-on. But then I wished I hadn't when his amazing blue eyes lasered into mine like a twin-barrelled Martian heat ray. I saw the raven dark wings of his eyebrows lift but I couldn't interpret the question they posed. Was he asking me how I really felt about Kyle? I was so sure that his thoughts lay somewhere within this vicinity that it came as an absolute shock when I saw his eyes move to my mouth in a flagrant signal of sexual attraction. So *this* was his unspoken question! I'd been so wide of the mark that my brain must have been vacationing on a different planet.

I was furious. How dared he have the nerve to try and flirt with me! A hot flush griddled my cheeks as I shot him an angry glare. But he merely smiled and looked away.

Holly plucked at his sleeve. 'Do you mind if we leave

now?' She'd come over pale and seemed a bit twitchy. 'I'm getting a headache.'

'Here comes mine,' murmured Harry as Alison returned to the table.

'Oh, you're not going, are you?' she wailed, seeing Gervaise helping Holly to her feet.

'Holly's not feeling too well,' he explained. 'I'm taking her home.'

'But the night is still young,' she protested.

'Then, by all means, enjoy it,' he said, taking out his wallet.

Alison flapped her hands. 'Put that away. This is my treat, darling. Are you sure I can't persuade you to stay? I'm sure that Holly wouldn't mind going home in a taxi.'

Gervaise narrowed his eyes. 'I wouldn't hear of it. But thank you for a pleasant evening.'

When they'd said their goodbyes and were gone, Alison heaved a wistful sigh. 'He's such a gentleman and so charming. Why don't they make men like that in England?'

'They don't have sufficient raw materials,' I said. 'A man that big takes a lot of constructing.'

'I was referring to his charisma.'

'I didn't notice he had any.' It wasn't true. For now that he was gone, there seemed a massive void at the table and it surprised me how keenly I was feeling his absence.

'I can't imagine what he sees in Holly,' Alison declared.

'What do you mean?' I challenged her.

'Darling, you know what I mean. He's got so much going for him, whereas she . . . well, she's just a stripper.'

'There's nothing wrong with stripping,' Kyle protested. 'Or with Holly for that matter – she's a peach.'

Alison gave a snort of derision. 'A trifle over-ripe, I'd have said.'

Annoyed, I defended Holly. 'She doesn't have to be a stripper; she has the brains to do almost anything. I don't know what we'd do without her in the office. I just wish that we could pay her more so she could give up stripping altogether.'

'But it's the perfect career for an Essex girl,' sniffed Alison. 'Taking their clothes off comes naturally to them.'

'Shut up,' Harry rumbled. 'That's enough.'

But Alison was into her stride. 'Why is an Essex girl like a great white shark? They both have big mouths and are happy to swallow seamen.' She hooted with laughter but the rest of us stayed silent.

'Are you going to shut up or do you want me to shove this empty bottle down your throat?' Harry warned.

'There's no need to upset yourself, my darling,' Alison said. 'You're not still carrying a torch for her, are you?'

Harry lifted his glass unsteadily and took a long swill of his drink. Then he wiped his mouth with the back of his hand and set down his glass. 'I should have married her,' he stated. 'I like a girl who strips to the buff and swallows my semen. When was the last time *you* did that, Alison? The answer is "never", isn't it?'

'Harry, you don't know what you're saying. You're drunk.'

He looked at her hatefully. 'Drunk or sober, I've never been more sure about anything. Alison, I want a divorce.'

I'd known it was coming and yet still it had shocked me to hear Harry telling his wife that their marriage was over. I felt a tiny ache of regret that he hadn't done it years ago, but otherwise strangely numb inside as Kyle drove me home.

Outside my house, I paid him for his evening's work. 'You did well,' I told him.

He looked at me hopefully. 'Do you want anything extra?'

I shook my head. 'No thanks.'

'What about Saturday?' he asked.

'Saturday?' I echoed. 'What about it?'

'I'm having a house-warming party. Holly's coming and I expect she'll bring Gervaise. It'll look strange if you're not there.'

I decided to be honest with him. 'I can't afford you, Kyle. Masquerade's in trouble and I need every penny I can get. I'll just have to pretend to be ill or something.'

He considered me a moment and then shrugged. 'Come anyway,' he said. 'If you lend me a hand with the food, I'll give you a cuddle now and then just to keep up appearances. What do you say?'

'I'll think about it,' I said, getting out the car. 'I'll let you know.'

When I saw Matt's car, which Gervaise had borrowed, parked on the driveway, I assumed that he'd dropped Holly off and come home alone. But when I entered the darkened house and began to climb the stairs, I heard some distinctly feminine sounds: erotic moans and whimpers that seemed to be emanating from Gervaise's bedroom.

His door was slightly ajar and I crept up to it like a burglar, tip-toeing on the balls of my feet, then stopped outside to listen. I was intrigued by the noises that Holly was making: the panting, the squealing, the breathless gasps. Her rapturous sounds were like siren calls to my ears.

I knew that I should walk on, go to bed, put my head under the pillow until they'd finished, but something compelled me to stay where I was. The longer I stood there, holding my breath, the stronger became the voyeuristic urge to put my head around the door and take a peek at what they were doing.

I convinced myself that, as Holly's friend, I ought, in any case, to see if she needed anything before I went to bed, such as a nightdress or make-up remover. I wasn't sure if she'd regard it as a plausible excuse to walk in on them, but I armed myself with it anyway and, taking a deep breath, fixed a friendly smile on my face and peered around the door.

In the dim light of the low wattage bedside lamp, I saw a sight that transfixed me. Gervaise was standing naked, with his back to me, at the foot of the bed, but all I could see of Holly were the tips of her toes peeping over his shoulders and a single flailing arm.

I hardly noticed what he was doing to her because I was staring so hard at him, my mind blown completely away by the sheer magnificence of his body. It was Herculean, a mighty physique that radiated strength and virile masculinity. This was no posing, muscle-bound freak with overblown biceps; this was Mother Nature's concept of male beauty and no amount of hours in the gym could emulate a body like this. He was the real thing and, as I looked at him, my reverent gaze delighted in the glorious breadth of his shoulders, the muscles that rippled in his flanks like a stallion's and the sculpted sinews of his powerful legs. Viewed from the rear, he was Superman, Batman, He-man, Ben Hur, Spartacus, and all seven of the Magnificent Seven.

It took another of Holly's squeals to snap me out my trance and wake me up to the fact that Gervaise wasn't displaying his body for my benefit or seeking my aesthetic appreciation. He didn't even know I was there.

I felt like a Peeping Tom but I couldn't withdraw. Instead, I became mesmerised by the clockwork motion of his hips. Their sliding thrusts seemed to call to my heart, making it beat to the same rhythm, making it skip with every sudden rotation of his pelvis. Watching his style, I could imagine how it must feel: the slow, slick movements of his cock, punctuated by twisting gyrations that must have stirred her insides like miniature tornadoes.

Holly threshed ecstatically as he lengthened his strokes. I could hear the slap of her flesh and her dog-like panting as the clenching, driving muscles of his arse drove his prick back and forth, again and again. There seemed no limit to his strength.

I could feel my whole body growing weak as I watched him. Then a fever-flush of lust crept over my skin as desire clutched my loins and my pussy contracted like a sponge being wrung. Wetness oozed into my panties and I had to bite on my knuckle to stifle a gasp.

Faster now, the impelling force of his pounding haunches made Holly's legs trampoline up and down on his chest. He grabbed her ankles and, turning his head to one side, pushed the slender columns of her legs apart. With his biblical black beard, his eyes squeezed closed and the strain of concentration on his face, he looked like Samson.

As I stood there watching the powerful jackhammer jerking of his hips, I yearned to move further into the bedroom for a better view, but I couldn't take the risk of being seen. So I summoned up my memories of his manhood and, in my mind's eye, added the long thick cock that had almost choked me to his broad, strong back and rutting rump. Then, with my eyes fixed firmly on his clenching bronzed buttocks, I imagined how his cock would feel inside me, shafting me, filling me, stretching me, making me raw with its merciless thrusts and remorseless friction.

I was with Holly in spirit, silently echoing her gasping cries, matching her body bucks; arms thrashing, head tossing. And when she froze, so did I. When her fingers clawed at the sheets, mine clawed at my dress. I shared her twitching orgasm and matched her sated groan with a soundless sigh.

Gervaise, still rampant, spread his legs wide and I could see his balls swinging as he continued his vigorous jabbing. But now he was jerking and jolting and making savage grunting noises in his throat. Then, suddenly, his head arced around his neck, his balls lifted, and he cannoned home his climax, using every muscle in his body.

I felt drained as I crept out, my limbs so heavy that I had to drag myself to my room. I flopped on to my bed, too exhausted even to undress, and went straight to sleep.

In the morning, I was woken up by the sound of talking on the landing. I crawled down to the end of my bed to listen. Hearing the rich, deep tones of Gervaise's voice, my stomach lurched and I felt sick with shame.

'I hope we didn't disturb you last night.'

Matt's voice answered. 'I didn't hear a thing. I remember going to bed with a bottle of whisky, but that's about it.'

'You won't find a job at the bottom of a bottle,' Gervaise told him.

'Give me a break,' Matt said. 'Do you know what it's like to be sitting on the scrap heap at my age?'

Holly's voice chimed in. 'I don't suppose it helps with Miranda being away.'

Somebody yawned. 'You look knackered,' Matt said (presumably to Gervaise). 'I can drop Holly off if you like. I'm going down to the Job Centre, so I'll need the car anyway.'

'That'll give me plenty of time to get changed for work,' Holly said. I heard the smack of a hand on bare flesh. 'You go back to sleep, lover boy. I'll give you a ring.'

Gervaise murmured something and then I heard a muted sound that might have been a kiss.

I glanced at the alarm clock and calculated that I could afford to stay another half-hour in bed in order to avoid him. I didn't want him to see the guilt that must be written all over my face.

Laying back, I tried not to think about what I'd seen last night, but the image of his fabulous body kept haunting me, luring my finger to the insistent little throb that was niggling my pussy. Before I knew it, my hand was inside my panties and I was pleasuring myself; thinking of his head between my legs; imagining his coarse black beard scratching my inner thighs; scraping my fanny; scouring my tender clit. I came quickly, fiercely, biting into my pillow. *Shit!*

This was getting ridiculous. First I had spied on him and now I was fantasising about him. I gave myself a mental shake. *You must be fucking joking!* This is Bluto, Guy the gorilla, bloody Chewbacca, for God's sake.

Having decided that the absurd inclinations of my libido had absolutely nothing to do with what was going on in my head, I felt a little better about myself. After all, if someone as loathsome as Luca Verdici could get me hot, then why not Gervaise? At least he had pretty eyes and a terrific ... *Oh no you don't!* I leapt out of bed. It was time for a cold shower.

As I walked quickly past Gervaise's door, I hoped he'd burnt himself out and would be sleeping like a baby for at least a couple of hours. With any luck, I'd be long gone before he woke up.

Inside the bathroom, I stripped off the clothes I'd been wearing all night and tossed them into the laundry, then

I showered in tepid water because someone had used up the hot. I didn't notice until I emerged, dripping wet, that all the bath towels were missing. Cursing, I wrapped the tiny hand towel around me and opened the door, intending to make a bolt for the airing cupboard. But instead I shrieked with shock when Gervaise tumbled in, apparently just about to knock. He spilled me backwards on to the toilet seat and I just managed to catch my towel before it burst open.

'Good morning, Sugarlips,' he chuckled. 'I heard you showering and I thought you might need this.' He lifted the bath towel he was holding. 'Me and Holly used the others.'

I couldn't look at his face so I stared at the dark sprawl of hair in between the lapels of his dressing gown. 'You used all the hot water too,' I grumbled.

'We were dirty,' he said.

I rose and made a grab for the towel but he flicked it behind him. 'On second thoughts,' he demurred, 'that skimpy little thing kind of suits you.'

'I'm not in the mood to play games,' I snapped. 'Just give me the bloody towel. And there's no need to look so pleased with yourself.'

'I had a very pleasing night,' he said. 'But you know that, don't you?'

I folded my arms around me. 'What do you mean?'

'Don't act the innocent.' He grabbed my chin and made me look into his eyes. They were deadly serious. 'I saw your reflection in the dressing-table mirror last night. I didn't realise you had voyeuristic tendencies, Selina. Did you get off on watching us?'

I gulped. 'It was idle curiosity,' I said. 'She was making so much noise I thought you were killing her.'

'It took you long enough to decide that I wasn't,' he pointed out.

I sidled towards the doorway but he stepped back, blocking it. 'Look, I'm sorry I intruded on your privacy,' I apologised. 'Could I have the towel please?'

'You know, it doesn't seem fair,' he said, running a hand through his thick black hair. 'You've had my cock in your mouth and you've seen me buck-naked. Don't you think it's time we evened up the score a little?' He hooked a lazy finger into the top of my towel.

'Get out of my way,' I demanded, pushing against his chest. It should have been a futile gesture, like trying to move an oak tree but, to my surprise, he yielded a step. Experimentally, I pushed him again. This time he tumbled back as if I'd hit him with a battering ram. Pretending to fall through the doorway, he grabbed my towel as if trying to save himself and yanked it from my body.

'You bastard!' I screamed, covering myself with my arms and hands.

'Go ahead and hit me,' he goaded. 'I'd like to see more of those breasts.'

Too outraged to speak, I bulldozed past him and legged it down the hall with my hands clamped over my buttocks.

'Hey, Sugarlips!' he shouted. 'Nice arse!'

12

By the time I'd dressed and made up my face, I'd calmed down a little. Under the circumstances, Gervaise could have done a lot worse than embarrass me and at least I had my virtue, if not my dignity, still intact. He'd let me off lightly considering that the violation of his eyes had lasted mere seconds whereas I had stood for minutes on end ogling his naked body and, worse still, judging his sexual prowess. I couldn't help wondering if his performance had been in any way enhanced by his knowledge of my presence, and it irked me to think that he might actually have enjoyed being watched.

I remembered his Samson-like pose – had he done that to impress me? But, after a couple minutes of trying to calculate the angle of his head in relation to Miranda's dressing table mirror, I gave up and accepted the pose at face value. I could hardly blame him for showing himself off to an audience as appreciative as I'd been.

My stomach rumbled a message to my brain: *stop thinking about Gervaise and bloody feed me!* I hadn't realised how ravenous I was.

Once again, I skipped past his bedroom door, but this time, unconcerned. I didn't care if he was in there or not. For now that he'd behaved almost as badly as I had, I felt acquitted of my guilt.

I was nonetheless relieved when I saw that he wasn't downstairs. In the kitchen, I grabbed a saucepan and some oats and started making porridge. He wandered in as it was thickening, wearing jeans and a T-shirt with the message 'Grrrr' distortedly stretched across the broad expanse of his chest.

'Oh, is this what they're wearing in Paris this season?' I commented sarcastically.

'I'm out of clean clothes,' he replied, sitting down. 'Any chance of doing my laundry?'

Fucking cheek! 'None at all after that execrable stunt you pulled earlier,' I seethed.

He looked at me narrowly. 'You don't think you deserved it?'

My brain had turned as lumpy as the porridge had become and I didn't know what to say. He let me off the hook by asking if he could share my breakfast. 'I don't care what it is, I'm starving,' he said. 'I must have burnt up a lot of calories last night.'

I looked glumly into the saucepan whose contents now resembled badly mixed wallpaper paste. 'You can have it all,' I offered generously. 'I'm not really hungry.'

As I fetched a bowl from the cupboard, I felt his eyes on me and got the unpleasant feeling that he was revisiting my naked arse. I swung round to confront him but he deflected me with a question:

'How did things go at the restaurant after we left?'

'You missed all the fireworks,' I told him. 'Harry asked Alison for a divorce.'

'I can't say I'm surprised,' he said. 'I don't know those two but it looked like the Marriage from Hell. I suppose this'll complicate things for you.'

'Huh?' I was trying to make the wretched porridge let go of the spoon.

'Harry ... Matt ... Kyle,' he went on. 'Do you know which one you want? Maybe it's all three at the same time; how would I know?'

I plonked the laden bowl in front of him. 'Is there

something wrong with your memory? You met my boy-friend last night.'

His blue eyes stabbed into mine. 'I met a man who didn't seem remotely your type,' he said. When I shrugged, he dug his spoon into the mound of porridge and let it stand up by itself. 'Selina, what the fuck is this?'

'What the fuck does it look like?'

He scratched his head. 'I don't know – a face pack?'

'Look, if you're going to be picky, don't eat it,' I snapped.

'Picky?' he echoed incredulously. 'Frankly, I've seen spunk that looks more appetising.'

'Your own, no doubt,' I retorted.

He put his head to one side to consider me. 'Either you can't cook or your mind's on other things. Do you know what I think? I think you can't stop thinking about my arse.' He gave his eyebrows a double lift.

'Don't flatter yourself,' I said loftily. 'Frankly, I've seen more appetising arses on rhinos.'

He shook his head. 'You can't hurt me that way. We rhinos have bloody thick skins.'

I spun away to conceal a giggle. 'Why don't I get you something else?' I opened the fridge and removed an egg. 'How about this?'

He looked at it like I was holding a grenade. 'You'd better put that down before it goes off in your hand,' he cautioned.

I tossed the egg from palm to palm. 'Are you suggesting that I can't cook an egg?'

'I'm suggesting that I'm too young to die of salmonella poisoning.'

It was an insult too far and, without even thinking about it, I smacked the egg down on his head just as Matt was walking in.

'What's going on here?' he asked.

Plucking eggshell from his hair, Gervaise squinted at him. 'Just don't ask for your eggs over easy.' Then he pursed his lips as a snail trail of yolk slid down the centre of his nose.

Matt looked at me askance, but I was laughing so hard that I could hardly breathe.

Gervaise stood up. 'If you're looking for breakfast, I wouldn't eat here,' he advised Matt. 'The food's lousy and the service would make a Turkish prison seem like the Waldorf.' He removed himself from the table with exaggerated dignity. 'I'm going to wash my hair.'

Still laughing as I watched him go, I realised, quite suddenly, that I liked him.

Matt smiled. 'What did he do to deserve that?'

'He insulted my porridge,' I said.

'What – this?' His face screwed up as he lifted the bowl and examined its glutinous contents. 'I hate to say it but he may have a point.'

I snatched the bowl from him. 'Are you looking for an egg shampoo yourself?'

'You're in a pissy mood today,' he observed. 'Did their shagging keep you awake last night?'

I went over to the sink and took a scouring pad to the gunk that had super-glued itself to the bottom of the saucepan. 'No, but they used up all the hot water.'

For a while, he watched me rubbing vigorously. 'That's a saucy little shimmy,' he said. 'Are you deliberately making your tits and arse shake?'

A peculiar chill came over me. 'No, I'm scrubbing a saucepan,' I answered flatly.

He came up behind me and ran his hands over the bare skin of my arms, giving me gooseflesh, but not from excitement. It shocked me how wary I'd become of him since he'd slapped me. 'Holly told me that she's taking

Gervaise to a party on Saturday night,' he murmured softly. 'We'll have the place to ourselves.'

I stopped scrubbing and stared into the soapy water. 'Matt, I think we should forget about us. I'm not really sure what I want any more.'

'What are you talking about?' he said, sliding his arms around my waist and nuzzling his groin into my butt. 'You can't imagine what I'm planning to do to you,' he breathed into my ear. One of his hands slid to my crotch and the other moved up to my breasts.

'That's just it,' I croaked. 'Your insinuations are starting to scare me. You keep saying you want more than you get from Miranda but you don't say what.'

The hand at my breast started squeezing, the one at my crotch began to rub. 'I'm going to fuck you like the devil,' he purred. 'I'm going to do dirty, filthy things until you scream your fucking head off. But you'll love it.'

His hands were undeniably persuasive, but I didn't like the content of his words. 'I'm not like that, Matt. You've got me all wrong.'

'We'll see if I'm right on Saturday.'

I winced as his fingers bit into my breast. 'But I . . . I'm going to that party myself,' I stammered.

'Like hell you are.' He wrenched me round to face him and, driving his tongue between my teeth, savagely kissed me.

He was still kissing me when Gervaise walked in. I was pinned against the sink with his tongue so far down my throat that my garbled cries of warning were as ineffectual as the frantic beating of my hands. I could do nothing but stare with bolting eyes as Gervaise strode over and clamped a heavy hand on his shoulder.

'Enjoying yourselves?' he snarled, yanking Matt off me and spinning him across the room. He glowered at us both. 'So this is what happens when I leave the two of you alone.'

'Damn it, I'm only a man!' Matt cried. 'The seductive little bitch keeps coming on to me. She refuses to leave me alone.'

I couldn't believe his treachery. 'That's not true,' I protested.

'Shut up,' Gervaise growled. 'I've seen what you do to men. You wear your tight little tops, your skimpy little skirts, that "fuck me" look in your eyes. I get the hots for you myself. There are names for women like you, but I dare say you've heard them all.'

Angry tears smarted at the back of my eyes. 'That's not fair. You're a bloody chauvinist.'

'Admit it, Selina,' Matt said. 'You've been teasing my prick since the day Miranda left. Look at her, Gervaise: that face, that fucking hair. She's a whole damn bowlful of lush forbidden fruit. Show me a man who wouldn't be tempted and I'll show you a faggot. All I've done is kiss her – and that's the truth.'

Gervaise glared at him with nostrils flared. 'It didn't look like kissing to me; it looked like you were performing a tonsillectomy.'

Matt eyed him fearfully. 'You can't tell Miranda about this. It'll break her heart.'

'Is it Miranda you're worried about? Or are you frightened of losing your meal ticket and the roof over your head? You had the cake and the icing, but you wanted the little cherry on the top. I call that greedy.'

'Hey, hold it a minute,' I objected. 'I'm no one's little cherry!'

'Are you *still* here?' Gervaise hurled at me. 'Get out. Go to work. This is man talk.'

'Correction – this is ape-man talk,' I returned. 'You've

put your cretinous jutting foreheads together and decided to blame the one with the tits. Well, fuck you both!' I stormed out with my head in the air, realised I'd forgotten my handbag, slunk back, retrieved it, and then stormed out again.

'Holly!' I hollered. 'The shit's hit the fan!' I found her sitting at Harry's desk.

She looked up and I saw concern in her eyes. 'Harry's put in a no-show. I'm worried, Selina, it just isn't like him.'

I sat down. 'Harry's shit has hit the fan as well,' I revealed. 'It happened after you left last night. He told Alison he wanted a divorce.'

She made me tell her word-for-word what had been said and, as she listened, her expression went through as many changes as a slide show. 'I can't believe he did it,' she uttered at length. 'She'll take him for every penny. He'll lose his home and his daughter; he might even lose Masquerade.'

'I don't think she can touch his livelihood,' I said. 'How else can he pay her maintenance?'

'But why now?' she wondered. 'If he was always going to leave her then why didn't he do it when you asked him to?'

I'd already figured that out. 'Because it was me doing the asking and not you.'

She bit her lip. 'Let's not talk about Harry. What were you going to tell me when you came in?'

I let my shoulders slump and pulled a dismal face. 'Gervaise caught Matt kissing me and went apeshit,' I explained. 'Matt played the innocent victim and made out that I'd thrown myself at him.'

'And had you?' she asked.

'Not this time,' I said. 'The truth is, Holly, I've gone

right off him. You were right when you said I was playing with fire. He's got these weird ideas and he's starting to scare me. I just want things back to the way they were.'

She lit a cigarette. 'Did you tell him this?'

'I tried to,' I stressed. 'But he shut me up with a kiss that wasn't a kiss: his mouth was raping my lips. God knows what he might have done if . . .'

'If Gervaise hadn't been there?' she surmised with a puff of smoke. 'I guess that makes him the good guy now. You won't want him out of the way any more.'

I gave my head a disbelieving shake. 'It seems crazy after all the trouble we've been to. But you're right – I need him firmly *in* the way, at least until Matt gets the message. I'm sorry to piss you about. You really like him, don't you?'

She nodded. 'Not only do I like him but he's the best bloody shag I've had in ages.'

Remembering what I'd seen, I had the grace to lower my eyes. 'Don't give him up on my account.'

She laughed. 'What's to give up? He's just amusing himself and so am I; we have a date booked for Saturday but, after that, I'll end it.'

I felt a queer sense of relief come over me. It must have shown on my face because Holly looked at me curiously. 'You're not starting to fancy him yourself, are you?'

'Gervaise?' I exclaimed. 'That's absurd! You know I'm beard-o-phobic.'

'All the same,' she muttered. 'Could be that your yin is not entirely in agreement with your yang about this.'

'Balls,' I said, castrating the conversation.

Holly let it go and revived the topic of Harry. 'He's picked a bad day not to come in. We're both out this afternoon.'

'We can't leave the office unmanned,' I said. 'We'll have to cancel our trip to Stratton's.' I was secretly glad of an excuse not to go through with the crazy scheme she'd devised to squeeze money out of Peter Stratton.

'Do you *want* to fuck Luca Verdici?' she asked me bluntly.

I shuddered and shook my head. 'I'd sooner carpet-munch Alison.'

'I'll ring Jack then, shall I?'

I pulled a face. 'Have you forgotten what happened the last time we left Jack in charge? He mixed up those two addresses and we ended up sending the big-booba-gram to the gay club and the Rocky-Horrorgram to the rugby club. The gays were furious, but luckily the rugby boys were too pissed to see past the suspenders and we only had one complaint.'

'I remember,' Holly replied, laughing. 'And even that was a request that in future could we please supply a woman with bigger tits and a smaller moustache.'

I chuckled. 'If Jack cocks up again, I'll dispatch him to one of those clubs in his pea costume. I wish you'd seen him in it, Holly. I haven't been able to look at a Brussels sprout since.'

'He deserves another chance just for having the nerve to wear the thing,' she said. 'I'll call him.'

Leaving Holly in charge of Masquerade Unmasked, I picked up my mail and took it to my office. It included two cheques that came to a total of £140 and two bills that came to a total of £144. It was a disappointing start to a day that went steadily downhill and then crashed at the bottom with a cancelled order. Holly came in at half past three carrying a bundle of clothes in her arms.

'Jack'll be here soon,' she said. 'We may as well start getting ready.'

But when I saw what she held, my mouth plopped open. 'You can't be serious, Holly!'

'I certainly am,' she insisted, dividing up the clothes. 'You're going to be Madam Whiplash and I'm going to be your nubile sex slave.'

'You said the idea was to dress up as call girls.'

She gave me a cunning smile. 'Trust me, this'll frighten Stratton a whole lot more than a couple of ordinary hookers.'

'We'll never get past the door,' I said.

'Don't worry,' she reassured me. 'I have it all figured out. I happen to know that Bopec Chemicals is one of Stratton Publicity's biggest accounts. So I rang Peter Stratton's PA and pretended to be speaking for their head of publicity. I told her they'd come up with an idea for a new advertising campaign and wanted Peter to look at it personally. I made a point of telling her to expect the unexpected. All we have to do is keep cool and tell them we're from Bopec.'

'I can't wait to see Peter's face,' I said, warming to the idea. 'He'll shit himself when he sees us.'

'Let's hope he shits money,' chuckled Holly.

My outfit was truly outrageous: a full dominatrix ensemble comprising black leather corset, laced at the front; thigh-high, spike-heeled boots attached to the corset by suspenders; tight leather armbands that covered my arms from wrist to elbow; a spiked dog collar and a miniature cat-o'-nine-tails that hung from a chain at my hip. Holly completed the picture by scraping all my hair up into a tall silver cone that added four inches to my height. Then she made up my face to look severe, emphasising my cheekbones with rouge, my eyes with black liner, and my mouth with blood-red lipstick. I didn't recognise myself in the mirror.

'What have you done to me?' I wailed.

'Stop whinging,' she said. 'At least try to sound like Madam Whiplash. How do I look?' She was wearing a black leather bikini, black stilettos, straps around her wrists and ankles, and had a choke chain round her neck with a long leash attached. 'Kinky,' I said, picking up the end of the leash. 'Time for "walkies", bitch.' Yanking on the chain, I dragged her with me into the corridor just as Jack was walking up it.

'Heavens!' he exclaimed. 'Have I blundered into a den of iniquity?'

I strode up to him with my elevated ponytail swinging like a pendulum. 'On your knees before your mistress,' I commanded.

He cowered before me. 'Er . . . should I take my anorak off first?'

Holly tittered. 'Go man the phones, Jack.'

'Yes, of course,' he muttered, trying not to look at the overspilling bulges of my breasts.

I followed him into Harry's office and, as he sat down, unhooked my cat-o'-nine-tails and let the thongs trail over his head. 'I don't want any mistakes, Jack.'

His thin face twitched. 'There won't be any, Miss King.'

'*Mistress* King,' I corrected him, flicking his bald patch.

He gulped. 'Oh, I say. This is awfully exciting.'

Holly handed me my coat. 'Stop tormenting him, Selina. We have to go now.'

But I couldn't resist a final tease. Lifting my foot on to the desk, I seductively stroked my leather-clad calf. 'These boots are dusty, Jack. Want to lick them clean with your tongue?'

He sneaked a peek at my black satin panties and rubbed his lips together. 'I don't quite know what to say.'

'Say goodbye,' I suggested, handing him my keys. 'Don't forget to lock up.'

'You realise you gave him a hard-on,' Holly said as we were getting into her car. 'Those corduroy trousers were definitely straining at the crotch. I reckon he's a closet masochist.'

'I could get used to being a dominatrix,' I said. 'I've always liked making men hot.'

Holly frowned at my naivety. 'I think it's more a question of whether you like making them yelp and bleed,' she counselled.

I smiled to myself. 'In Peter Stratton's case, I think I shall.'

Holly's plan went like clockwork. The receptionist at Stratton's looked strangely at us but rang through to Peter's office to announce the arrival of Bopec's representatives. His personal assistant, Yolander, was dispatched to meet us. She was a tiny Jack Russell terrier of a woman with small, pointed features and no-nonsense eyes.

'Are you sure you're from Bopec?' she yapped as we took off our coats and handed them to her. Her nostrils twitched in a sneer of disapproval as she stared at our costumes.

'Mr Stratton *is* expecting us,' I said, picking up Holly's leash.

Still shaking her head doubtfully, Yolander opened the door to Peter's office and I strutted through like a catwalk model, dragging Holly behind me. He was a short, fat man in his forties with greying combed-over hair pulled back into a stubby ponytail, who was dressed too young for his age in a collar-less designer jacket and turtleneck sweater

He took one look at us and wheezed with laughter. 'This is Mike's idea of a joke, right?'

Holly nudged me and I thwacked my leather whip against the gleaming surface of his vast mahogany desk. 'This is no laughing matter, Mr Stratton.'

He looked at me uncertainly. 'Mike Randell didn't send you?'

'No one sent me,' I said.

His forehead buckled with incomprehension. 'I don't get it.'

I leaned across the table to glare at him. 'Don't you? Well, it's perfectly simple, Stratton. I'm here to whip your arse.'

'Yeah, right.' He laughed again but unconvincingly. 'So, what's the gag? Are you hookers?'

'We're from Masquerade,' Holly said.

'Masquerade?' He rubbed his cheek. 'I know them. Hey, don't tell me Randell's actually serious about this.'

'Mike Randell has nothing to do with us,' I stressed. 'We're representing Masquerade.'

He stared at us both. 'What the fuck is going on here? Are you saying you're not from Bopec?'

I yanked on Holly's choke chain. 'We used their name to get an appointment,' she confessed. 'But we've come to deliver Masquerade's final demand for settlement of your overdue account.'

'What!' His round cheeks splotched with colour. 'You're wasting my time chasing up a piffling debt for some piddling little company with a turnover smaller than our annual budget for paperclips?' He rounded on me furiously. 'Who the fuck do you think you are?'

I glared wrathfully at him. 'My name is Selina King and I'm a partner in that piddling little company that you, Peter Stratton, are indebted to, to the tune of one thousand, two hundred and thirty-six pounds.'

'And fifty-eight pence,' chipped in Holly.

I slapped my whip across my palm. 'I intend to beat it out of you if I have to.'

'You're threatening me?' He looked astonished. 'Don't be ridiculous. Get out of here!'

'I'm not leaving without my money,' I insisted.

He stretched his hand towards the intercom. 'Then I'll call security and have you thrown out.'

'That's OK,' Holly said quickly. 'We don't mind hanging around outside, attracting media attention. The press will lap up the costumes and everyone loves a David and Goliath story. It'll be great for Masquerade. But I'm not so sure about Stratton's. I mean, a publicity company that can't manage its own publicity? Still, I'm sure Mike Randell of Bopec will see the funny side of it. He sounds like a man with a sense of humour.'

Peter's hand hovered above the intercom as he considered her words. Then he looked me straight in the eye and turned it on. 'Yolander, ring through to accounts and have Mark draw up a cheque for the full amount owing to Masquerade. Tell him to sign it and send it down to reception.'

'Masquerade?' she queried.

'You heard what I said,' he snapped. 'I want it done immediately.' Releasing the button, he leaned back and folded his arms. 'Satisfied?'

I smiled broadly. 'It's good of you to be so reasonable.'

'You didn't exactly give me a choice.' He looked at me with grudging respect. 'I have to admire someone who's willing to go to such lengths to keep their business solvent. But I warn you, Miss King, I wouldn't try bending me over a barrel more than once.' He gestured towards the door. 'Go on, get out of here.'

'Do you think he'll close the account?' I asked Holly as we headed down to reception.

She shook her head. 'Not if I know Peter Stratton. A move like that would make him look like a wanker and that wouldn't fit in with his corporate image of himself.'

The cheque, as promised, was waiting in reception.

'This calls for a celebration,' I declared, storing the precious slip of paper inside the pocket of my coat.

'I can't,' Holly said. 'Tonight I'm being a traffic warden at a taxi driver's fortieth.'

'Damn.' I was disappointed. I felt exhilarated and ready to party. Madam Whiplash had triumphed over the mighty mogul and carried off the prize. Bring on Luca Verdici! I'd flay him into submission with my miniature cat-o'-nine-tails.

Holly was a little more cautious and, as we drove home, pointed out, 'You still don't have enough money to pay Luca in full.'

'The hell with him!' I bellowed. 'He'll take what he's given and bloody well like it.'

'You're drunk on power,' Holly cried, stomping the brakes on outside my house. 'Go and sober yourself up with a drink.'

'As luck would have it,' I informed her, 'there's a whole bottle of vodka with my name on it stashed in a cupboard in the kitchen. I'm going to have myself a nice hot bath with an ice-cold glass of Russian potato juice.'

With this in mind, I went inside, tossed my coat on to a hook and made a beeline for the vodka. I was a woman on a mission. I wasn't going to take any shit from any man, and I'd whip the arse of anyone who stood in my way.

Gervaise was standing in front of a shirt-covered ironing board, biting into an apple as I flounced into the kitchen. He glanced up, did a double take and then choked on his apple, looking as shocked as if I'd zapped him with a stun gun. It took a split second before the mallet of realisation thumped down on my head to remind me that I was dressed as Madam Whiplash. *Oh please let the earth swallow me up right now!*

Hysterical laughter bubbled in my throat but I swallowed it down and conjured an expression to match my attire. 'Men doing the laundry – that's what I like to see,' I stated stridently.

He was still spluttering and spitting apple, but he managed to croak, 'If you're looking for Matt dressed like that, he's gone out.'

I deliberately misunderstood. 'Matt went out dressed like *this*?'

He scowled. 'That would be funny if I hadn't caught the pair of you swallowing each other's tongues this morning.' Dropping his eyes to my feet, he let his gaze trawl slowly up my black leather legs to my saucy suspendered thighs where it paused to caress my bare flesh and satin covered crotch before dragging itself upward to the pushed-up globes of my breasts.

I stood firm beneath his scrutiny, holding myself magnificently erect as I prepared to meet his gaze with a glare of bold defiance. But the look in his eyes when they finally reached mine was not at all what I'd expected. Instead of contempt, instead of steely disapproval, there was a raw sexuality that sent a shiver down my spine.

'No wonder Matt can't keep his hands off you,' he murmured huskily. 'Is this how you torment him?'

'It's just a costume,' I answered defensively. 'I'm not wearing it for pleasure; I've just come home from work.'

He snorted sardonically. 'Was it "casual day"? I'm beginning to think that Masquerade is just a front. Sex is the only thing you could possibly be promoting in that outfit.'

I grew nervous as he moved around the ironing board and my fingers grabbed hold of my whip. 'What are you planning to do with that,' he asked, 'tickle my testicles?'

'Back off, Gervaise,' I warned him.

'Or what?' he laughed. 'Come on, Sugarlips, how much do you charge for a spanking?'

'How dare you!' I cried, stepping back as he crowded in on me. 'What the hell do you take me for?'

'If you really want to know,' he said, 'I think you're a cheap little whore: a slut, a slapper. Am I getting my message across?'

I swung back the cat-o'-nine-tails and lashed it across his face. 'Here's a message for *you*,' I yelled vehemently.

'*Merde!*' he exclaimed, wrenching the whip from my hand. Then, grabbing me round the waist, he pushed me against the fridge. 'You've let that costume go to your head. You're making a grave mistake if you think I'm the kind of man you can dominate.'

I knew I was in danger but I wanted to hurt him still more. Grasping his beard, I yanked on it spitefully. 'It strikes me that you could use a little discipline, you arrogant fur-faced bastard.'

'You're the one who needs discipline,' he snarled. Then he grabbed the two edges of my corset and, with a single powerful jerk, tore them apart. As my breasts spilled out, he grasped them in his hands and rubbed his face into their soft creamy flesh.

The shocking roughness of his beard took my breath away as it scraped against my skin like a nailbrush. I yelped and hammered him with my fists, but he only gripped me more tightly and continued his savage 'bearding' of my breasts.

It was meant to be a punishment but his sex drive overtook him and, suddenly, I felt his lips surrounding my sensitised nipple, deliciously warm and soft in contrast to the harsh bristles digging into my aureole. Then, as his tongue curled wetly around my stiffening bud, the sensational merging of textures drove me wild.

Ablaze with lustful fury, I dug my fingers into his hair, wanting to tear it from his head but instead pressing his face even harder to my breast and squirming as I strained towards his body.

Misreading my reaction, he lifted his face to kiss me. But I craned my head away, cringing with beard-o-phobia. Summoning scorn to my voice, I gritted my teeth and rasped, 'Get that stinking beard out of my face.'

Jolted from his sexual daze, he released me instantly, muttering first in French and then in English, 'I'm sorry, I shouldn't have done that.'

Covering myself, I shoved him aside. 'No doubt you'll say it was my fault,' I raged.

'*Non.*' He shook his head. 'This time, it was my fault.'

13

Despite Gervaise's admission, I was convinced that he held me responsible for what had happened and, in the morning, I was still furious with him and determined to give him a hard time. My temper was exacerbated by the discovery that Matt, who'd come home drunk, had left a trail of vomit in his wake.

I'd cleaned it up and was soaking the cloths in bleach when Gervaise came into the kitchen and asked me what I was doing.

'Fuck off,' I snarled, without turning round. 'Don't even talk to me.'

I heard him sigh and then he said, 'Don't be angry with me, Sugarlips.' He sounded contrite. 'I'm sorry for what I said last night.'

'I don't care about what you said,' I seethed. 'But I *do* care about being brutalised by that rabid hedgehog on your face.'

'I can't explain why I did that,' he said. 'For some reason, I had a crazy urge to maul you. It must have been that kinky outfit.'

'Don't try shifting the blame on to me,' I growled.

'I wasn't. It was my fault and I've said I'm sorry. Just look at me, Selina, and you'll see how sorry I am.'

I turned reluctantly to face him and got the shock of my life. He'd shaved off his beard, every trace of it!

I watched him in a daze as he lifted his hand and rubbed his smooth cheek. 'The damn thing had taken on a life of its own and had to go,' he explained.

I was speechless. I couldn't believe how handsome he was or how stupid I'd been not to see it. I should have guessed he'd have a strong, masculine jaw and sexy dimpled chin. What else would have gone with those amazing blue eyes? And why hadn't I noticed the sensual shape of his mouth before?

'Do you realise you're gawping?' he asked.

'You . . . you look so different,' I murmured.

His smile was utterly gorgeous. 'I told you I was handsome, didn't I?'

I recalled that he had, and that I hadn't believed him. 'If you admire your face so much then why did you cover it up?'

'Because I was attracting the wrong kind of women: the kind who thinks a man's face is more important than his mind.' I realised that he was more confident than conceited about his looks. He knew he was attractive but it hardly seemed to matter to him at all.

For my part, it made a world of difference. Now that I was seeing him without his 'mask', my senses were bombarding me with physical attraction. I had to look away because I knew that my pupils were dilating and that my skin had begun to flush. I couldn't let him see how much I fancied him.

I busied myself cleaning the sink. 'Matt came home in a state last night,' I commented. 'He's in a real mess.'

I felt Gervaise's eyes boring into my back. 'If you cared for him at all, you'd leave him alone.'

I didn't rise to the bait. 'I know you'll find this hard to believe but I didn't encourage him yesterday.'

'Then why did he say that you did?'

'To get himself off the hook, I suppose.'

'He could have said it was a moment of madness.' He uttered a dry laugh. 'Lord knows, I couldn't blame him for that.'

'Madness?' I echoed. 'You may have put your finger on it. He's certainly behaving irrationally. What he needs is a job.'

'As a matter of fact, I'm taking him to London with me today,' Gervaise informed me. 'I have an uncle there who owns a couple of printing plants, and Miranda's his favourite niece,' he added meaningfully. 'I expect we'll stay overnight.'

I felt relieved. I didn't want to be in the same house as that handsome face a minute longer than I had to.

Later that day, when I told Holly what he'd done, she looked disappointed. 'Looks like I've shaved off my pubes for nothing,' she complained.

'Holly, you didn't!' I squealed.

'Just kidding,' she giggled. 'However, I do admit to fantasising about that beard and my denuded pussy.'

'This sounds like my kind of conversation,' declared Harry, strolling in. 'Mind if I join you girls? My office is still crawling with Bavarian folk dancers and Daisy's ordered me to make myself "bleedin' scarce" because, apparently, I'm "in the bleedin' way".'

It just so happened that we'd both been waiting for an opportunity to ask him about his absence. Holly bowled straight in with, 'Where were you yesterday?'

'More to the point, where were you two?' he countered. 'And whose stupid idea was it to leave that toffee-nosed twit in charge again?'

'We were debt collecting,' I told him. 'It may please you to know that we successfully persuaded Peter Stratton to pay his account.'

He nodded, impressed. 'Well done. How did you manage it?'

'Oh, it was easy,' said Holly. 'We took a testicle apiece and walked in different directions.'

Harry winced. 'On second thoughts, maybe I don't want to know how you did it.'

'So, that's our story – what's yours?' Holly probed.

He plopped himself on to a chair. 'I spent the morning nursing the motherfucker of all hangovers. Then, after I'd sunk enough aspirin to kill a lesser mortal, Alison and me started talking. Then Alison stopped talking and started shouting. Then her mother came on the phone and started screaming. I think my head blew up at that point. I threw my collection of novelty underpants into a suitcase and fucked off. I'm dossing round a mate's house for the time being.'

'That's it then,' said Holly, 'the end of the road.'

'The end of a nightmare,' he groaned. 'Holly, why did you ever let me take that road?'

'Don't try and blame me for your cock-ups,' she answered angrily.

'Ah, speaking of cock-ups,' he said, 'it may interest you know that Gentleman Jack took a booking for Rudolph the Red-knobbed Reindeer for tomorrow night.'

'But Rudi doesn't work for us any more,' Holly said.

'Precisely,' said Harry. 'Anybody know where I can get a pair of antlers in the middle of May?'

'If I knew where to get 'em, I know where I'd bleedin' shove 'em,' grizzled Daisy, trundling in. 'Hello, ducks,' she greeted me and Holly.

'What's up now, you sour old dragon?' Harry asked her good-humouredly.

'There are two fat birds and one of the blokes is a dwarf,' she moaned. 'Three of the costumes don't fit.'

'That's why you're here to do the fitting,' he reminded her. 'We knew there'd be alterations.'

'I can't make a bleedin' silk purse out of a bleedin' sow's ear,' she grumbled.

'Of course you can, my darling,' he cajoled as he

steered her out, 'because you're an absolute bleedin' marvel.'

After he'd gone, Holly said, 'Who'd have thought it, Harry back on the singles' market again?'

'Are you thinking of going shopping?' I asked.

She pulled a face. 'Oh, please! That's a ticket to hell in a handcart. Don't let's talk about Harry; tell me about Gervaise. How do you like him without his beard?'

'It's an improvement,' I said grudgingly.

She peered at me closely. 'Oh ho? Do I detect a smidgen of attraction?'

I endeavoured to sound indifferent. 'Who cares if he's handsome? It's still the same Gervaise.'

'So, it's handsome now, is it?'

There was no fooling Holly. 'And then some,' I admitted. 'He even has a dimple in his chin. I feel like I've been conned.'

She scratched her head. 'How do you work that out?'

'How could he let me be such a bitch to him knowing that he was *that* bloody handsome?' I whined. 'I had his cock in my mouth and spat it out, for God's sake.'

She laughed. 'That'll teach you not to judge a bloke by his cover-up, be it facial hair or mask of Zorro.'

'I'll bear that in mind when I next meet a mugger in a ski-mask,' I said. 'Anyway, it doesn't matter what I think about Gervaise. What he thinks about *me* is unprintable.' I dismissed the topic with a nonchalant gesture. 'To hell with him. I've more important things to think about, such as money, money, money. How much can I give Luca tomorrow?'

Holly reckoned it up. 'I'll have to pay your phone bill as they're threatening to cut you off. So that's fifteen hundred tops. That leaves you a thousand short. How lucky do you feel?'

I certainly didn't feel as confident as I had in my

dominatrix outfit, but I put on a brave face. 'It should buy me the extra time I need. After all, what's a thousand pounds to Luca? He probably spends more than that on hair gel each week.'

'Or on garrotting wire,' Holly muttered forebodingly. 'I hope you know what you're doing, Selina.'

'Don't worry,' I told her. 'Harry's in tomorrow, so I won't be on my own.'

But I was wrong.

At one o'clock on Friday, Harry broke the news: 'I'm off to see my solicitor.'

'What, now?' I exclaimed.

'Yes, now,' he confirmed, puzzled by my tone. 'Do you have a problem with that?'

'No ... it's just that ... are you coming back?'

'I shouldn't think so,' he said, 'there's a lot to discuss.' He studied my face. 'Are you OK, Selina? You look a bit pale.'

'I'm fine,' I said dully.

'Good, then I'll see you at Kyle's party tomorrow night.'

'You're still going?' I asked him in surprise. 'With all this turmoil in your life?'

'My first party as a free man; are you kidding?' he replied. 'I wouldn't miss it for the world.'

And so he left me all alone, watching the clock with dread anticipation. By quarter to five, the suspense was killing me; Luca still hadn't shown. I'd spent the last hour jumping whenever the phone rang and twitching to every little sound. My nerves were in tatters.

I was speaking on the phone when he finally swaggered in. My cheery tone became tight and my heart began to bang against my rib cage as I watched him prowling around my office, waiting for me to finish. I clung to the conversation like a lifeline, but eventually the caller hung up and Luca sat down in front of me as I put down the phone.

'Business is good?' he queried.

'So-so,' I replied.

His dark brown eyes, soulless as a shark's, surveyed the baggy jumper that I'd worn to hide my figure, along with a pair of jeans two sizes too big for me. My face was free of make-up and I had my hair scraped back into a ponytail. 'I like this new look,' he pronounced. 'You could be fifteen or sixteen years old.'

'Don't flatter me,' I said. 'I know I look a mess.'

His crooked smile materialised on his thin lips. 'You've tried to look a mess, but beauty like yours needs no adornment and you'd still look sexy in a dustbin liner.'

'Do you rehearse these corny lines?' I scoffed.

He ran a fingernail down the white scar on his tanned cheek. 'Would you prefer to be insulted?'

'Actually, I'd prefer it if we didn't speak at all,' I said, handing him the cheque I'd written out. 'Why don't you take this and leave?'

He glanced at the cheque and then screwed it up. 'I thought I made myself clear last week – I want all of it or nothing.'

'But it's only a thousand short,' I protested. 'Give me one more week and I'll have it.'

'No.'

'Please, Luca.'

'No.' He'd set his mouth into a thin stubborn line, leaving barely enough room for the negative to squeeze out. He had his arms folded and the manicured fingers of his right hand were tapping on his sleeve. 'If you begged, if you crawled on all fours, the answer would still be *no*. Your time is up, Selina, it's pay-day.'

I looked at him nervously. 'What do you want? You

had your pound of flesh last week. Is it my blood you're after now?'

'To have your blood racing perhaps.'

'With fear?' I submitted.

He shook his head slowly. 'With desire.'

I gave a harsh laugh. 'That'll never happen.'

His eyes lit up with sudden passion. 'Have you forgotten how your body responded to me? How your breasts swelled and your nipples hardened like rose-hips?'

'I explained that to you,' I countered. 'My breasts would react that way if a puppy licked them.'

He leaned towards me and spoke softly. 'What if a puppy licked your clit?'

I gulped. 'I beg your pardon?'

His tongue slithered out of his mouth and circled around his lips. 'I think you know what I'm talking about. Give yourself a moment to consider the idea of my tongue and your pussy.'

'I won't let you do that!' I cried.

'My wriggling tongue and your hot little pussy.'

'Shut up! You disgust me!' But deep inside, I could feel the stirring of a grotesque excitement.

'My tongue and your pussy,' he repeated once more, lewdly licking into a circle that he'd made with his finger and thumb. Then he held out his hand, palm upward. 'Give me your keys.'

I stared at him blankly. 'My keys?'

'We don't want to be disturbed,' he murmured. 'I'll lock the door while you get undressed.'

Needing time to think, I picked up the keys, hating his gleeful smirk as he snatched them from me. When he'd gone, I tried to convince myself that I didn't have to do what he wanted. I could call his bluff, refuse to submit to his blackmail, tell him to go ahead and do his worst. Yet I feared what his worst might be.

When he returned, he looked annoyed to find me still fully dressed. 'I thought I told you to take off your clothes.'

I gathered my courage. 'What if I don't? What if I refuse to do what you want?'

'That would be unwise,' he said, coming up beside me and twining his hand into my ponytail. I yelped as he yanked me to my feet by my hair and forced me to stand on tiptoe. 'It would be a shame for someone to find Masquerade's offices reduced to smoking remains,' he said, releasing me.

'I don't believe you,' I whimpered. 'You're just trying to frighten me.'

'Am I?' To my horror, he grabbed some papers from my desk, took a gold lighter from his pocket and set fire to them, his eyes blazing as fiercely as the flame. Then, holding me back, he waited until the fire was almost to his fingers before dropping the paper to the floor and stamping it out with his foot. 'Don't test me,' he rasped. 'Others have tried. Some have lived to regret it but the rest weren't so lucky. That's right, Selina, I'm a bad boy.'

I couldn't tell if he was faking his menace or not but, right at that moment, it hardly seemed to matter if he was a mobster, an arsonist, or some kind of demented Walter Mitty. He was scaring the bloody shit out of me.

There was only one way to get him out of my life as quickly as possible and for good. 'All right,' I said. 'You win.'

'That's a sensible girl,' he murmured, lifting his hands to my belt. 'Very soon you'll be wondering why you made such a fuss.'

In a daze, I watched his long, tapered fingers unfastening my buckle. He drew the belt slowly through the loops so that it felt like a snake creeping around my waist. Then, with ever deepening breaths, he unbuttoned the waistband of my jeans and pulled the zip, tooth by tooth, to my crotch. A tremor went through my body as his two hands parted the material, exposing my belly and the top of my white nylon briefs.

A croak of laughter issued from his lips. 'Are you wearing these unattractive panties on purpose? Did you think they'd put me off if I got this far?'

I looked away from his mocking eyes, angry that he'd guessed correctly: I'd deliberately worn my plainest underwear as potentially a last line of defence.

'You knew it would end this way,' he accused me. 'Perhaps you even wanted it to.'

Denial flushed hotly in my cheeks. 'I wouldn't want this if you were the last man alive.'

'Let's see if that's true.' He grabbed my jumper and, pulling me close, thrust his hand into my pants. I struggled as his finger pushed into the valley of my sex. 'Keep still,' he commanded.

Knowing it would only prolong the ordeal to resist him, I stiffened my body, squeezed my hands into fists, and let the invading finger explore me.

'Look at me,' he whispered urgently. 'Let me see the hatred in your eyes.' When I glared at him, he exhaled his hot breath into my face. 'How disgusted you look. You want to claw and spit and scratch. You'd like to bite off my finger, wouldn't you? This finger I'm using to tickle your clit. Can you feel it tormenting your hot little bud? Do you like it slow and sliding like this ... or do these teasing little flicks turn you on? Do you know what I think? I think you'd like this –'

His experiment, to my horror, was atrociously stimulating and I had to bite on my lip and dig my fingernails into my palms to suppress my body's primeval response.

However, the shallowness of my breathing gave me away and he plundered deeper into my pussy, seeking evidence of arousal.

'What did I tell you?' he murmured triumphantly, withdrawing his hand to show me my dew on his fingertip.

'That's piss,' I sneered. 'I peed on your finger, you dirty bastard.'

'Stay angry,' he purred, sliding my jeans over my arse. 'You'll enjoy it much better that way.' As he peeled the fabric from my thighs and I felt his warm hands caressing my skin, I offered no resistance but stood still while he knelt, took off my shoes, and then removed my jeans completely.

When his eyes drew level with my crotch again, I saw him clench his fingers as if restraining an urge to simply tear off my panties and plunge his face into my sex. Anticipating such a move, I felt a shaky tremor of excitement flinch my body as spurs of lust jabbed into my loins.

But instead of pulling them down, he thrust his thumbs into the leg-holes and pushed up, forcing the crotch-piece so tight into my crack that my clit was constricted and my pussy numbed. Then, keeping the fabric pulled taut, he rubbed hard on the thin strip of nylon until the friction heated my sex. When it was sizzling, he ripped down my pants and, just as sensation was flooding back into my pussy, thrust his tongue between my thighs and licked me right on the button. I must have leapt a foot into the air.

The exquisite thrill sent a shock wave through my body and, trembling, I grasped his shoulders and expelled a whistling breath as he parted my pussy lips and licked me again.

The sensational wriggling moistness of his tongue

produced one rapturous ripple after another until my aching clit could stand no more. Wildly angry that he'd made me so horny, I clutched his hair and ground myself into his face. Pushing, shoving, smothering his mouth with my soaking wetness.

'You filthy pig,' I gasped between shivery groans. 'Eat my pussy, you bastard. I hope it fucking chokes you.'

His fingers gripped my thighs as his slippery tongue thrust deep inside me and then raked across my throbbing flesh, stabbing and lapping, delving and licking. I could feel my climax coiling inside me like a spring. My limbs grew rigid with tension as I waited for the snap of its release. Sensing how close I was, he sucked hard on my clit, firing a trigger that injected molten lava into my veins. My body jolted and shook as a spasm of ecstasy galloped from my loins to my brain.

I sagged to my knees just as Luca was rising to his feet. My head slumped and I felt sick inside.

I heard him laugh. 'Do you know how easy it would be for me to fuck you right now?'

'That wasn't part of the deal,' I croaked, trying to ignore the aching emptiness inside me that demanded a cock to fill it.

He pulled me to my feet and pressed his visible erection to my still twitching pussy. 'That may be so,' he agreed, grinding his hardness into my pubis. 'But what will you do to stop me?'

I couldn't speak. My exposed and sensitised clit was loving the prodding hardness of his cock and the rough chafing of his trousers.

'Come on,' he urged me, 'unfasten my zip.' His hand slid under my jumper and, kneading my breast, he whispered, 'Come on, Selina . . . take my cock out and let me fuck you.'

'Why don't you just go ahead and do it?' I hissed.

'Because I want you to do it.'

I was torn between revulsion and desire. I was desperate to be fucked but, dear God, not by him! I made myself focus on his gloating face and then viciously rammed my knee into his groin.

A groan blasted out of him and he staggered back, clutching his balls. While he was doubled-up in pain, I hurriedly put on my clothes.

'You little bitch!' he snarled.

'You asked for that, Luca.'

Still wincing, he straightened. 'I almost had you begging for it then. Next time, you will be.'

I shook my head vigorously. 'Oh no. There won't be a next time. I'm finished with you. I've paid you in full.'

He looked at me coldly. 'I don't recall that we discussed any terms.'

'But you said if...' I realised I couldn't remember what he'd said. 'Damn it, Luca, you know what I thought we'd agreed.'

'Do I?' he asked. 'As far as I'm concerned, you still owe me two and a half thousand and I want it by next Wednesday. All you've done is bought yourself a little more time. Don't look so hard done by. You enjoyed it. You can try and pretend that you didn't but, someday, when the angels ask, you'll have to confess that you did.' He picked up my keys and rattled them. 'You don't mind if I let myself out, do you?'

14

I slunk into the house like a bedraggled alley cat that had crawled in with its tail between its legs after a pasting from the local ginger tom. I intended to go straight upstairs for a shower but Gervaise came into the hall and beckoned me to the lounge.

As I flopped on to the couch, he gave his head a little shake. 'It's amazing,' he commented. 'Today you look like the little tomboy from next door who climbs trees and plays football. That's quite a change from Widow Spanky.'

I ignored the observation. 'When did you get back?'

He dipped his head, trying to catch my evasive eye, but I simply couldn't bring myself to look at him. 'This afternoon,' he murmured.

'Uh huh.' I nodded. 'Where's Matt?'

He sat down in the armchair. 'Next door with Alan, watching rugby.'

Still avoiding his gaze, I stared down at the carpet. 'How was London?' I asked.

Muttering something in French, he lobbed a cushion that bounced off my head. 'Hey!' I exclaimed, looking up.

'That's better,' he declared. 'I find it unsettling when people avoid making eye contact with me.'

'You've a distrustful nature,' I grumbled, picking up the cushion and looking at that instead. 'When you were a baby, were you tossed up and dropped, by any chance?'

'Selina,' he sighed, 'if you can't look me in the eye,

what am I to think? You're not still angry with me, are you?'

'I don't believe in staying angry,' I said. 'I consider it a waste of energy.' Reluctantly, I dragged my eyes to his face and once again felt a thwack of sexual attraction. I found myself wishing that he hadn't shaved his beard off after all. 'So, how was London?' I repeated. 'Did you fix Matt up with a job?'

Returning my look with one that contained an encrypted message that I couldn't decipher, he answered, 'We've arranged an interview at my uncle's Norfolk plant for Monday morning. Matt's travelling up on Sunday to get an early start. I'd say he has a fair chance of getting the job.' Looking suddenly weary, he closed his eyes and pinched the top of his nose. 'But I didn't call you in here to talk about Matt. I'm worried about Miranda. There's something weird going on.'

'What do you mean?' I asked.

'Don't you think it's strange that we haven't heard from her?'

'She sent me that e-mail at work saying that she'd arrived safely,' I pointed out.

He raked a hand through his hair. 'But she hasn't telephoned once.'

I shrugged. 'She said she had a packed itinerary. She didn't want to be bothered with phone calls.'

'Nevertheless, Matt's been trying to ring her at the number she left – the Carlton Hotel – but she hasn't returned his calls.'

I sat up, intrigued. 'Perhaps she doesn't want to speak to him. They had a row before she left. Have you tried the number yourself?'

He nodded. 'She'd already checked out without leaving a forwarding address.'

I spread my hands. 'I still don't see what's so weird about it. She's probably incommunicado.'

'I was just getting to the weird bit,' he said. 'I rang her office to see if they had a number for her. They didn't.' He paused for effect. 'She resigned more than a month ago.'

'She what!' I exclaimed. 'But what about John Lyons – the man she went away with? He's one of their chief executives.'

'They'd never even heard of him.'

'Never heard of him?' I was shocked. 'So, who the hell is he?'

He bobbled his head. 'Her lover perhaps?'

'How typically French,' I snapped. 'Why does it always have to be *amour* with you people?'

'Can you think of a better explanation?'

I couldn't. 'Does Matt know all this?'

His face became stern. 'No he doesn't and, clearly, she doesn't want him to just yet. I'm only telling you because I hoped you might know if she has a friend that she confides in. I just want to know if she's OK.'

I could see that he was genuinely concerned. 'She has plenty of casual friends,' I replied, 'but no one intimate as far as I know.'

He stroked the indentation in his chin. 'I suppose she's never been what you'd call a woman's woman,' he said.

'No, but she's certainly a *man's* woman,' I emphasised bitchily. 'It's ironic, isn't it? All this time you've been worrying about Matt cheating on her when it's she who appears to have done the dirty on him.'

'We don't know that yet,' he insisted. 'There could be another explanation.'

'I'm sure you'll hear it before anyone else if you're as close as you claim to be,' I said. 'Personally, I wouldn't put it past her to jump from cock to cock. She's done it before.'

'Why do you always pretend to be so hateful?' he asked. 'I know it hurt you when Miranda brought Matt into the house, but if you'd seen the letters she wrote to me after your father died, you'd know how heartbroken she really was. Matt was just someone to fill a void, someone to ease the pain. Why do you suppose she continues to care for you, you idiot? Because your face reminds her of your father. He was the love of her life, didn't you know that?'

His words brought tears to my eyes. 'Then why couldn't she tell me this herself? Why does she let me go on hating her?'

'She feels guilty,' he answered. 'She still blames herself for your father's tragic death and maybe she thinks that your hatred is something she deserves. But she's wrong. Matt came along when she needed someone. It wasn't a callous substitution; how could it be?'

'Supposing you're right and she's found someone else now. Where does that leave him?' I wondered.

He looked at me severely. 'If my suspicions are correct then he's a free man and you can have him. I'll get out of your lives and the two of you can live happily ever after for all I care.'

It suddenly hit me like a train that this was the last thing I wanted. He couldn't leave. Not now! 'But ... I don't want you to go,' I uttered softly. 'I ... feel differently about you now.'

He lifted his handsome black eyebrows. 'What you mean is you're attracted to me now,' he surmised.

'A little,' I admitted, lowering my lashes.

'Oh, a little more than that, I think,' he said. 'But let's assume it's a passing fancy and let's believe that you'll get over it.'

'Do you really think I'm as fickle as all that?'

'Put it this way,' he said, 'you're not the type to waste too much time tilling soil that you know to be barren.'

'Barren?' I echoed. 'Who's kidding who now, Gervaise? If you were that indifferent, I'd know it.'

'Hostile then,' he conceded.

I allowed the distinction. 'Hostile is something else. Hostile is –'

'Horny?' he suggested.

'Justified,' I said. 'But I know what you mean and, yes, I'd sooner have you hostile than indifferent.'

'You don't think I can be both?'

'Not a chance.'

We looked at each for a long moment and the carpet seemed like an ocean between us. I would have crossed it if he'd uttered a single word of encouragement. But he didn't.

In fact, we hardly spoke to one another for the rest of the evening. We ate our food separately, watched television in silence, and then went, separately, to our rooms.

The next day followed a similar pattern of careful avoidance. Matt, buoyed up by his impending interview, seemed unaware of the sexual tension in the air. He appeared, for the moment, to have lost interest in me, and I was grateful for that. Gervaise made no mention of his suspicions concerning Miranda, and I kept my mouth shut.

I left the house at five o'clock and took a taxi to Kyle's to help with the preparations for his party. He was surprised to see me so early but glad of my assistance. I spent a couple of hours cooking pizzas and cutting sandwiches and then commandeered his bathroom.

I took extra care over my appearance; setting my hair

into rivulets of glossy Pre-Raphaelite curls; painting my finger- and toenails gold to match the slinky jersey-silk dress that clung to my body as if I'd been sprayed with an aerosol can. I dusted my eyelids with glitter and put my feet into dainty gold sandals.

'Wow!' exclaimed Kyle, when I emerged at last. 'You look like a goddess.'

His reaction pleased me. 'It's just some old thing I sprayed on,' I joked.

As the guests began arriving, I found that I was drinking a lot to steady my nerves and that my eyes were scanning faces with the eagerness of a child awaiting Father Christmas. Harry, who'd turned up alone, wondered hopefully if my efforts had been for him.

'You needn't have gone to so much trouble,' he said; 'I'd have fancied you in a sack. Mind you,' he demurred, running his hand over my arse, 'some sacks are sexier than others. You're not wearing knickers, you saucy little minx. Do you want to slope off upstairs for a fuck?'

For once, his lecherous green eyes had no effect on me. 'Sorry, Harry, you'll have to celebrate your independence in some other way,' I said.

Disappointed, he looked me up and down. 'This wasn't for me then?'

'Why should it be for anyone? Can't a...' I broke off as I saw Gervaise walk through the door, and my heart cannoned into my chest. Harry followed the line of my gaze. 'Well, well,' he said, 'looks like Bluto's transformed himself into the incredibly handsome hulk.'

Feeling a sudden rush of colour to my cheeks, I sidled into a crowded corner where I could look without being seen.

From my vantage point, Gervaise was easy to spot. He was *so* tall, *so* big and *so* impossibly gut-wrenchingly handsome in his stylish black suit and an open-necked silk shirt that exactly matched the colour of his eyes. I hardly noticed Holly standing next to him until Harry, who'd followed me, commented, 'She looks lovely, doesn't she? They make a stunning couple, don't you think?'

I skewed him a look. 'Are you jealous?'

He sighed. 'Considering my track record with Holly, that would be a damn fool thing to be.'

'Answer the question, you coward,' I ribbed him.

He scowled at me. 'Yes, OK, I'm jealous. Will you get off my case now?'

'Oh, my God!' I exclaimed. 'He has feelings after all! And there was I thinking they'd removed your heart at birth and put an ice cube in its place.'

'That's not my heart talking,' he insisted, 'that's just my dick being sentimental.'

I peered at him curiously. 'Which bit of you was talking when you said you wanted me back?'

He gave a mystified shrug. 'My foreskin perhaps, who knows? What do *you* think?'

'I think you were looking for a legitimate excuse to leave little Katy,' I told him, 'and I was the nearest thing to hand that you happened to be fond of.'

He nodded slowly. 'You could be right. But, if that's the case, then why didn't I use Holly? She was near to hand as well.'

I looked at him sagely. 'Think about it, Harry. You couldn't possibly use her like that.'

His gaze wandered over to Holly, looking gorgeous in red satin capri pants and a skimpy black top. I noticed her face light up when she saw him. 'You're right,' Harry muttered, raising a hand in greeting.

Holly and I exchanged friendly waves. Then she tugged Gervaise's arm to draw his attention to us. Instantly, his eyes swooped across the room to single me out. He stared and I stared back, sexual attraction crackling between us like lightning. *Barren soil indeed!*

The four of us came together in the middle of the room. 'God, it's crowded in here,' Holly said.

Gervaise and I now studied one another in close-up: His eyes scanning my hair, mine examining his beardless dimpled chin and chiselled jawline. Then he looked at my mouth and I looked at his. When our eyes met, he grunted hoarsely, 'Where's your boyfriend?'

'Who?' I uttered stupidly.

'The host,' he reminded me.

'Kyle,' Holly said.

'Oh, he's . . . er –' I didn't have a clue '– circulating?'

Someone put on some smoochy music and Harry grabbed Holly by the hand. 'What do you say we take my two left feet and your canoe feet for a trundle around the room?' he invited her.

She tried to pull away. 'I'd have to be drunk to take part in that toe-crushing ritual you call dancing.'

He swung her into his arms. 'Just press your nipples tight to my chest and you'll forget you even have toes.'

I laughed as he steered her away, but it froze on my lips when I realised that everyone around us was drawing into pairs. I looked awkwardly at Gervaise. 'Shall we – get a drink?'

'No, we'll dance,' he decided. But his hand reached out slowly, inflicting nanoseconds of nervousness as I watched it advancing towards my waist. When he touched me, I almost jolted, appalled by how acutely conscious I was of the warmth and the weight of his hand through the thin material of my dress.

I took a step towards him and placed my own hand on his powerful chest, letting it slide slowly upwards to the sweeping ledge of his shoulder. He captured my other hand and, as our palms pressed together, I could feel a surge of electricity between us.

Perhaps aware of it himself, he seemed agitated and held me awkwardly at arm's length. 'What's on your mind?' I asked, after a moment or two of uneasy silence. 'You seem bothered by something. Is it me?'

'You don't bother me,' he said.

'Then look at me,' I urged him. I thought I'd be ready to meet his gaze, but I wasn't. The dazzling blueness of his eyes, so beautifully echoed by his shirt, took my breath clean away. I swallowed, lowered my sights to his mouth, and then looked up again through the screen of my lashes.

He shook his head. 'Don't flirt with me.'

I pulled a petulant face. 'Oh, lighten up, Gervaise, it's a party. Everyone's flirting with everybody else. What are you worried about? Don't tell me some little seedlings of desire have started sprouting in that hostile soil of yours. Is that what's troubling you?'

He rolled his eyes. 'I might have known you'd turn that comment into a challenge. I didn't say it to tantalise you.'

'But it has,' I admitted.

'Oh, I get it,' he realised, with a sweeping glance over my hair and attire. 'This is all for me. You really know how to pull out the stops, don't you?'

I tilted my head. 'Has it worked?'

'Not at all.'

I moved my hand to the nape of his neck. 'Liar.'

A muscle quirked in his cheek; 'Coming on to me won't work either.'

'Are you sure?' Moving closer, I nuzzled against his cheek, breathing in his sexy, masculine fragrance. Then, with my fingers stroking his hair, I pressed my pubis to his groin and whispered teasingly into his ear, 'I want to fuck you, *mon cheri.*' But when his hand slid to my hip and his hot breath purred against my skin, I pulled back sharply. 'You're getting a hard-on,' I coolly advised him. 'Still think you're indifferent?'

Unabashed, he smiled charismatically. 'Maybe not. Perhaps I'd better confer with my prick in future. I'm not sure if you've won your point though. Hitting a man below his belt is hardly fair play.'

'The object wasn't to score a point but to prove one,' I enlightened him.

'The only point you've proven is – you do.'

'Do what?'

'Want to fuck me, *ma cherie.*'

'Mind if I cut in?' It was Kyle. 'You seem a little too cosy with my girlfriend, pal.'

'I apologise,' Gervaise said, releasing me into his arms.

I was furious at being dragged away at such a point. 'What the hell did you do that for?' I scolded Kyle.

His eyebrows knitted together in a puzzled frown. 'I thought he was the one that you wanted convincing?'

Seeing Gervaise watching, I coiled my arms around his neck. 'Yes, you're right. I'm sorry. I ought to be grateful.'

Kyle's wandering hands were extremely convincing. 'Don't get carried away,' I warned him, lifting his palms from my buttocks.

'I stopped play-acting five minutes ago,' he told me, kissing my shoulder. 'I've really got the hots for you tonight.'

I didn't know what to say. 'Oh ... well ... that's very flattering but ...'

'But you fancy the big guy, right?' *Was it that bloody obvious?*

I dismissed his deduction with an airy toss of my

head. 'Absolutely not. As a matter of fact, the only thing I fancy is a drink.'

We went out to the kitchen, where I found Holly chatting to George. 'You remember Arse Number One?' she giggled.

I bent my head to hers. 'The one who doesn't need a pole to pole vault?' She nodded and so did George who'd overheard. 'Still thinking about my ebony love snake, sweetheart?'

'You've got a white man's python, you demented liquorice all-sort,' muttered Kyle.

'Where's Gervaise?' I asked Holly.

She shrugged. 'Last time I saw him he was dancing with a girl who had tits like inflated air bags.'

'Honeydew Helen,' Kyle and George said simultaneously.

'Are they real?' Holly wondered.

'About as real as red bananas,' chuckled George. 'Uh-oh, don't look now, torpedoes at twelve o'clock. She's coming in behind you.'

I took a sneaky peek and saw a skinny brunette tottering on heels like tent pegs, who looked as if she'd shoplifted a couple of Christmas puddings and stashed them under her blouse. I couldn't imagine why Gervaise had asked it to dance. 'She's not even pretty,' I grumbled.

'Who cares about pretty with momma-fruit like that?' declared George.

'I do,' contested Kyle. 'Big isn't *always* best.'

'Get outa here!' cried George. 'The bigger the better – just ask the ladies. That's why we brothers make the beast-with-two-backs better than you bleached guys.'

'Bollocks,' snorted Kyle. 'That's a bloody myth put about by black blokes.' He looked at Holly. 'Isn't it?'

'If you ask me,' she said, 'I think Frenchmen make the best lovers. They're certainly the best kissers.'

'That's another crock of shit,' whined Kyle. 'Just because the frogs invented the Frenchie doesn't mean they still own the copyright. What do you think?' he asked me.

I spread my hands. 'I wouldn't know,' I said. 'I've never kissed a Frenchman.'

'I bet you'd agree with me if you had,' Holly said.

Kyle squinted at her. 'How much?'

'How much?' she echoed.

'How much are you willing to bet?' he replied, peering over my shoulder. 'I've got a tenner that says Selina wouldn't agree with you.'

Holly cast her eyes in the same direction as his. 'I see what you're getting at.'

I turned my head and a wallaby jumped in my stomach when I spotted Gervaise endeavouring to disengage himself from Honeydew Helen who was clinging to his arm.

I was horrified when I heard Kyle challenging Holly, 'Are you willing to put your money where his mouth is?'

To my chagrin, she was already beckoning Gervaise. 'Absolutely,' she affirmed.

'Hey, hold on a bloody minute,' I protested. 'You're not expecting me to kiss him, are you?'

Holly smiled and nodded. 'It'll be the easiest tenner I ever make. Don't be a spoilsport, Selina.'

Arriving at her side, Gervaise slipped an arm around her waist. All of us looked at him. 'What?' he enquired.

I could feel my cheeks getting redder and redder as Holly explained about the bet. 'You'll be representing your countrymen,' she concluded. 'Are you man enough for the job?'

He moved his eyes to my face and for a long moment didn't say anything. I knew he was contemplating what would be more embarrassing for me: to refuse or agree.

Eventually, he murmured, 'OK, I'll do it.' *Oh, that subtle hint of bravery and reluctance – rotten sod!*

But now the ball was in my court and everyone was looking at me. 'This is stupid,' I said. Gervaise smiled. 'Childish.' The smile grew broader. 'It won't prove anything.' Now he was grinning like a bastard.

'I thought you liked proving points,' he said.

My heart was racing as I searched his eyes, wondering what he was thinking. Was he hoping I'd refuse and let him off the hook? His face, as he held my gaze, was such a picture of absolute nonchalance that I was completely caught out by the sudden lift of his eyebrows. Though no more than a fleeting shrug, I knew what it meant. He was daring me to kiss him.

I had no choice but to pick up the gauntlet. 'All right, I'll do it,' I consented.

Gervaise looked at Kyle. 'Are you sure about this?' He nodded and nudged me towards him.

Then suddenly I was in his arms: a large hand cupping my face, another holding me close. He brushed his thumb across my cheek, drawing back a wisp of hair. Then his eyes grew misty as his dense black lashes lowered over them. I knew a moment of panic as his lips descended on mine. Then I was lost.

I grew conscious only of his mouth moving over mine, of feeling warm, firm lips so incredibly sensual that my spine was tingling from top to bottom.

He was teasing my mouth, coaxing my lips into soft, pliant readiness until, flushed and swollen, they parted and responded: I was kissing him back. I couldn't help myself. His mouth was like a magnet, compelling my lips to follow its every move and as the pressure deepened, excitement mounted in my body.

At the first touch of his tongue, my legs turned to liquid and, as he tasted and tormented my lips with just its tip, I had to cling to him to stop myself from crumpling.

In a distant corner of my mind, I heard Holly yell, 'Hang on to your hat, Selina, here comes the best bit!'

Gervaise tightened his grip and, with his fingers scrunching my hair, slid his tongue inside my mouth and released the full potency of his passion.

I was overwhelmed by the sheer intensity of his kiss. It swept me into a swirling tornado of ravenous sexual desire and, as our tongues made love in the sultry cavern of our mouths, I wanted him so badly that every bone in my body ached with the urgency of my need.

With starbursts of ecstasy exploding in my head and fireworks spluttering in my loins, I forgot myself completely and let my hands rake into his hair and clutch at his body. Groaning, he murmured, 'Easy tiger,' and gently released me.

Robbed of his lips, I plummeted back to Earth with a bump, suddenly realising that everyone in the kitchen was watching us. I stared at Gervaise in wonder. What had he done to me? What right had a man to kiss like that? Flustered, and annoyed with myself for losing control, I stepped back shakily.

Gervaise accepted a drink from George. 'You got any black in you, brother?' George asked. 'That was one helluva demonstration.'

Kyle looked at me glumly. 'I guess I've lost my bet.'

Deciding not to be churlish, I said, 'You have.'

'Told you!' tooted Holly, holding out her palm to receive his ten pound note. She kissed Gervaise on his cheek. '*Vive La France!*'

I decided I needed a stiff drink myself and so, detaching from the group, I went over to the drinks table and helped myself to a wineglassful of vodka to which I added a spit of tonic. Holly followed me.

'So what do you think?' she asked. 'Fourth of July?'

'Bastille Day,' I muttered. 'You might have warned me.'

'Would you have kissed him if I had?'

'Probably not,' I admitted, taking a long swig of my drink.

'You can't deny you enjoyed it,' she said. 'Your nipples are sticking out like ball bearings.'

'Gervaise must be laughing his head off,' I moaned.

'If it's any consolation, he was sporting a massive erection,' she said.

I smiled. 'I know, I felt it. Yet he claims he's not interested.'

She laughed. 'Who's he kidding? Is he playing hard to get?'

'Oh, he isn't playing,' I said. 'He's put himself off limits. He thinks I'm bad news; I guess he ought to know, he's a journalist after all.'

'He'll come round,' she said. 'You just got off to a bad start, that's all.' She tilted her head to look at me. 'How could he possibly resist you?'

'Quite easily,' I answered morbidly.

'What makes you say that?'

'Because he's just gone back into the lounge with Honeydew Helen!' I looked at her despairingly. 'Do you see what you've done? I'm so jealous I could spit.'

She peered at me closely. 'Good God, you've really fallen for him! This could get serious.'

'Frankly, I haven't a clue what's going on inside my head,' I declared. 'It's a quagmire in there.' I told her about Luca Verdici. 'What the hell is wrong with me if a creep like that can turn me on?'

'Oh, come on, you'd have to be pretty frigid not be aroused,' she said. 'I don't think women are any different to men really. Given the right stimulation, we're away with the fairies whoever the fuck is doing it. I've had terrific orgasms with men I don't fancy. I think it's called self-indulgence.'

'I suppose so,' I agreed. 'But I wish I could lobotomise my libido. I'd sooner have no sex drive at all than give Luca the satisfaction of hearing me gasp again. If I don't get that money by Wednesday, heaven alone knows what he'll do next.'

'Don't worry, we'll get it,' she said. 'Cheer up, it's a party. Finish your drink and forget your cares. I see Arse Number Two over there. You'll feel much better once you've snogged his face off.'

But kissing Dane after Gervaise was like drinking scrumpy after a glass of champagne. I tried Kyle and then George, but he'd jaded my palate and left me no appetite for flirtation. I kept seeing him everywhere, talking, dancing, flirting, but he was like a will-o'-the-wisp: every time I drew near he'd disappear. Fed up with trying to accidentally bump into him, I hijacked him in the hallway.

'You're ostentatiously avoiding me,' I said, wishing I'd picked another word when I heard myself slurring my Ss.

A smile tugged the corners of his mouth. 'You're imagining things, Sugarlips.'

'You're the one with the sugar lips,' I reproached him. 'What the hell did you kiss me for?'

He lifted his fabulous shoulders. 'For a bet.'

Unfazed, I asked him boldly, 'Are you planning on doing it again?'

He shook his head. 'Uh-uh.'

'Why not?'

He looked at me regretfully. 'Because I know what you are – and that's poison.'

'You've got me all wrong,' I said. 'I'm not nearly as bad as you think I am.'

'Why don't you tell that to someone who gives a fuck?' came his acrid response. Wounded, I turned away, but he spun me back round. 'I didn't mean that,' he growled. We both looked at his hand on my arm and he released me as if I'd caught him trying to steal it. 'The funny thing is – I kind of like you,' he said. 'But that's as far as it goes.'

'Have you conferred with your prick about this?' I enquired.

He laughed. 'This may be news to you, but we don't *all* keep our brains between our balls.'

'Maybe you should try to be a little more relaxed about letting Mother Nature have her way,' I suggested.

He looked at me archly. 'Like you are?'

I gazed longingly at his mouth. 'Why are we even having this conversation? We should be fucking.' I'd meant to say 'kissing' but my tipsy brain had cross-wired my tongue to my subconscious.

Consequently, my bluntness made him wince. 'Goddamn it! Do you think all men are playthings? Do you think all you have to do is wind them up and away they go? Well, I'm not a toy, Selina, and I won't be played with. Go find yourself some other chump.' He shoved me aside and stomped off down the hall.

Oh, buggerfuck! I'd really cocked that up! Furious with myself for making such a hash of things, I marched upstairs, intending to sluice my face and sober up. But when I reached the landing and heard familiar voices coming from one of the bedrooms, my curiosity was aroused.

'Holly, please.'

'Don't do this to me, Harry.'

'Just one little kiss. What harm can it do?'

Intrigued, I peeped in. He had her pinned against the wardrobe, his hands gripping her wrists, his mouth seeking her lips, his body pressed tight against hers. 'Baby, please,' he begged, kissing her cheek, her hair, her neck. 'Just one little kiss and I swear I'll let you go.'

She had a tortured look on her face, but I could see her resistance crumbling. Then, all at once, the fight drained out of her and she gave herself up to his kiss.

It was a strangely magical moment as I realised I was watching the inevitable conclusion of a romantic saga. It pulled on my heartstrings and, smiling wistfully, I withdrew to let the picture fade and the credits roll.

But I hadn't gone five paces down the hall when I heard Holly shout, 'Let go of me!' She sounded so distressed that I instantly tracked back. Harry came out of the bedroom, looking distraught. I grabbed his arm. 'What's wrong?'

Declaring himself an arsehole, he shrugged out of my grip and pushed me aside. I went in and found Holly sitting on the bed with tears streaming from her eyes. 'Jesus Christ!' I exclaimed, rushing over to cuddle her. 'What the bloody hell did he do to you?'

She shook her head, unable to speak, so I let her cry for a while and then probed her again. 'Did he try it on with you?'

She laughed bitterly through her tears. 'Of course he did. It's what he does. He can't help himself, poor sod.'

'If you know what he's like then why are you so upset?'

She sighed. 'I stupidly thought that for once in his life he wasn't thinking about sex.'

I knew what she meant. In a romantic saga, the hero didn't grope the heroine right at the end. But Harry wasn't a conventional hero. 'I know he loves you,' I said. 'Why won't you give him a second chance?'

'We'd only hurt each other again,' she whimpered.

'Life's too short to be so obstinate,' I advised her. 'It couldn't have been so bad if you still love each other after all this time. You do still love him, don't you?'

'Yes,' the affirmative racked out of her. 'Yes, I love him. But you loved him too and where did it get you?'

'Nowhere,' I admitted. 'But now I know why I couldn't reach his heart. He didn't have one after he'd given it to you. I don't know what you did with it, Holly, but you sure as hell didn't give it back.'

Another sigh wheezed out of her. 'I'll tell you the story and you can judge for yourself if I'm being too hard on him.' She drew a deep breath. 'We were deeply in love, or so I thought. Then Harry did what Harry does – with my best friend. When I caught them in bed together, my whole world collapsed. He said it was nothing. Nothing! Isn't that just typical of Harry?

'I tried to forgive him but I couldn't get it out my head. I felt I needed revenge, so I started sleeping with a friend of his called Bill. And then I got pregnant. Harry had always worn a condom, except just after my period, but Bill didn't like them and we'd taken a couple of risks, so naturally I assumed that the baby was his. I didn't tell him about it because our fling had run its course and the last thing I wanted was a souvenir like that! But when I tried to ditch him, he got nasty and told Harry he'd been screwing me. Harry went crazy and I really thought I'd lost him but, after a while, he cooled down and we agreed to bury the past and try again. I went ahead with the abortion.

'I met a girl at the clinic. I don't remember her name. We cried on each other's shoulders, like you do, and we told our sad little stories. Well, it's a small world after all, because it turned out she knew Harry Lambert; he'd dated her sister a few times – her sister, Alison. You can guess the rest, well almost. There's a sting in the tail. When Alison spilled the beans, Harry was devastated that I'd kept the pregnancy a secret because he knew something I didn't: he knew the baby had to be his. He told me that Bill had had a vasectomy that he liked to keep quiet because it's a turn-off to single women. I really know how to pick the bastards, don't I?' She paused to let out a sob. 'Harry accused me of killing his kid. The things he said to me.' She shook her head. 'I suppose I deserved them. But I wouldn't have had the abortion if I'd known it was Harry's child. You believe me, don't you?'

I squeezed her hand. 'Of course I do.'

'Well, Harry didn't,' she said. 'He married Alison to spite me; got her pregnant to spite me; even had an affair with my new best friend right in front of my nose. Still think I should give him a second chance?'

'Whatever he's done, you still love him,' I said, 'and you can't get away from that fact. You love him because he's sexy and funny and charming. He stirs your blood and makes you laugh like nobody else. You see, I know what it is to love Harry. He's a bloody hard act to follow, and it would take a big man to fill his shoes.'

'A big man?' she queried. 'You mean someone like Gervaise?'

I'd meant larger-than-life but I found myself nodding. 'Yes, someone like Gervaise.'

15

I'd spent an uncomfortable night on Kyle's couch, but it was worth the crick in my neck just to see the look on Gervaise's face when I drifted home at lunchtime. I knew he'd assume that I'd slept with Kyle, which was exactly what I wanted him to think, my intention being to convince him that his incredible kiss had meant nothing to me.

I'd changed back into the jeans I'd worn the day before and all that remained of my 'golden goddess' creation was a few limp curls and my painted nails.

He was eating cheese-on-toast in the kitchen and, after glancing up to administer a surly look, his eyes returned to the Sunday paper he was reading.

'I notice the car's gone,' I commented. 'Has Matt left for Norfolk already?'

'Yes,' he grunted.

I began collecting ingredients for a sandwich. 'It's starting to rain,' I observed.

He didn't respond.

'Anything interesting in the paper?'

'No.'

'I'm making some coffee, would you like some?'

'Yes.'

'Name the seven ancient wonders of the world.'

He furrowed his brow and looked up. 'What?'

'I'm trying to make conversation,' I said, slapping butter on to my bread. 'Do you know what that is? You talk, I talk. It's like tennis only you play it with words.'

'I don't feel like talking,' he said.

'Hung over?' I suggested, tousling his sleep-ruffled hair as I passed. He swatted my hand and grunted irritably.

I finished making my sandwich and joined him at the table. While I ate, my eyes made a leisurely tour of his features as he continued to read in silence. He endured my scrutiny for a full five minutes, then his hand lifted to his forehead and he rubbed it with his fingers. 'Is the plan to keep on staring at me until I say something?'

'Pretty much,' I agreed. 'It seems to have worked so far.'

He gave a sigh of resignation and closed the newspaper. 'What do you want to talk about?'

'Last night.'

He stretched his arms and the broad expanse of his chest strained against the fabric of his tight-fitting polo shirt. 'Yesterday is a crazy place, are you sure you want to go there?'

'Only to revisit something you said,' I specified. 'What exactly did you mean when you said I was poison?'

He pulled a wry face. 'I think you know what I meant.'

'No I don't, I'm not a mind-reader.'

'Aren't you?' Rubbing his chin, he leaned back to consider me. 'What do you suppose I'm thinking right now?'

His eyes scrolled over me in a way that made my nipples tighten. 'I don't think I care to guess,' I said.

'You don't need to guess – you *know* what I'm thinking. But do you know why?'

I shrugged. 'Why does any man think about sex? Were you looking at the tits in the tabloid?'

He brushed aside my flippant response. 'I'm thinking about sex because you want me to,' he said. 'Your eyes want me to, your lips want me to; everything about you is an open invitation. I don't think I've ever met a woman who exploits her sexuality quite as ruthlessly as you do. You're as seductive as a cobra: you mesmerise, strike without thinking, and then inject your victims with that poisonous venom called desire.'

'It's the weakness in men that women exploit,' I argued defensively. 'Is it our fault if nature designed us to be alluring? Being attractive to men doesn't make me a sexual predator.'

'But that's exactly what you are,' he pronounced. 'And you're very, very good at it.'

I hadn't thought about it before but I suspected he was right. 'Does that threaten you?' I asked.

'On the contrary, it excites me.'

'Enough to impair your judgement?'

He shook his head. 'Not if I can help it.'

I plucked absently at a button on my shirt. 'The thing about snakes, cobras in particular, is they're sly. You could get bitten when you least expect it.'

His eyes focused on my fingers. 'Then I shall have to keep my wits about me.'

Beneath the table, I slipped off my sandal and rubbed his leg with my foot. 'Most men keep their wits in their underpants,' I informed him.

'Undoubtedly,' he said.

'So –' I lifted my foot to his fly '– what do you keep in yours?'

'That's very good,' he murmured, watching my gold-painted toes caressing his crotch, 'but you and I both know that you can do a whole lot better.'

Confused, I dropped my foot. 'You're inviting me to try?'

His smile was ambiguous. 'Sure, why not?'

I tried to match his smile, but I couldn't match his self-assuredness. 'You realise I'm only teasing you, don't you?'

His smile grew wider. 'If I was teasing *you*, I wouldn't tell you.'

'Are you?' I demanded.

'Maybe.'

'That isn't teasing, that's just being annoying.'

He laughed. 'What really annoys you is not being able to piss higher up the wall than I can.'

'I didn't realise it was a contest,' I said sulkily.

He looked at me shrewdly. 'I see it more as a battle of wills.'

'I have an idea,' I submitted. 'Why don't we call a truce? I'd like to have a stab at reforming your opinion of me.'

He arced an eyebrow. 'Why would you want to do that?'

'Because I like you.'

'That must be a novelty for you,' he said. 'You don't always seem to like the men you fancy. What do you propose?'

'Just that we spend the rest of the day getting to know each other.'

'I can't,' he declared, glancing at his watch. 'I have a cab picking me up in half an hour.'

'Where are you going?' I asked jealously.

'I said I'd call round Holly's after lunch. She was in a state last night and I've offered her my shoulder.'

I had a disturbing flashback of Holly's foot bouncing on his shoulder. 'How long will you be?' I asked mournfully.

He lifted his hands. 'You know her better than I do. How long does she normally take to pour her heart out?'

'You'll be there all day,' I forecast glumly.

Smiling, he leaned forward and chucked me under my chin. 'Cheer up, Sugarlips. It's not like I'm being unfaithful.'

'Why don't you bring home some wine?' I suggested. 'I could order a Chinese takeaway, say for seven o'clock?'

He rose and his eyes twinkled mischievously as he lifted my hand and brought it to his lips. 'Very well, *à tout à l'heure, mon petit serpent.*' The touch of his mouth brought the memory of his kiss flooding back to me and I felt a chilly tremor of nerves as he turned my hand over and erotically brushed his tongue across its palm.

I looked at him confusedly. 'I'm not sure what you said, but that gesture is universal. Does it mean what I think it means?'

'If you think it means I want you,' he softly replied, 'then you're absolutely right.'

Long after he'd gone, I sat looking at my hand, trying to figure out the reason behind his admission. It had come as no surprise to me, and he must have known that I already knew. So why had he said it? Had he voiced his desire in order to deal with it? Or was he mind-fucking my head again? Pissing even higher up that wall?

I took the problem into a bubble bath with me and, after soaking for almost an hour, arrived at the conclusion that he'd said it precisely to torment me in exactly the way that it had.

Annoyed that I'd fallen for his ploy, I resolved to turn the tables on him by making him want me even more than I wanted him. After getting out of the bath, I rubbed fragrant body lotion into every square inch of my skin: spent an age blow-drying my hair into soft rippling waves and then made up my face as cunningly as I could so that it would look like I hadn't bothered. Choosing what to wear proved more difficult. I tried on and discarded a dozen or more outfits before settling on a simple cherry-red top and a calf-length black skirt with a seductive side split. I put on stockings and then took them off – too obvious. It was enough that I was wearing my most expensive black lace underwear underneath. But, to add a touch of sauciness, I slipped my feet into fluffy red mules.

Once downstairs, I ordered the takeaway, but after laying the table for dinner, I stripped it again – too formal. I set out lighted candles and then blew them out – too romantic. Eventually I settled for dimmed lights and mood music. The Chinese food arrived and I was just putting it on the coffee table when Gervaise came in.

'I thought we'd sit on the floor,' I said, throwing down some cushions.

'Smells good,' he murmured, coming up behind me and nuzzling my hair. 'So do you.' His arms surrounded my body and he swayed me to the music. 'I like this song.'

What the damn fuck was he playing at, holding me like this? 'The food will get cold,' I uttered shrilly, practically leaping from his arms.

He took a bottle of wine from a carrier bag containing half a dozen and filled up the glasses while I finished unpacking the food. As he took off his jacket, I positioned myself on the cushions in what I hoped was a sexy sprawl and was rewarded with a trawling gaze and some muttered words in French.

'What did you say?'

'I said I'm ravenous,' he answered, kneeling down. Then he handed me a folded piece of paper. 'I want you to have this, Selina.'

Puzzled, I opened it up. It was a cheque for two and

half thousand pounds made out to Luca Verdici. I sat up with a jolt. 'What the hell is this?'

'It's just a loan; it's no big deal.'

'Holly told you about Luca?'

'Only that you owed him some money and that he was getting a little nasty about it.'

I was furious. 'She had no damn right to involve you in my business.'

'She has every right as your friend to try and help you,' he said. 'But, if it makes you feel better, she didn't tell me any details.'

'You must have asked questions.'

He gave me an old-fashioned look. 'Of course I asked questions.'

'And?'

'She wouldn't tell me anything but I got the distinct impression that she was worried about you. Take the money, Selina. Pay me back when you can.'

I stared at him in wonder. 'But why would you do this?'

He shrugged. 'You're family.'

'We're not remotely blood related,' I pointed out.

'Nevertheless, if Miranda were here, she would help you. You must allow me to act in her place.'

'I don't know what to say,' I muttered numbly.

He waved his hand dismissively. 'Say, "Thank you, Gervaise," and hand me that tub of chow mien.'

'Thank you,' I said gratefully.

His gesture and my acceptance of it created an ambience of goodwill between us and, for the first time, I allowed myself to relax in his company. Listening to him talk, I discovered a man I hadn't met before: a lucid, intelligent thinker with fascinating views and ideas. I found myself being drawn into discussing things that I hadn't even thought about before. Yet his charismatic personality didn't allow him to stay serious for too long and, every so often, his eyes would sparkle with sudden humour and he would say something witty that would set me off laughing again. But as the wine continued to flow, the conversation became surreal until finally descending into the blur of intoxication.

While I still had the power of rational thought, I got up to change the CDs. When I came back to the table, I saw that he'd refilled our glasses for the umpteenth time and was lighting up a joint.

'Is that a good idea?' I fuzzily enquired, doing a belly flop back on to the cushions.

'Compared to what,' he asked bemusedly, 'the wheel?'

'No, not the wheel.' I flapped my hands. 'That's just silly.'

He took a deep inhalation. 'Compared to what then?'

'I don't know. something not so important, like ...' I couldn't think of anything so I said the first thing that came into my head. 'Fishfingers?'

He gave me a condescending look. 'You can't get a buzz out of smoking fishfingers, at least, I don't think so.' He handed me the joint, but as I drew the sweet smoke into my lungs it made me cough.

'Bloody amateur,' he said.

With some difficulty, I focused on the spliff between my fingers. 'This stuff ... doesn't affect me ... a bit,' I declared, taking another short puff before handing it back.

He nodded his head like it was made of lead. 'That's what *I* said.' He took another drag. 'But he didn't believe me.'

'Who didn't?'

'The goat I said it to.'

We both started giggling and then couldn't seem to stop. Eventually, I wheezed, 'I think I'm pissed.'

'I must be getting pissed as well,' he said, 'I'm beginning to like you.'

Pathetically pleased, I asked, 'What do you like about me?'

'Your face,' he decided.

'What about my face?'

He considered a moment. 'I kind of like the way it fits on your head.'

Absurdly flattered, I probed him further: 'Do you still think I'm a shnake?' *Did I say 'shnake'?*

'What's a shnake?'

'You know ... a shnake.' *What the fuck was the matter with my tongue?*

He chuckled. 'I don't know what a shnake is, but I was bitten by a snake once.'

'Oh, really? Where?'

He screwed up his face and with great effort pronounced, 'Ag-fan-is-tan.'

'No, I mean ... *where*?'

'On my buttock,' he answered.

'Wow! Did you have to ... suck out the poison?'

He gave me a quizzical look. 'How do you suck your own buttock?' he wondered.

'I don't know,' I said, mystified. He passed me the joint and with a wobbly hand I steered it into my mouth. 'Finish it,' he instructed, laying down and closing his eyes.

I was feeling decidedly woozy by the time I stubbed out the roach and accidentally knocked over a gloopy pot of sweet and sour congealed glue. 'Bugger,' I moaned, staggering to my feet to weave a winding path to the kitchen for a cloth. When I returned, Gervaise was helpfully stowing the half-empty cartons into the bag they'd arrived in.

'These leftovers could feed a starving family for a week,' he commented earnestly.

'It's mostly water chestnuts and bamboo shoots,' I said, listlessly wiping up the mess. 'They'd have to be seriously hungry to eat those. I don't know anybody who does.'

'Believe me, Sugarlips, there are people in the world who'd eat the cartons.'

'How awful,' I said. 'Who *are* these people?'

He crawled back on to the cushions. 'They live in muddy rivers,' he slurred, 'and have to walk miles to a hut in the blistery heat without any shoes on.'

'What – not even flip-flops?'

He shook his head slowly. 'When you're starving even a flip-flap is a delicacy.'

'They eat their own flop-flops!' I exclaimed. 'That's terrible. We have to do something.'

'Like what?' he asked. 'Make a donation? You're up to your deck in net, Selina.'

'Then I'll send them my shoes,' I pronounced, unsteadily removing my red fluffy mules and slapping them on to the coffee table. 'There!'

'That's sweet,' he said. 'They'll like those.'

'Don't patronise me,' I growled. 'At least I'm giving *something*. You wouldn't give a jelly bean if you owned a jelly bean factory.'

'Are you saying I'm a skinflint?'

'Yes, I'm saying you're a flinskint.'

'I'll show you who's a flinkstink!' He sat up angrily. 'I'll call your slutty tart's shoes with my Moroccan leather loafers.' He yanked them off and thumped them on to the table. 'And I'll raise you a pair of –' spilling over sideways, he grappled with his feet '– socks. Now who's a stinkflin?' he demanded, balling them up and lobbing them like a grenade.

Annoyed that he'd gone one better, I shimmied out of my tights. 'I'll see your cheap supermarket socks with my very expensable dulux tights.'

'Is that ... bloody ... so!' he cried, dragging his polo shirt over his head and tossing it on to the pile. 'Then I re-raise! Ha!'

To our pissed and hash-fuddled brains, it seemed perfectly natural to gamble with the currency of our clothing and so we carried on playing until my knickers and his pants had been added to the pot, creating an honourable stalemate. By this time, the exertion of undressing had tired us both; his head was drooping and I had double vision, plus the room had started spinning.

Somehow, I managed to climb on to the sofa and although I was conscious of feeling chilly, my brain hadn't registered that my body was naked and so failed to propose a solution. 'S'cold,' I murmured into the cushion I'd buried my head in.

I must have dozed off for a second or two because my next conscious thought was that I'd been covered by something warm, something weighty like a mattress, but sort of clingy like cling-film. It was smooth in places, yet furry in others, and had a built-in warm air fan that was purring against my shoulder. The idea of it being a human body didn't occur to my foggy brain until I heard a husky male voice in my ear and felt a hand slide under my belly. Even then, as realisation clinked in my skull, it didn't ring an alarm bell, for I reasoned it must be Gervaise keeping me warm with his body. *How sweet of him.*

I drifted into a horny dream in which a faceless man, who I assumed to be Harry because he was dressed in black leather lederhosen and a matador's hat, was rubbing sweet and sour sauce into my buttocks and licking it off with his tongue. A small part of my brain was appalled by the act because it knew with utmost certainty that I needed that sauce to go with my fishfingers. 'Harry, my fishfingers,' I muttered.

Ignoring me, he parted my thighs and wriggled his fingers between my pussy lips. It felt so good that I knew it must be wrong. 'Harry,' I moaned. My voice sounded muffled and distant, and when I levered open an eye, I couldn't see a thing. My face was buried in a cushion!

Suddenly, I was lucid again and aware that something impossibly large was being squeezed into my pussy and that a heavy weight was bearing down on my back. I struggled feebly against the invader but it kept on coming, pushing inch after inch into the tight, moistened tunnel of my sex. Then, slowly and gently, it began to slide back and forth, creating a glorious sensation of being languidly made love to.

I tried to stay awake but the lazy, steady rhythm kept rocking me off to sleep and, in the end, I succumbed to the darkness of oblivion.

16

I had the strangest feeling when I woke up. I felt that my skull had a blancmange inside it and, each time I lifted my head, the blancmange would wobble, causing my bleary eyes to boggle out of focus.

Forced to lie back on my pillow, I tried to piece together the fragmented bytes of my memory. I had a million questions to ask the blancmange but, fearing it might collapse under the stress of interrogation, I restricted myself to one at a time. First: When and how did I get into bed? Answer: *Search me.* It was not a good start. I tried another: How, in the name of quantum physics, did I manage to get undressed? *Buggered if I know* came the vapid response.

Now listen to me, you solidified lump of custard, start talking! But it was no use. The blancmange couldn't remember anything beyond the point where Gervaise had lit up a joint.

What had happened thereafter? Had we slept together? I tentatively explored between my legs. I couldn't find any stickiness but my insides felt strangely raw as if either I'd enjoyed a marathon sex session or had been forcibly fucked. The latter proposition seemed the most unlikely bearing in mind how much I wanted Gervaise, so I was drawn to the conclusion that I'd probably had the best sex of my life but couldn't remember a sodding thing about it.

I was furious with myself. How could I forget such a momentous event? I searched my brain again but encountered the same void of nothingness. All I had to go by was the evidence of my pussy and even that was inconclusive. For all I knew, I might have taken my dildo to bed and had a bloody good time on my own. The absence of semen perplexed me. Had he worn a condom or simply failed to come? Neither of these premises appealed to me. On the one hand, a condom suggested premeditation on his part and, on the other, a lack of enthusiasm.

There was only one way to find out – I had to get up. I eased myself gently out of bed and, taking care not to shake the blancmange, carried my head like a china bowl to the bathroom. I half expected it to fall off my neck when I finally let go. But, remarkably, it stayed where it was and somehow I managed to wash.

The stairs were a trickier affair. I had to take each step very slowly, clinging to the banister all the way, and when at last I reached the hall, it seemed to lurch underneath me like the deck of a ship in a gale. I heaved as the smell of bacon wafted down the hall from the kitchen.

I found Gervaise cracking eggs into a frying pan. Hearing me ricochet off the fridge as I staggered in, he slew me a look. 'Want some?'

I screwed up my face and swallowed. 'Do I look like I want some? What's the best thing for a hangover?'

'Drinking heavily the night before,' he quipped. 'Sit down and I'll get you some seltzer.'

I felt too nauseous to question him while he was eating so I took my fizzy drink into the lounge, hoping to find some evidence of how the evening had concluded. But he'd cleared everything away and tidied up the room.

Presently, he joined me. 'You've cleared up,' I accused him.

He glanced at me warily. 'I'll mess it up again if you like.'

'Gervaise . . .' *How did I broach the subject?* 'What happened last night?'

'You don't remember?' I hated his sly smile.

'Would I bloody well ask if I did?'

He furrowed his brow. 'No need to be tetchy.'

'Just tell me what happened,' I urged him. 'Did we – you know?'

'Get to know each other?' he finished for me. I nodded. 'Yes, I think you could say that,' he confirmed. 'Or did you mean in the biblical sense?'

'Goddamn it, did we fuck or didn't we?' I stormed.

My frustration amused him. 'What difference does it make if you can't remember?'

'It may not make a difference to *you*,' I ranted, 'but if I've been to bed with someone then I damn well want to know about it.'

'Actually, we slept in our own beds,' he told me. 'We did the fucking on the couch.'

'Oh shit,' I groaned, sinking my head into my hands. 'I don't remember.'

'I wouldn't worry about it,' he said. 'People are fucking people all the time. It's what the human race is good at. Nobody's keeping tabs any more, Selina.'

It enraged me to hear him speak so casually. 'How do I know that you didn't take advantage of me?'

He raised his eyebrows. 'Take advantage of an open goal? I should bloody well think so! Correct me if I'm wrong, but weren't you the one playing footsie with my balls yesterday? And wasn't it you who said: "I want to fuck you, *mon cheri*"?'

'I was teasing!' I exclaimed.

'To what end?' he contested.

Unable to meet the challenge of his gaze, I glanced

away. 'OK, I was being seductive. I suppose I can't blame you for thinking that I was offering you my body in gift-wrap. But you might have had the courtesy to wait until I was conscious before you took it.' He didn't answer. 'What baffles me,' I continued, 'is that yesterday you seemed to have made up your mind that I was some kind of man-eating serpent. All that talk about snakes and poison. Was it bollocks?'

'I'm still of that opinion,' he answered coolly. 'But don't get me wrong, I'm attracted to danger; it's written in my résumé. I've learnt to be cautious, however. For example, I wouldn't fuck with a snake when it's wide-awake, I'd sneak up on it when it's asleep.'

My hands flew to my cheeks. 'Oh, you coward!' I cried. 'You used me.'

'You didn't seem to mind at the time,' he advised.

'I've only *your* word for that,' I said scornfully. 'How can you be such a self-preserving bastard?'

'I warned you I wanted you,' he said.

I gaped at him. 'That hand-licking thing was a warning?'

'What did you think it was?'

'A statement,' I uttered stupidly.

He cocked his head to one side. 'Why would I bother stating the obvious?'

I felt wretchedly disappointed. 'I thought I was getting through to you. You even said you were starting to like me. But all the time you were working out how you could nail me without putting yourself at risk.'

'It was still a high risk strategy,' he said. 'After all, you could have woken at any time and sunk your fangs into me. That's why I dumped you in your own bed, incidentally.'

'You bastard!' I seethed.

'Now you're getting monotonous.' He made a gesture

of dismissal. 'Can't we just forget about this? You wanted me on your terms: I took you on mine. Is that so terrible?'

The blancmange in my head was finding it hard to follow his reasoning. 'But considering the state I was in, unless you're into necrophilia, it couldn't have been much fun for you.'

He laughed. 'Believe me, Selina, you weren't *that* unresponsive: corpses don't moan and wriggle with pleasure. Not that I'm claiming any credit for that.'

'Why not? Did you slip in a third party to get me prepped for you or something?'

'You were the one who made it a threesome,' he said.

'What are you talking about?'

'You kept muttering Harry's name.'

I thought I detected an edge to his voice. 'That must have offended your ego,' I judged.

'Frankly, my ego was too pissed to be offended,' he retorted.

Without realising it, he'd handed me a lifeline. Snatching it up, I waded out to salvage my pride. 'No wonder I was wriggling and moaning if I thought it was Harry. How well did you play his role? Did you give me a rapturous orgasm?'

'Not that I can remember,' he answered gruffly.

I twisted the knife. 'Then you can't have been aping his style too well. What else did I say in my sleep?'

His lips twitched with restrained humour. 'You mumbled something about fishfingers. Is that a fetish of his?'

'Fishfingers?' *Fish bloody fingers – how drunk had I been?*

He glanced at his watch. 'Shouldn't you be at work by now?'

'Oh shit!' I sprang to my feet. 'Harry will kill me.'

* * *

But Harry scarcely raised an eyebrow when I hurtled into the office forty minutes late. And when he mumbled a listless greeting and attempted a wooden smile, I knew that something was wrong.

Drawing up a chair, I sat down. 'What's the matter, Harry? You've a face like a trodden-on frog.'

He looked at me dispiritedly. 'Notice anything missing?'

'Where's Holly?' I asked.

'She's quit,' he uttered morosely, 'and she isn't coming back.'

I flapped my hands. 'Oh, for heaven's sake, if I had a quid for every time she's walked out on you, I could buy myself a pair of Gucci shoes and a matching handbag.'

'It's different this time,' he stressed. 'I made a prick of myself on Saturday night and if I could lay my hands on an orthopaedic boot, I'd shove it on my foot and give myself a right good kicking up the arse.'

'I'd buy tickets to see that,' I said keenly. 'Holly told me what you did. For God's sake, Harry, what's the matter with you? Are those tentacles growing out of your arms?'

'I didn't mean to grope her. It just happened.'

'I'll bet you've been using that same adolescent excuse ever since you started shaving,' I sneered. 'I'm only surprised that Holly didn't sock you one in the kisser, considering the history between you.'

He nodded contritely. 'I wish she had! I'd feel a whole lot better if I had a fat lip and a multicoloured scrotum to show you. How much of our history did she tell you?'

'All of it,' I said.

He cast his eyes downward. 'It's not a pretty tale, is it? I suppose she said it was all my fault; that if I hadn't cheated on her in the first place, none of it would have happened? Well, she's right: I had a great thing going and I ballsed it up.'

I shook my head. 'Actually, she wasn't half as hard on you as you're being on yourself; she took her share of the blame.'

He heaved a heavy sigh. 'I should have left things alone. It's taken us years to bury the past and rebuild our friendship. Asking her to try again must have seemed as inviting as someone offering to give her a second dose of the clap. I should have known she'd run a mile.'

'She's only running because she's scared,' I said. 'That doesn't mean she doesn't want to.'

He perked up. 'Why, what did she say?'

I hesitated. Should I betray Holly's confidence for the sake of her happiness? Harry was drilling me with his eyes. I could see the desperation on his face, the flicker of hope that he hadn't quite blown it. The words whispered out of me, 'She loves you.'

His face crumpled as if I'd slapped him. 'She said that?'

I clenched my fists, wanting to pummel his stupidity. 'You bloody fool, didn't you know?'

'I'd hoped,' he murmured, 'but I didn't really think I stood a chance. I don't deserve it.'

'Yes you do,' I insisted. 'You both do. But you have to say it, Harry, that four-letter word you've been avoiding all your life. You have to admit it to yourself and then to her.'

'I do . . . love her,' he declared.

'Welcome to humanity!' I cried. 'Now all you have to do is tell Holly.'

'But if she's as scared as you say, won't she just keep running?'

'Probably,' I concurred. 'So you'll have to keep on

chasing her until she runs out of steam or pulls up.' I rolled my eyes heavenward. 'What are you sitting there for? Get your Reeboks on and go get her!'

He stood up, lifted me out of my seat, and planted a smacker on my cheek. Then, squeezing my bum, he smiled wolfishly. 'Just for old time's sake.'

'Piss off,' I said, giggling as he speed-walked out the door.

I felt inordinately pleased with myself, as if I'd engineered the entire romance and, with a wave of my magic wand, put everything right. I had a vision of Harry going down on one knee to declare his undying love and – providing he didn't take it into his head to stick his hand up her skirt while he was down there – of Holly erupting into joyful tears.

I floated into my office on a pink cloud of happiness only to be brought swiftly down to earth by a telephone enquiry from a local sandwich company seeking to promote their new menu with someone dressed up as a bagel.

Later on that day, I heard from Matt. Apparently, a fire had broken out during his interview and they'd had to postpone it. 'Bloody typical,' he grumbled. 'I finally get a crack at a decent job and some stupid wanker sets fire to the premises.'

'Was anyone hurt?' I asked worriedly.

'No,' he replied, 'the only casualty was a box of leaflets on soffits and facias – hardly a loss to mankind. But it means I'll be stuck here another night.'

The news set my pulses racing as I considered the prospect of another night alone with Gervaise. After the unscrupulous way that he'd used my body for his own selfish pleasure, I should have been angry with him, but each time I pictured him screwing me, it brought a sultry smile to my lips and a twinge of erotic desire. In truth, I was more annoyed with myself than with him for having foolishly flunked a golden opportunity to hold and caress him, to know and enjoy his body, to experience the thrill of his kiss and the thrust of his cock. It infuriated me that I'd been too pissed to do anything but lie there impassively, babbling incoherently about fishfingers and fantasising over a man that I didn't want any more. How could I have been such a lousy lay? No wonder he hadn't come!

The more I thought about it, the more determined I became to demonstrate my sexiness and dispel any notion in his head that, by fucking me once, he'd satisfied his carnal curiosity and could write me off as an apathetic lover with whom he'd shared a thoroughly forgettable one-night stand.

Goddamn him – I had to prove myself. If he thought of me as a snake then I'd be a bloody snake. I'd sharpen those fangs that he feared so much, sink them deep into his skin and inject him with a lethal dose of lust! I spent the rest of the day making sneaky snaky plans for his seduction.

I was so wrapped up in my campaign that I scarcely did any work, but I did remember to ring Luca Verdici: 'You'll be pleased to know that I have all your money,' I told him.

'Is that so?' he replied, sounding not very pleased at all.

'I could put the cheque in the post,' I suggested. 'It'll save you the trouble of coming in.'

'Put the cheque in the post?' he uttered cynically. 'How many times have I heard that one? No, Selina, I won't be fucked about with. You'll deliver it to my home on Wednesday evening. I'll give you the address.'

Knowing better than to argue with him, I agreed to his demand.

Since the first phase of my plan was to put Gervaise at ease by being nice to him, I walked into the lounge with a big, friendly smile on my face, but he wasn't there. When he wasn't in the kitchen either, I sprang up the stairs with the smile still fixed to my face and knocked on his door.

His deep voice answered, 'Come.'

He was sprawled across the bed typing on his laptop. His long legs encased in arse-hugging black jeans, his bronzed chest exposed in an unbuttoned black shirt with the sleeves rolled up. He looked so gorgeous that I felt like throwing my plans out of the window and myself on top of him.

'What do you want?' he asked brusquely.

'Hmm?' My eyes had been captivated by the dark sprawl of man-fur on his chest. What did I want? I wanted to rub my breasts against it, of course. But I said, 'I thought I'd cook something.'

He looked at me as if I'd offered to unicycle across a tightrope. 'You? Cook? What did you have in mind – beans on toast?'

'Oh, I think I can be a little more adventuresome than that,' I said. 'It's just the two of us tonight, by the way.'

When I explained about Matt, he drew his eyebrows together. 'Don't bother cooking for me – I thought I'd go round Holly's,' he said.

I strolled into the room and peered over his shoulder at his computer screen; he was writing a letter in French. 'She's entertaining Harry,' I advised him. 'I don't think you'd be welcome.'

'Then maybe I'll go for a drink instead.'

I laid my hand on his shoulder. 'Is it my cooking you're trying to avoid – or me?'

He twisted his head to look at my hand and then his laser blue eyes zapped into mine. 'Last night was a one-off,' he told me bluntly. 'If you're looking for a repeat performance – forget it.'

I removed my hand. 'I was just trying to be friendly,' I said.

He smiled sardonically. 'I've never met a friendly cobra yet.'

'Will you quit with the snake talk!' I fumed. 'Don't you realise, Gervaise, it isn't me you don't trust – it's yourself. What are you scared of? Are you afraid that if we get too close I'll drag you out of your depth?'

'You're distracting,' he said, looking back at his screen. 'Sometimes I forget that I have a girlfriend back home.'

'Is that who you're writing to?' He nodded. 'Be sure to mention Holly, won't you,' I reminded him frostily.

'Veronique would understand about Holly,' he said. 'We don't expect each other to be celibate.'

'Would she understand about me?'

He gave a humourless chuckle. 'No, I don't suppose she would.'

My heart gave a flutter. 'Why not?'

He merely shrugged. 'Because I don't.'

It was the most annoyingly ambiguous thing he could have said and, to make any sense of it, I was tempted to make a move on him then and there. But my inner voice warned that he was much too guarded at present and would probably fend me off. Collecting myself, I feigned indifference. 'Suit your bloody self what you do. I've offered you the olive branch – you can stick it up your arse for all I care.'

'Oh, for God's sake,' he sighed. 'Go and cook if you must. I'll eat it if it kills me.'

Contented, I withdrew. Although phase one hadn't quite gone according to plan, I was determined to pull off phase two without a hitch. A romantic meal for two must surely make him more receptive to me. But unfortunately, in drawing up my plans, I'd neglected to take the contents of the fridge into account. What possible gourmet offering could I conjure out of one egg, some iffy-looking cheese and half a pint of milk? In the freezer, I found a packet of fishfingers and a bag of frozen broccoli but after toying with the idea of presenting *cod in breadcrumb avec calabrese au gratin*, I decided to use the fishfingers as a starter and to prepare a broccoli cheese for the main course.

After painstakingly removing all the breadcrumbs from the fishfingers, I nuked them in the microwave and then covered them in some thick tomato sauce that I'd nicked from a can of pilchards. I didn't know how to make broccoli cheese but I was pretty sure that it ought to contain egg, milk and cheese, so I whipped together the ingredients and then poured the mixture into a dish on top of the frozen broccoli. I stood vigil by the oven because I didn't know how long it would take to cook. Presently, to my surprise, my cheese sauce grew firm and began to rise like a soufflé. It looked quite impressive until I opened the oven door to take a closer look. Then it sank like a pricked balloon. I wasn't sure what I'd made but it had browned quite nicely and looked edible.

After laying the dining room table and lighting a candle, I summoned Gervaise downstairs and while he poured out the wine, I served the first course.

He poked it with his fork. 'What is it?' he asked sceptically.

'It's cod in a fish and tomato sauce,' I pronounced.

He lifted the plate to his nose and sniffed. 'Are you sure? It smells of pilchard.'

'I may have used some pilchard flavouring in the sauce,' I admitted demurely.

A smile twitched the corners of his lips. 'Then, I'm sorry, I can't eat it; it looks wonderful but I really hate the taste of pilchard.' He pushed back his plate. 'Aren't you having any?'

'I don't like pilchard either,' I confessed. 'It's just that the recipe called for it.'

'What recipe book would that be?' he chuckled. 'One hundred and one things to do with a pilchard?'

I loved the way his eyes sparkled when he laughed. 'I'll fetch the main course,' I uttered nervously.

In the kitchen, I realised that my heart was pumping in frenetic anticipation of phase three and that my hands were shaking as I dissected two bricks from the thing that I'd made and served each of them up with a dribble of Worcester sauce.

'You're kidding,' he said, as I placed his in front of him.

'It's a deep-dish broccoli omelette,' I submitted hopefully.

He screwed up his face. 'This is an omelette? It looks more like a bath sponge.'

'Yes, well, it's how we like them in England, nice and thick,' I flannelled feebly.

'And do you also like your broccoli hard?' he wondered, sawing his knife through a stalk.

'As a matter of fact,' I insisted, chewing bravely, 'the ... crunchiness is supposed to ... enhance the smooth texture of ... bugger-fucking bollocks!' I slammed down my knife and fork. 'It's shit, isn't it?'

He nodded, laughing. 'Can I make a suggestion? Why don't you get the beans while I make the toast?'

Although phase two had meandered off course, it wouldn't have mattered too much if I'd served up bits of cardboard. The most important thing was the romantic candlelit ambience I'd created. As I sat, sipping wine and stabbing beans on to my fork, with the sound of John Coltrane's smooth arrangements in the background, I was reasonably pleased with the way things were progressing.

Gervaise had relaxed and was beginning to respond to flirtation. 'You cook a mean piece of toast,' I commended him.

'You cook a mean bean,' he returned, making an OK circle with his finger and thumb and kissing it off his lips. 'Even though you had the microwave on defrost.'

'I wish I could put *you* on defrost,' I murmured wistfully.

He narrowed his gaze into a wary look. 'What I can't understand is why Miranda never taught you to cook,' he commented.

'Oh she tried, but I didn't really take to it,' I said. 'I was much more interested in other things.'

'Such as Matt?' he suggested.

'Such as music,' I replied. 'I used to take dancing lessons. My teacher said I had a natural sense of rhythm.'

'Yeah, I noticed it at the party,' he concurred. 'You move like a table dancer.'

I leaned forward. 'It's all in the hips, don't you think? In the rhythmic movement of the pelvis?'

His eyes strayed to my mouth. 'Are we still talking about dancing?'

I licked my lips. 'I don't know – are we? What were you thinking of?' I'd dropped my voice to a husky purr.

He sucked in his cheeks and looked at me severely. 'That's very good, Selina. You've got me thinking about sex.'

I made an innocent gesture. 'Men think about sex

238

every few seconds,' I pointed out. 'You can hardly blame me for the predilections of your species.'

'It's the female that keeps us thinking that way,' he said. 'Take you, for example. You've been offering to fuck me ever since I sat down.'

'I didn't hear myself say that,' I said.

'Not in words,' he agreed. 'But wouldn't it be more honest if you just came out and said it? You remember how it goes: "*I want to fuck you,* mon cheri, *only, this time, I damn well mean it.*"'

'All right then. I do,' I admitted.

'Well, I *don't*,' he said firmly. 'I'd sooner slam my dick in a door. Is that clear enough for you?'

'Whatever,' I acknowledged, with an unconcerned lift of my shoulders. 'You have the dick and I don't. If you choose not to use it then, I guess that's up to you.' I leaned back and shook my long hair.

'Oh, that's beautiful,' he sighed. 'You're so incredibly good at marketing your assets – that was hair and tits together.'

'But you're not buying,' I said petulantly, 'so what's the point of window-shopping?'

'It doesn't do any harm to speculate,' he said.

'About what?'

'About whether I could kiss that pouty mouth of yours without getting an erection.'

'You couldn't do it,' I said scornfully.

'Why not?'

'Because you're French.'

'I'm half English,' he reminded me.

'In your head perhaps, but your lower half is definitely French.'

He stood up. 'I have a niggling feeling that you might be right.' He lifted my chin and touched his lips teasingly to mine. 'But I don't think I'll put it to the test.' He picked up the dinner plates. 'Why don't you go and relax? I'll clear up.'

I flapped my long eyelashes. 'Are you sure you don't want me to ... do anything?' I flicked my eyes to his crotch.

I detected the memory of my mouth around his cock flashing in his eyes. But he blinked and drew his lips into a tight smile. 'No thank you, *Sugarlips*. I think I can manage.'

Despite his apparent determination to resist me, I knew that he was weakening and that, with any luck, phase three would nuke the last of his defences. Excitement mounted in me as I stole upstairs to execute the final part of my plan.

I didn't have much time, so I flung my clothes all over the place as I stripped them off. I gave my hair a brutal brushing and, after refreshing my lipstick and perfume, took a negligée from my wardrobe and slipped it on.

Actually, it wasn't much more than a cobweb: a flimsy black veil that only pretended to cover my nakedness. It gave a soft focus to my figure, clinging to my shapely breasts and rounded hips in a way that enhanced their voluptuousness and, through the filmy fabric, the dark inverted triangle of my pubic hair pointed, like an arrow, to my sex.

My eyes were shining with anticipation, their pupils large and sexy, their irises constantly shifting colour from aquamarine to turquoise. The heightened colour in my cheeks had given my face a sensual glow and my reddened lips were softly swollen.

Giving my hair a final shake so that it rippled over my shoulders, I took a deep breath and, like a witch, summoned all my powers of seduction. There was nothing more I could do. Whatever happened next rested firmly in the hands of fate.

17

As fate would have it, we met in the hall: Gervaise coming out of the kitchen just as I was stepping off the last stair. We both stopped dead in our tracks.

'*Mon Dieu!*' he exclaimed, slamming his hand to his forehead and half-turning away. The hand scrubbed over his face and then stopped at his mouth. 'Selina,' he rasped from behind it, 'what the hell have you done?'

As I floated towards him in my see-through night-gown, his hand crawled into his hair, raking unsteady fingers through it while his darkening eyes devoured me. 'Gervaise,' I uttered softly, cupping my breasts. 'I can't bear it any more, I want you so much.'

I saw him chew on his lip as he watched my thumbs caressing my stiffening nipples. I saw his cock stir and his chest rise to accommodate his deepening breath. I saw the fire of lust igniting in his eyes as his voice ratcheted out of him, 'Dear God, you're so beautiful,' he croaked.

When I'd closed the distance between us, he reached out and touched my hair, his eyes locking with mine as his fingers trailed down its silky length to the rounded swell of my breast and then beyond to the curve of my waist. Then with sudden fierce roughness he jerked me into his arms and, with fingers gripping my face, crushed his lips to mine in a bruising, angry kiss.

Completely overwhelmed, I offered no resistance as he slammed me against the wall and, pinning me with his body, ground the hardening wedge of his manhood against my sex. Then, for a few frenzied seconds, he let the beast of his passion run wild, savagely assaulting me with cruel mouth, ravishing hands and steamy, snorting breath. Like a rag doll in his arms, I could do nothing but gasp and moan, and cling to him.

Now utterly the master of me, he gathered me to his chest and, holding me close, let his fury shudder out of him. When he sought my lips again, his mouth was firm and gentle and his kiss so penetratingly sexy that my bones dissolved into liquid. At the touch of his hands, now incredibly sensual, the longest sigh groaned out of me as I realised he'd finally surrendered.

He let me kiss his face, run my fingers through his hair and caress his fabulous body. He let me twine myself around him like a snake. Then, all at once, we were kissing as if our lives depended on it: tongue fucking tongue, bodies pressed together, nature's imperative swamping our thoughts, driving our hands to tear at each other's clothes.

When my pussy, drenched and dripping, encountered his throbbing cock, our mutual desire combusted into a fireball. Neither he nor I could bear the touch of hands on our scorching genitals or endure another moment's delay. We were hopelessly, helplessly, out of control.

There was no time to lay me down or choose a comfortable position; it was all about urgency and doing it right then and there. Now, right now, up against the wall. I didn't need to guide him in and he didn't need to feel his way. With a single, powerful thrust, he'd imbedded himself inside me.

It was the ultimate joy, the ultimate relief. We both groaned and shivered in rapture. 'OK?' he uttered hoarsely. I nodded, eager and breathless.

Burying his face into my hair and whispering words in French, he clamped his hand around my thigh and, lifting my leg, began to move his hips. *Oh my God! Oh wow!*

I came so quickly and so out-of-the-blue that I almost collapsed. He had to grit his teeth against my vaginal spasms to stop himself from coming. 'Damn it,' I heard him say. 'Couldn't you at least wait until I was into double figures?'

'I can't help it,' I gasped euphorically. 'I'm having the most incredible sensations. Bloody hell, is this what love is?'

'No,' he growled, 'this is what sex is. So will you just shut up and let me get on with it?'

'Catch up with me,' I urged him, biting into his neck as my rippling inner muscles squeezed his shaft.

But he wouldn't be rushed and eased into his rhythm, controlling his powerful haunches to release their energy little by little. He played me like a maestro, leading me, making me follow, until our bodies were moving as one: hearts beating together, breath purring an erotic duet.

I had never been so totally in tune with a man before and the feel of his slick cock sliding inside my silky tunnel was almost unbearably exquisite. Then, as my insides began to tighten as if bunching into a fist, he unleashed the stallion strength of his hips and with a force that ripped the breath from my lungs, began ramming home his thrusts with feral grunts.

I grasped his arse, gasping as his cock pounded into me with a clit-tugging friction that swamped my brain with Morse-coded messages of pleasure until wails and screams of ecstasy were jumping from my throat. Then, suddenly, the tension within me snapped like a bone breaking, and instantly the rumbling quake of an orgasm shook my body. In the cataclysm of its wake, my mind was only dimly aware of his semen flooding into me as his groan, like a thunderclap, blasted in my ear.

It was a long time before either of us could speak. We stood, slumped together, with our hearts hammering for what seemed like an age. But, eventually, he disengaged himself and zipped up his trousers. I saw that he was frowning.

'Gervaise?' I ventured softly. 'What's wrong?'

'This – this is wrong,' he fumed, glaring at me angrily. Then, abruptly, he slammed his hand against the wall beside my head. 'Damn you!' he cried. 'Fuck you!' Then he stomped down the hall, yanked his jacket off the peg and threw it at me. 'Cover yourself up for God's sake.'

'What's got into you?' I exclaimed. The jacket was like a tent on me and despite his annoyance, I could see that my appearance amused him.

He brought his hand to his neck. 'You bit me,' he raged. 'I damn well said you would, didn't I?'

At first I thought he was speaking metaphorically until he showed me the actual teeth marks on his skin. *Did I do that? Bloody hell!*

'There's no need to look like that,' I said. 'I didn't do it on purpose.'

'Oh yes you did,' he accused me. 'You've been trying to get your fangs into me ever since I shaved off my beard. You just couldn't take "no" for an answer, could you?'

'It's a little late to cry rape,' I protested. 'You weren't exactly fighting me off, Gervaise.' I followed him as he marched into the lounge. 'I can't understand why you're being like this. I thought it was fantastic.'

'I didn't say I didn't enjoy it,' he said, sitting down, getting up, and then marching out to the kitchen. I followed him like a puppy, watching his every move as he went to the fridge and poured himself a glass of milk.

Presently, I said, 'So – let's go upstairs and do it again.'

'You what!' he exclaimed, spluttering milk.

'Only this time let's make love,' I suggested.

'Make love?' he echoed cynically. 'You don't know how to love; all you know is how to fuck.'

'That's not true!' I objected. 'I was deeply in love with Harry.'

'You loved fucking Harry,' he corrected me. 'That's why you couldn't stop. You don't want Kyle, or Matt, or me. You've just been looking for a substitute. You were even prepared to bust up my sister's relationship just to try Matt out in the sack. When I got in your way, you thought you'd try me instead. Well congratulations – you've succeeded. How do I measure up? No – don't tell me, I don't give a shit.' He stormed off again only, this time, I didn't follow but sat staring into space.

Was it true? Had I been lying to myself all these years? Was I really incapable of feeling anything more than physical love for a man?

At last I understood why Gervaise had been resisting me. He hadn't liked the idea of being part of a chain of experimental lovers, of being tried out and found wanting. And, right at this moment, he was furious with himself for submitting to my seduction and allowing himself to be tested.

What he didn't know was how well he'd passed the test. How his skill as a lover had Harry trumped in spades: how the taste, the touch, and the feel of him had left me craving for more. He was everything I wanted. And if this wasn't love then it damn well ought to be!

Hearing the front door slam, I gave my head a rueful shake. It wasn't going to be easy trying to tell him how I felt.

In the morning I woke up on the sofa after waiting up all night for him. But he hadn't come home. He'd run out on me, and I was forced to confront the painful truth that he despised me for what I'd done and bitterly regretted what he'd done. Feeling maudlin and depressed, I washed and dressed lethargically and then dragged myself to work.

But when I walked into Harry's office, I forgot all my troubles in an instant when I saw he and Holly in a loving embrace, kissing each other tenderly. It made me happy to know that romance was still alive in the world and to see Holly's face wreathed in smiles. 'Do you think I'm crazy?' she asked me.

'No, but I think you're a glutton for punishment,' I said.

'She says she never stopped loving my dick,' Harry commented. 'What do you make of that?'

'It's a nice dick,' I declared. 'She could do a lot worse for herself. But I can't say I'm too sure about the rest of you.'

Holly grinned. She looked radiant. 'I'm probably making the biggest mistake of my life but – what the heck – you only live once.'

'I'm a one-woman man from now on,' decreed Harry, giving her a squeeze. 'And, if it takes the rest of my life, someday I'll convince you that you haven't made a mistake.'

I stabbed my finger into my mouth, pretending to make myself sick. 'I think I'm going to throw up.'

Holly nodded. 'Me too,' she agreed, patting his hand. 'Gooey doesn't suit you, darling. I like it better when you're a shit.'

'Oh, bugger off the pair of you,' he grumbled good-naturedly.

Later on, in my office, Holly asked me what had happened between Gervaise and me. 'He spent last night on my couch,' she informed me.

'With Harry there? Didn't he mind?'

'Oh, you know Harry – he suggested a threesome.' She laughed. 'But, seriously, he likes Gervaise; they get on really well.'

'Did he talk about me?' I asked tentatively.

'Not in so many words,' she replied, 'but I got the impression that you'd fallen out over something. He didn't seem in any hurry to go home. I said he could stay for as long as he likes.'

'Cheers,' I muttered glumly.

'Did I do wrong?' She looked dismayed.

I waved my hand. 'No, of course not. It's just that I had a few things that I wanted to say to him.'

'Should I tell him that?'

I shook my head. 'If he's still peevish about what happened, he's unlikely to listen right now.'

'So – what *did* happen?' she probed me.

'Take a guess.'

'You had sex with him,' she deduced. 'But why would that make him peevish?'

'I'm not sure how you're going to take this,' I said, 'but he thinks I only shagged him to see how he compares to Harry.'

She screwed up her face. 'Is that true?'

'I suppose if I'm honest with myself I *have* been searching for someone like Harry,' I admitted. 'But that was before I fell for Gervaise. Oh Holly, I think I love him. But I just don't know how to tell him and I doubt if he'd believe me if I did. He doesn't think I'm capable of loving. He thinks I'm all about sex.'

'Which you refuted by screwing him?' She gave her head a solemn shake. 'Didn't it cross your mind to simply ask him out on a date?'

I pulled a rueful face. 'I didn't think of that.'

She sighed. 'Then maybe he has a point. When you next get a chance to talk to him, try sitting on your hands and looking into his eyes instead of his flies.'

Holly's advice made sense. Instead of throwing my body at Gervaise, I should have started out by trying to win his friendship. I should have charmed him first and bedded him later. As it dawned on me that every relationship I'd ever had with a man had been centred on the physical, I began to see myself as the sexual predator that Gervaise had described. Effectively, I'd been a female version of Harry.

Maybe it was too late to alter his opinion but perhaps if I told him how I felt, I could make him understand that I wasn't quite as heartless as I seemed. If Harry could persuade Holly of his capacity to love, then surely I stood a chance of convincing Gervaise.

With this as my mission, I spent most of the day rehearsing what I would say to him. But when I got home, he still wasn't there. Without his presence the house seemed cold and empty.

I wandered from room to room, remembering little things about him: like the way he smiled and the way his long legs took up so much room and his body filled a chair. Like the charismatic dancing of his eyebrows when he talked and the lively intelligence in his sparkling blue eyes.

I longed for him to come home but as the hours slipped by, I grew more and more anxious. What point was he trying to make? What was I supposed to read into his prolonged absence? Didn't he trust himself to be alone with me again?

When, at last, I heard a key in the front door, I raced into the hall, ready to throw myself at his mercy. But the smile slipped from my lips when I saw that it was Matt.

'Oh, you're back,' I blurted, trying to hide my disappointment. 'How did you get on?'

He flicked his blond hair from his eyes and held up a bottle of scotch. 'Come and have a drink with me,' he ordered, pushing past me into the lounge.

'Are we celebrating?' I asked.

He threw himself down on the couch, unscrewed the bottle and took a long swig from it. 'Not exactly.'

'You mean you didn't get the job?'

'No,' he snarled, 'I didn't get the job.' He quirked his chin. 'Where's that fucking French son-of-a-bitch?'

'I don't know, he's ... er ... out,' I answered awkwardly. 'What went wrong, Matt, did the interview go badly?'

He took another swig. 'Yeah, you could say that. I kind of lost my temper.' His eyes grew wide and furious. 'It was a waste of fucking time. They said the stuff in my portfolio was out of the ark because I hadn't done anything on a computer.'

'Didn't you tell them that you're willing to learn?'

He laughed contemptuously. 'Oh, they said they'd train me. But when they told me what I'd be earning – that's when I lost it. I'm not some kid out of art school that they can pay in fucking peanuts.'

'But surely it's only while you're training?' I said.

'I don't give a shit!' he raged. 'I've worked hard in my profession to earn a decent living and I won't accept a penny less than I'm worth.'

'But don't you see that you're not worth all that much to them until you've acquired the skills they need?' I pointed out. 'It was a chance for you, Matt.'

'It was a waste of time,' he grumbled, 'a wild fucking goose chase. I ought to lamp that French bastard for setting it up.'

'Gervaise was only trying to help you,' I snapped, aggressively defending him. 'But now you've made him look a fool by letting him down.'

Matt's eyes leapt to my face. 'You sound as if you've changed your tune about him,' he accused me. 'Am I missing something here?' Whatever he saw in my expression made him angry. 'There's something going on between you and Gervaise. I suspected it before I went away. Those little looks you keep giving each other. And I've heard what he calls you – *Sugarlips*. Is that a reference to your pussy lips, huh? Has he been going down on you, Selina?'

'Stop it!' I cried. 'It's just a joke.'

'And sending me to Norfolk – was that a joke?' He jumped up and grabbed my arm. 'Did he get me out of the way so he could screw you? Did you spread your legs the minute my back was turned?'

I winced as his fingers bit into me. 'You're being ridiculous, Matt. If I wanted to fuck him, I would. I don't need anyone's permission, least of all yours.'

He clamped his hand around my jaws and brought his face close to mine. 'So, did you? Did you fuck him? Come on, you horny little bitch. What did he do? Did he take you up the arse?'

I wrestled my face from his grip. 'I think you're getting me mixed up with Miranda. I'm not answerable to you. I'm your girlfriend's stepdaughter, remember?'

'Her wicked stepdaughter,' he said, turning back to the table to swill another drink from the bottle. 'You threw yourself at me the minute she was gone. Did you spare her a thought when you were playing around with my cock or I was fingering your pussy – no! You wanted me for yourself and you didn't give a shit about her.'

'I made a stupid mistake,' I said. 'You're right, I wanted you, but for all the wrong reasons. I was looking for something that was missing in my life but I didn't know what until ... recently. But at least things haven't gone too far between us. All we have to do is forget what happened and go back to the way things were. It's what I want, Matt.' Then, leaving him to his bottle, I went upstairs to bed.

Sometime later, I was roused from a deep, dreamless slumber through my skin prickling with cold. Believing I'd thrown off my covers, I fumbled drowsily for my duvet. When I couldn't find it, I reluctantly opened my eyes to the unexpected glare from my bedroom light. Confused, I blinked the room into focus and that's when I saw him, standing at the foot of my bed, clutching my covers in his fists.

'Matt!' I exclaimed, covering my naked breasts. I had nothing on but a pair of skimpy panties. 'What the hell are you doing?'

'Just looking,' he slurred, letting go of the covers and staggering around the edge of the bed.

'You're stinking drunk,' I hurled at him. 'Get out of my room!'

He flopped on to the bed and leaned over me. 'Let's fuck – I want to fuck.' His breath stank of whisky, his eyes seemed half-crazed and his lips were curled back into a tooth-baring snarl.

I cowered from him. 'Go away, Matt, please. You're frightening me.'

He plucked at my hands. 'Why are you covering yourself up?' He gave a sinister laugh as I fended him off. 'Oh, I get it – you want to play rough.' He grabbed my wrists and, spreadeagling my arms, clambered on top of me.

'No, Matt, no!' I screeched, averting my head as his slobbering mouth tried to ravish my lips.

When I tried to bite him, he grunted ecstatically. 'Go

on, scratch me, hit me, bite me, you spiteful little bitch.' Then he grabbed hold of my breast and, squeezing it like putty, sucked and chewed on my teat.

'Ow! You're hurting me,' I yelped, tugging his hair with my free hand as I tried to pull his head from my chest. Shaking free of my grip, he smashed his face against my cheek and, with his stubble scraping my skin, growled fiercely into my ear, 'Is this rough enough for you, baby?' Then, thrusting his hand inside my panties, he scrunched his fingers into my pubic mound and viciously twisted his wrist to bring wincing tears of pain to my eyes. A cold rush of panic flooded my brain. Bucking and struggling frantically, I lashed and clawed at him. But my resistance seemed only to incite him. Cackling with manic glee, he captured my flailing hand and pinned it underneath me.

I tried to scream but his weight was crushing down on my ribs and I could barely draw breath. Translating my muted cries as groans of pleasure, Matt spouted filth from his mouth as he grappled with his fly: 'I'm going to come in your cunt. I'm going to spunk in your face, spit on your tits and make you lick out my arsehole.'

He forced my legs apart but, in his frenzied desire to enter me, he'd forgotten I was still wearing panties and rammed his cock into the gusset. 'What the fuck?' he exploded, jabbing fiercely but ineffectually. His fuddled brain seemed unable to grasp his mistake.

I took advantage of his confusion to effect a change of tact. 'Oh Matt,' I groaned sexily, 'I want you so much. Lift yourself up and let me take off my panties.' My intention was to knee him in the balls if he did, but I never got the chance. For, just as I'd finished speaking, an angry voice boomed out, 'What the fuck is going on here!'

'Gervaise!' I cried out joyfully as, with superhuman strength, he plucked Matt from my body and flung him across the room like an inflatable male sex doll that, after crashing into my wardrobe, seemed to puncture and shrivel up. Shielding himself with his arms, Matt whimpered pathetically, 'Don't hit me, please don't hit me. It's all her fault; she lured me into her bed. You heard what she said. She was begging for it.'

Standing over him like a bear, Gervaise glowered at his cowering form. 'How little you must care for Miranda if you can't even find the willpower to resist her slut of a stepdaughter. Get out of my sight, you cringing piece of shit, before I kick your head up your arse.'

As Matt slunk out of the room, I grabbed my duvet and hauled it up to my chin. 'Oh, thank God you came home,' I gushed gratefully.

He didn't seem to be listening. He was staring at me with an expression of utter contempt on his face. 'You just move right along, don't you?' he murmured. 'One man after another.'

'No, you've got it all wrong,' I protested. 'I didn't invite him into my bed. He was trying to rape me.'

'Oh, please,' he sneered, 'do me a favour. Do I look like I have a diploma from the dumb-arse school for dickheads? You forget I've been on the receiving end of that horny seduction routine of yours. He didn't stand a chance, any more than I did.'

'But you have to believe me!' I wailed. 'It's not what you think. Matt came home in a foul mood because he didn't get the job. He downed a bottle of whisky and tried to force himself on me.'

'I heard what you said to him,' he flung at me. 'You tell a man you want him and then accuse him of rape? Only an evil witch or a demented bitch would do a thing like that.'

I stared at him unbelievingly. 'Is that what you think of me?'

He nodded slowly. 'Yeah, that's what I think of you.'

'I see.' I reached down the side of the bed and picked up my handbag. 'In that case,' I said, opening it up, 'I don't want your lousy money.' I removed the cheque he'd given me and held it out with a shaky hand.

'Don't be stupid,' he snapped. 'How else are you going to pay?'

'Oh, I'm sure I'll think of something,' I said. 'Go on – take it! I don't need your money and I certainly don't need your scowling disapproval.'

'I don't want it,' he declared.

'Neither do I!' I ripped up the cheque and threw the pieces like confetti. 'Now, get out of my bedroom, you pig!'

18

'You did what!' Holly exclaimed.

'I tore up the cheque,' I repeated guiltily.

She threw up her hands in despair. 'Are you crazy?'

'Don't look at me like that,' I beseeched her. 'If you'd heard the things he said to me last night, you'd have done the same. He made me feel like bacteria.'

She gave me a critical look. 'Considering the compromising situation he discovered you in, I'm not exactly surprised about that.'

'I told you what happened,' I said sullenly.

'But think how bad it must have looked,' she reflected. 'Try imagining the scene from Gervaise's point of view: You were lying on a bed with Matt on top of you, telling him how much you wanted him and offering to remove your own panties.'

My shoulders sagged and I sighed. 'He had to walk in right at that moment, didn't he? If only he'd come in earlier when I was fighting him tooth and nail.'

'Why don't you let me call him for you?' she offered. 'Let me explain what really happened. Damn it, Selina, you can't go to Luca's without that cheque! He'll eat you alive.'

'I might enjoy being eaten,' I said stubbornly. 'I did before.'

She scowled at me. 'Is that meant to be funny?'

'No, I'm serious,' I insisted. 'Gervaise thinks I'm all about sex and maybe he's right. Who knows, I might have enjoyed the sex with Matt if Gervaise hadn't come back when he did. There's no accounting for my sex drive; it's a law unto itself.'

'Let me speak to him,' she urged me again. 'Hanging on to your pride will only cost you your self-respect. Can't you see that?'

'You've been in corners like this yourself,' I levelled at her sharply, 'and used your body to get out of them. But I'll bet you never took a handout from someone who despised you.'

'Maybe I was never that desperate,' she said. 'But, I'll tell you this, if I was in your place, I wouldn't sell myself to Luca. That's like giving up your soul.'

I glanced at my watch; it was nearly five o'clock. 'That's why I put off telling you about this until now. I knew you'd disapprove and I didn't want you spending the entire day trying to talk me out of it. There's a taxi coming in five minutes to take me to Luca's. By tomorrow this will be over and I won't be indebted to anyone.'

'Let me talk to Harry,' she pleaded. 'There must be something he can do.'

'Harry's got enough on his plate. When Alison finds out he's with you again, she'll make sure that he ends up penniless.' I laughed. 'You may have to go on the game to support him. Have you thought about that?'

'We'd probably earn more money if I put him out to stud,' she said. 'Underneath that business suit, he's all gigolo.' She grew serious again. 'Selina, you can't really mean to go through with this. Luca Verdici is a –'

She was cut off by the arrival of a middle-aged man. 'Someone order a cab for number five, Elderberry Close?' he enquired.

I nodded. 'That's me.'

'Hold it a minute,' begged Holly. 'I'm not happy about this at all.'

'I don't expect you to be,' I told her, following the man out the door, 'but stop worrying; I'll be fine.'

'I'm not happy!' she called after me.

I wasn't so happy myself when the cab dropped me off outside a vast redbrick house, one of only three in a cul-de-sac. It looked severe and imposing, and the herringbone driveway seemed half a mile long as I walked up to the covered porch.

The door was opened by a thick-set brute of a man who looked like an all-in wrestler, his features cartoonishly flattened as if, at some point in his life, he'd been smashed in the face with a flat iron. His name, I discovered later, was Bulldog Baxter and he was, in fact, a former boxer who'd been forcibly retired from the ring due to his uncontrollable temper and his penchant for punching referees.

As a butler, he was unimpressive. 'What do you want?' he asked gruffly.

I refused to be intimidated. 'Mr Verdici is expecting me. My name is Selina King.' The lummox nodded as if I'd uttered a magic password and permitted me into the house.

He showed me into a minimalistic lounge, which had stark white walls and varnished floorboards. The furniture, such as there was of it, was black and the only ornamentation was two large paintings of black circles on two of the walls. They reminded me of black holes.

I sat down on the black leather sofa and after a minute or two Luca came in. 'You look as if you've come to sell me insurance,' he said, casting a critical gaze over my smart, businesslike trouser suit; his eyes reminded me of black holes.

'You seem to have all the insurance you need,' I commented. 'The man who let me in – is he your bodyguard?'

He gave a qualified nod. 'He looks after me.'

'Do you need looking after?'

He sat down in one of the armchairs and gave a nonchalant lift of his hands. 'We all have enemies. Can I offer you some refreshment?'

I shook my head. 'No thank you.'

He went on to tell me about Bulldog. 'I found him left for dead after an illegal bare-knuckle fight,' he explained. 'He's lived with me ever since.'

'Funny, I can't seem to picture you as an altruist,' I said.

'I'm not,' he replied. 'I only hired Bulldog because I needed a new man after his predecessor was convicted of GBH and went down for ten years. I'm afraid there isn't a benevolent bone in my body.'

'That's a pity,' I said darkly. 'I was rather hoping you might have a soul instead of a . . . black hole.'

He smiled lopsidedly. 'Why would you nurture such a hope?'

I took a deep breath. 'Because I don't have your money after all.'

He tapped his fingertips together. 'I see.' There was a long pause before he spoke again. 'You present me with a dilemma,' he said. 'How do you propose that I solve it?'

'I don't know,' I answered defeatedly. 'I suppose you could set your Bulldog on me; have him rip out my guts and cook them up for you on a plate.'

'I could,' he agreed. 'You might actually prefer that to some of the alternatives I have in mind.'

I shuddered inwardly. 'Such as?'

He stood up and opened the lid of an ebony cube of furniture. 'I think we should discuss this over a drink. You need to relax a little. A brandy, I think.' He removed two crystal balloon glasses and poured a generous measure of golden liquid into both. I tried not to shrink from him as he sat next to me on the sofa and handed me my glass. The liqueur burnt my throat, but I gulped it down like water. He put a restraining hand on my arm. 'You should savour the taste,' he advised.

Ignoring him, I drained my glass. 'I loathe brandy,' I declared, 'but I find if I swallow it fast enough, I can hardly taste it at all.' I thrust the empty glass into his hand.

He set it down. 'You may not like the taste,' he said, 'but I've no doubt you'll relish its intoxicating effect. We both know you have a capacity to enjoy the things you despise.' He slid his hand between my thighs.

'What do you want from me?' I whispered tightly.

Sipping casually from his glass, he dug his fingers into the crease of my crotch and scratched at my clit through my clothes. I made no attempt to stop him because I wanted it over with.

If Gervaise was right and I was 'all about sex' there should be nothing to stop me from getting aroused, especially if I imagined it was him.

'Open your eyes!' snapped Luca, slamming down his glass. 'Do you think I'd let you escape into a fantasy?'

'I'll fantasise if I want to,' I said. 'You can fuck my body but you can't fuck my brain. Don't you get it, Luca? You're just not doing it for me.'

He removed his hand. 'Then I won't trouble myself any longer. You see I've a fantasy of my own in which I've imagined you as both a willing and an unwilling participant, so it really makes no difference to me at all. Would you like me to tell you about it?'

'Do I have any choice?'

'It may interest you to know what I have in mind for you,' he said. He put his elbow on the padded arm of the sofa and rested his head on his hand. His voice grew soft as a purr. 'I imagine that I'm fucking you on the floor.

You're naked as a baby and your soft, white thighs are slapping against my flanks because I'm fucking you so hard. Your back is arched and your arms are flailing; you hate yourself because you can't get enough of me. Your eyes are full of hatred. You spit, and claw, and lash at me, but you're loving the pounding of my cock. Your juices are flowing like a river.

'Then into the room walks Bulldog. He stares at your naked body. He drools and salivates like a hungry pig. He begs me to let him join us. He falls to his knees and begs me like a dog. You are horrified. You struggle to escape. But I raise my hand and beckon him.

'He takes off his clothes and unfurls his massive cock. It's ugly, and fat, and gnarled as the bough of an oak tree. Your eyes are on stalks as he straddles your face with his back to me. I start fucking you again as he rubs his hairy arse on your breasts and feeds his cock into your mouth inch by inch. You gobble him down until his fat balls are slapping on your chin. Then his body starts to shake and I know he's going to come. "On her face!" I shout. "On her face!" And he obeys me. He lifts himself up and through the arch of his legs I see the jets of white spunk splashing on your face.

'I feel my own climax rising and pull my cock from your pussy, then I spurt on your body and I spurt on his arse. What do you think of my fantasy?'

I felt sick. 'I think it sucks,' I croaked. 'You're disgusting.'

He gave a sinister laugh. 'What did you expect, Selina? A bit of oral sex, an hour or two of screwing? Surely it must have occurred to you that I might want more for my money?'

'No,' I shook my head vigorously. 'I wouldn't do what you've described for a million pounds.'

He looked at me with eyes like pieces of granite. 'The

way I see it, you really don't have much choice in the matter: it's payday.'

I tried to get up but he gripped my throat and pushed me back down. 'Don't be a fool,' he snarled. 'Is my fantasy worse than looking in the mirror each day and being horrified by your own reflection? It would be a shame to mess up this beautiful face with acid.'

I was terrified. 'Please, Luca,' I stammered. 'I'll sell my share of the business. I'll pay you twice what I owe you.'

'You've had your last chance,' he said. 'Your time's up.'

'Not quite, pal.'

For a second I thought I'd imagined Gervaise's voice, but as Luca swung round and I pulled out from under him, I saw him fighting his way into the room with Bulldog hanging off his back.

'I'm sorry, boss, he burst right in,' Bulldog panted. 'I couldn't stop him. He says he's come for *her*.'

'Let him go,' Luca said calmly.

As Bulldog released his arm-lock and Gervaise shrugged him off, I yearned to throw myself into the protective circle of his arms, but Luca had my wrist in a vice-like grip. 'Who the fuck are you?' he demanded of the Frenchman.

'I'm her uncle.'

As Luca took a moment to absorb the information, Gervaise crossed the floor and thrust a cheque in front of his face. 'Here's the money she owes you.'

'You're too late,' Luca said.

'Do you hear any clocks chiming midnight?' asked Gervaise. 'Has anyone mislaid a glass slipper? No? Well then, it must still be Wednesday.'

'How do I know this cheque won't bounce?' Luca rasped.

Gervaise looked at him sternly. 'How do I know your head won't bounce? I guess I won't until I kick it. Let go of my niece, arsehole. I get angry when people mistreat my family, especially right in front of me. As an Italian you ought to know better.'

Luca released me. 'The girl can go, but you and I need to have a little chat.'

Gervaise nodded fearlessly. 'That suits me just fine.' He grabbed my hand and tugged me out of my seat. 'There's a cab outside – get in it and wait for me.'

'I'm not leaving you with him,' I said. 'The man's a psycho.'

'So what?' he retorted. 'Most of my pals in the SAS are psychos. Don't worry, Selina, this won't take long.' He turned to Luca. 'Why don't you have your man escort her from the house?'

Luca nodded towards Bulldog who stepped forward and clamped his sausage fingers on my arm. 'Gently,' growled Gervaise as he dragged me away.

I was flung out the door by my britches and as I picked myself up from the path, I heard it slam behind me with a grim finality. The taxi driver got out of the car and hurried over to me. 'Are you all right?'

'Please,' I begged him. 'You have to help me. My … boyfriend's in trouble.'

'Your boyfriend told me to get you into the cab if you came out alone,' he informed me. 'Come on, lady, let's do as he says.'

I hung back. 'They could be beating him up in there. You don't know what these people are like.'

'Listen, love, it's none of my fucking business,' said the driver. 'I'm not a bloody cop. Now, if you don't get in the car, I'll drive off and leave the pair of you.'

'Oh, God!' I wailed. 'I don't know what to do.'

'Get in the car,' he coaxed me, softening as he saw how distraught I was. 'He's a big lad; he can take care of himself. But he might need to make a fast getaway, so get into the car and I'll start up the engine. It's the best I can do, love. I've a wife and kids to think of.' Reluctantly, I let him lead me away.

It was agony waiting for the front door to open and, as the minutes ticked by, I grew more and more fearful.

What were they doing to him? Dear God, don't let them mess up his beautiful face!

When, at last, Gervaise stumbled out, holding his hand to his cheek, I thought the worst. I flung open the car door to jump out but he waved me back inside. Yet he seemed in no hurry to get into the car.

'Are you OK, mate?' the driver asked.

He nodded. 'No problem. You can take us home now.'

As soon as he sat down, I threw my arms around him, overwhelmed by emotion. Tears of relief flooded from my eyes as I clung to him tightly. 'Oh, Gervaise, I was so frightened for you. What happened in there?'

He answered in the matter-of-fact way that was so wonderfully Gervaise. 'He set his Bulldog on me.'

I snatched his hand from his face. 'You're bleeding.'

'It's nothing,' he said. 'He clipped me with his pinky ring when he tried to take a swing at me.'

'But he must have landed some punches – he's a boxer,' I declared.

'Just one in the stomach,' he admitted. 'He's got a neat left hook; it took the wind out of my sails. It was almost a pity to have to break an arm like that.'

'You broke his arm?' I exclaimed.

He rolled his eyes. 'What else could I do? He was hitting me with it.'

He was being impossible and I loved him so much for making so little of it. 'What about Luca?'

He shrugged. 'Luca's a pathetic little wimp who wasn't worth bruising my knuckles on. I don't think he'll be bothering you again.'

Almost timidly, I laid my little hand on top of his mighty one. 'I can't believe you walked out of there with just a scratch. Are you really in the SAS?'

He looked at me archly. 'What would I be doing in the SAS? I'm French, you ninny.'

'Of course you are,' I agreed with a sigh. 'Only a foreigner would use a word like "ninny".'

'But you don't work alongside the Special Forces for as many years as I have without picking up a thing or two,' he explained. 'I *do* have a lot friends in the SAS.' He removed his hand from under mine. 'I'm not a hero, Selina. I just know how to fight dirty.'

'Why did you come after me?' I asked. 'And, come to think of it, how did you get Luca's address?'

He looked out of the window. 'Holly rang me and told me everything,' he said. 'She thought you might need rescuing from a fate worse than death. Was she right?'

'She was right,' I confessed. 'I underestimated Luca. He isn't just a slime-ball, he's an evil son-of-a-bitch.'

He swung his blue gaze at me. 'But you were willing to sleep with him.'

'I didn't have any choice.'

'Yes you did.'

As we fell into silence, I felt the weight of his accusation bearing down on my head. He must have thought I was pond-life even to consider bedding a man like Luca.

Sick with shame, I ran indoors as soon as the taxi pulled up. I'd intended to flee to my room but, as I passed the lounge, I noticed a broken lamp on the floor and signs of a scuffle. I went inside to investigate.

When Gervaise came in, I enquired, 'Where's Matt?'

He wiped his hand over his face. 'He's gone. I threw him out.'

'You threw him out?'

He spread his hands and grinned sheepishly. 'It's been one of those days.'

'Did he confess what he tried to do to me?' I asked.

He shook his head. 'That's not the reason I threw him out. Take a seat, Selina, I've something to tell you.'

Mystified, I plonked into an armchair. 'What is it?'

He reached inside the pocket of his jacket and took out an airmail letter. 'It's from Miranda,' he explained. 'It's been all over the place but it finally caught up with me today. It tells me everything. This guy she went to America with – he isn't her lover, he's just a friend. She didn't run off with another man; she was running away from Matt. He's been brutalising her: slapping her about and forcing himself on her . . .' he paused to look at me accusingly. 'Didn't you notice anything? Were you totally blind?'

Shocked, I clamped my hand over my mouth. 'I had no idea, I swear it,' I gasped.

'You didn't see anything at all?' he asked incredulously.

'No . . . I . . .' I broke off as I remembered the bruises. 'Oh, God!'

'What?' he prompted.

'I saw some bruises on her arm once. I asked her about them but she laughed them off; she said she'd been clumsy.'

'And you believed her?'

'I had no reason not to,' I stressed. 'Matt never showed any signs of brutality. He always seemed so loving and caring towards her. Why do you think I went after him? I thought he was perfect and wanted him for myself. I hated Miranda and I was convinced that she didn't deserve him. Believe me, Gervaise, if I'd known the kind of man he was –'

'You'd probably have fucked him anyway,' he deduced. 'After all, you knew what Luca was, didn't you?'

'Your precious sister isn't so much better than me,' I said. 'She left me on my own with a man that she knows is a brute. It's hardly the act of a doting stepmother, is it?'

He referred to the letter. '"Selina is strong",' he quoted, '"if Matt tries to abuse her, she'll know how to deal with him. I wish I could be like that. But I'm not. I was too weak to live without a man after her father died or to care for her on my own. I thought that Matt could provide the security we needed but, instead, my feebleness has left me trapped in an abusive relationship with flight as the only way out. I don't have the strength to stand up to him and I've become so scared of him, dear brother, that I must turn to you for help".' He put the letter back into his pocket. 'She didn't know how to get in touch with me but she was sure that the letter would reach me eventually. She's sitting tight until she hears from me. I'm to call her as soon as it's safe to come home.'

'What did Matt say when you confronted him with the letter?' I asked.

'He blamed her, of course; said she'd ridiculed him after he lost his job.'

'That's isn't true!' I exclaimed.

'He seemed to think that she needed a smack now and then, just to keep her in her place.'

'That's outrageous,' I fumed. 'How did you react?'

'I nodded,' he replied.

'You nodded!' I cried.

'Yes, I nodded,' he confirmed. 'Unfortunately his head got in the way of me nodding.'

A strangled laugh choked out me. 'You mean you head-butted him?'

He shrugged. 'It was my way of telling him that I didn't agree with him.'

I gave my head a disbelieving shake. 'Tell me, Gervaise, what do you do when you're not beating up all the bad guys? I had no idea you were such a thug.'

He pulled a wry face. 'Neither did I. I suppose you'd better keep an eye on me in case I turn green and start ripping off my clothes.'

'I wish you would,' I urged him longingly.

He cocked an eyebrow. 'Turn green or rip off my clothes?'

'Take a guess,' I murmured, craving him so much that I could taste it. He was my hero, my champion, my Hercules, to be worshipped with my hands and adored with my heart.

He heaved a heavy sigh and flopped into the other armchair. 'Don't you ever think of anything but sex? I thought that was a man's job.'

'Well, if it is, you're not doing it very well,' I pointed out.

He smiled. 'Oh, yes I am. I'm just a little more sneaky about it.'

'Are you saying I'm too obvious?'

He peered into my eyes. 'You have a certain way of looking at a man that licks his dick and tickles his balls. So, in some respects, you're substantially more obvious than a hooker in hot-pants.'

Wishing I hadn't asked, I went over to the cabinet and opened the drawer where I kept the first aid kit. 'Let me see to that cut,' I said, tearing open an antiseptic wipe.

'It's nothing,' he grumbled, waving me away.

'Don't be a baby,' I scolded, dabbing at the cut. 'You're right – it's just a nick. But it could have been a lot worse.' I knelt down in front of him and rested my head on the arm of his chair. 'I want to thank you for what you did.'

He tousled my hair. 'Forget it.' Then he yawned and, slumping wearily back, closed his eyes.

I let him doze so that I could study his handsome features in repose. I wanted to cover his face with kisses, but I let my eyes caress him instead, smiling to myself as his five o'clock shadow evoked a ghostly reminder of the beard he'd once had. Struck by a sudden revelation, I rattled his arm excitedly. 'Gervaise, I've something to tell you.'

He jolted awake. 'What – what is it?'

'I can prove myself to you.'

His face sagged. 'Oh shit,' he groaned. 'Please don't offer to cook.'

'I want you to grow back your beard,' I said brightly.

He screwed up his nose. 'Right this minute?'

'I mean it,' I said. 'You see, I've realised I'd love you even if you grew it all back and dyed it purple or green.'

'I like blue,' he grunted.

'Well, blue then.' I clasped his hand. 'Don't you see what this means? Lust alone wouldn't cure me of my beard-o-phobia, would it? I *must* be in love with you.'

'Then you'd better get out of it,' he said, 'because I'm leaving in the morning.'

'What!' I was mortified, horrified, terrified. 'Why?'

His face became a mask of indifference. 'Now that I know that Matt and Miranda are finished, I have no reason to stay.' He gave my hand back to me. 'It's time I went home.'

My lip was trembling so much that I could hardly speak. 'Back to France, back to *her*?'

He nodded slowly. 'I'm sorry, *ma petite*.'

'But you don't love that Veronique,' I muttered tremulously. 'Why are you running away from me? Do you still think I'm poison?'

'For fuck's sake!' he exploded. 'Of course you're fuck-ing poison. You wind men up, you can't keep your knickers on, and you cook like a crackpot scientist who's trying to invent a new form of rubber. If I stay here, you'll creep into my bed and crawl into my head like a bloody infestation. I don't want you under my skin, Selina, you'd only bring me out in hives!' He thumped his head on the back of the chair. 'I don't want you.'

He was lying. Suddenly, I knew he was lying. I could see it now in the slumping of his shoulders and in his battle-weary demeanour. My darling Gervaise was all but defeated. I had broken through his defences and he was making his very last stand. 'I'm going to bed,' he said, rising wearily to his feet.

'But it's still early,' I protested. 'Please stay and talk to me.'

'I'm tired,' he sighed. 'It's been a helluva day and I want to make an early start.'

I let him go. I let him think he'd survived. I'd give him a chance to rest before launching my final assault upon the last of his resistance. Yet the victory wouldn't be mine. For, although he didn't realise it, he'd conquered me more thoroughly than he would ever know.

It was still light when I went upstairs and all was quiet in his room as I tiptoed past. I was surprised by how nervous I felt; my hands were shaking as I took off my clothes, trying not to think too far ahead because I felt like such a novice. I had seduced a man's body before but never his heart and mind. And, although I'd sought pleasure many times, I'd never once set out in search of happiness.

I opened the door to his room with a tingling sense of déjà vu and crept in noiselessly. The curtains were half-drawn, blotting out some but not all of the evening light. He had his back to me and, beneath the cover, the rugged mound of his body lay still. His breathing was shallow and steady.

I peeled back the cover, sighing inwardly at the magnificent landscape of his broad, tapered back. There was so much of him to explore, so much rolling golden territory. I felt shivery with pleasure just looking at him and my fingers were itching to run themselves through his raven black hair so dark against the pillow.

Slowly as a snake, I slithered into bed with him and snuggled up to his body. He jerked and I heard him take a sharp intake of breath; then his body went as rigid as steel.

'This is just about where I came in,' he murmured huskily. 'It all started with you sneaking into my bed. I take it you know that it's me this time?'

'Oh, yes,' I uttered softly, kissing the tense muscles in his back. 'I know it's you.'

He rolled over to face me. 'Are you sure? I wouldn't want you making another mistake.'

'Oh, shut up,' I groaned, clasping his head and crushing my lips to his. The combination of my hot, hungry kisses and horny wriggling body were simply too much for him.

'Oh, fuck it!' he cried and, grabbing me, he kissed me back.

As our tongues made languid love, the bones in my legs seemed to curl right up and a delirious dizziness suffused my brain. I was ready to give up breathing so that he'd never stop kissing me. Our hands were going crazy, as if we wanted to touch every part of each other at once. But, suddenly, he tore himself away from me. 'Hey, hold it a minute,' he said.

'What is it?' I simpered.

'What's going on here? Are you trying to seduce me like that time when you thought it was Matt?'

'Yes I am,' I admitted.

'I seem to remember that you used a pretty effective technique.'

'As a matter of fact, I was just about to do that again,' I told him, 'because I simply can't think of a better way to show you how much I love you.'

'I see.' He lay back and his blue eyes considered me for a moment. Then a slow, sexy smile spread across his features. 'In that case,' he said, pushing my head down towards his cock, 'I guess you'd better get on with it ... *Sugarlips*.'

LOOK OUT FOR THE ALL-NEW BLACK LACE BOOKS – AVAILABLE NOW!

All books priced £6.99 in the UK. Please note publication dates apply to the UK only. For other territories, please contact your retailer.

LIBERTY HALL
Kate Stewart
ISBN O 352 33776 1

Vicar's daughter and wannabe journalist Tess Morgan is willing to do anything to pay off her student overdraft. Luckily for Tess, her flatmate Imogen is the daughter of infamous madam, Liberty Hall, who owns a pleasure palace of the same name that operates under a guise of respectability as a hotel. When Tess lands herself a summer job catering for 'special clients' at Liberty Hall, she sees an opportunity to clear that overdraft with a bit of undercover journalism. But when she tries to tell all to a Sunday newspaper, Tess is in for a shocking surprise. **Fruity antics aplenty in this tale of naughty behaviour and double-crossing.**

DRAWN TOGETHER
Robyn Russell
ISBN O 352 33269 7

When Tanya, a graphic artist, creates Katrina Cortez – a sexy, comic-strip detective – she begins to wish her own life were more like that of Katrina's. Stephen Sinclair, who works with Tanya, is her kind of man. Unfortunately Tanya's just moved in with her bank manager boyfriend, who expects her to play the part of the executive girlfriend. In Tanya's quest to gain the affection of Mr Sinclair, she must become more like Katrina Cortez – a voluptuous wild woman! **Unusual and engaging story of seduction and delight.**

Coming in March

EVIL'S NIECE
Melissa MacNeal
ISBN 0 352 33781 8

The setting is 1890s New Orleans. When Eve spies her husband with a sultry blonde, she is determined to win back his affection. When her brother-in-law sends a maid to train her in the ways of seduction, things spin rapidly out of control. Their first lesson reveals a surprise that Miss Eve isn't prepared for, and when her husband discovers these liaisons, it seems she will lose her prestigious place in society. However, his own covert life is about to unravel and reveal the biggest secret of all. **More historical high jinks from Ms MacNeal, the undisputed queen of kinky erotica set in the world of corsets and chaperones.**

LEARNING THE HARD WAY
Jasmine Archer
ISBN 0 352 33782 6

Tamsin has won a photographic assignment to collaborate on a book of nudes with the sex-obsessed Leandra. Thing is, the job is in Los Angeles and she doesn't want her new friend to know how sexually inexperienced she is. Tamsin sets out to learn all she can before flying out to meet her photographic mentor, but nothing can prepare her for Leandra's outrageous lifestyle. Along with husband Nigel, and an assortment of kinky friends, Leandra is about to initiate Tamsin into some very different ways to have fun. **Fun and upbeat story of a young woman's transition from sexual ingénue to fully fledged dominatrix.**

ACE OF HEARTS
Lisette Allen
ISBN 0 352 33059 7

England, 1816. The wealthy elite is enjoying an unprecedented era of hedonistic adventure. Their lives are filled with parties, sexual dalliances and scandal. Marisa Brooke is a young lady who lives by her wits, fencing and cheating the wealthy at cards. She also likes seducing young men and indulging her fancy for fleshly pleasures. However, love and fortune are lost as easily as they are won, and she has to use all her skill and cunning if she wants to hold on to her winnings and her lovers. **Highly enjoyable historical erotica set in the period of Regency excess.**

Coming in April

VALENTINA'S RULES
Monica Belle
ISBN 0 352 33788 5

Valentina is the girl with a plan: find a wealthy man, marry him, mould him and take her place in the sun. She's got the looks, she's got the ambition and, after one night with her, most men are following her around like puppies. When she decides that Michael Callington is too good for her friend Chrissy and just right for her, she finds she has bitten off a bit more than she expected. Then there's Michael's father, the notorious spanking Major, who is determined to have his fun, too. **Monica Belle specialises in erotic stories about modern girls about town and up to no good.**

WICKED WORDS 8
Edited by Kerri Sharp
ISBN O 352 33787 7

Hugely popular and immensely entertaining, the *Wicked Words* collections are the freshest and most cutting-edge volumes of women's erotic stories to be found anywhere in the world. The diversity of themes and styles reflects the multi-faceted nature of the female sexual imagination. Combining humour, warmth and attitude with fun, imaginative writing, these stories sizzle with horny action. Only the most arousing fiction makes it into a *Wicked Words* volume. This is the best in fun, sassy erotica from the UK and USA. **Another sizzling collection of wild fantasies from wicked women!**

Black Lace Booklist

Information is correct at time of printing. To avoid disappointment check availability before ordering. Go to www.blacklace-books.co.uk. All books are priced £6.99 unless another price is given.

☐ THE HOUSE IN NEW ORLEANS Fleur Reynolds	ISBN 0 352 32951 3
☐ NOBLE VICES Monica Belle	ISBN 0 352 33738 9
☐ HEAT OF THE MOMENT Tesni Morgan	ISBN 0 352 33742 7
☐ STORMY HAVEN Savannah Smythe	ISBN 0 352 33757 5
☐ STICKY FINGERS Alison Tyler	ISBN 0 352 33756 7
☐ THE WICKED STEPDAUGHTER Wendy Harris	ISBN 0 352 33777 X
☐ DRAWN TOGETHER Robyn Russell	ISBN 0 352 33269 7

BLACK LACE BOOKS WITH AN HISTORICAL SETTING

☐ PRIMAL SKIN Leona Benkt Rhys	ISBN 0 352 33500 9	£5.99
☐ DEVIL'S FIRE Melissa MacNeal	ISBN 0 352 33527 0	£5.99
☐ WILD KINGDOM Deanna Ashford	ISBN 0 352 33549 1	£5.99
☐ DARKER THAN LOVE Kristina Lloyd	ISBN 0 352 33279 4	
☐ STAND AND DELIVER Helena Ravenscroft	ISBN 0 352 33340 5	£5.99
☐ THE CAPTIVATION Natasha Rostova	ISBN 0 352 33234 4	
☐ CIRCO EROTICA Mercedes Kelley	ISBN 0 352 33257 3	
☐ MINX Megan Blythe	ISBN 0 352 33638 2	
☐ PLEASURE'S DAUGHTER Sedalia Johnson	ISBN 0 352 33237 9	
☐ JULIET RISING Cleo Cordell	ISBN 0 352 32938 6	
☐ DEMON'S DARE Melissa MacNeal	ISBN 0 352 33683 8	
☐ ELENA'S CONQUEST Lisette Allen	ISBN 0 352 32950 5	
☐ DIVINE TORMENT Janine Ashbless	ISBN 0 352 33719 2	
☐ THE CAPTIVE FLESH Cleo Cordell	ISBN 0 352 32872 X	
☐ SATAN'S ANGEL Melissa MacNeal	ISBN 0 352 33726 5	
☐ THE INTIMATE EYE Georgia Angelis	ISBN 0 352 33004 X	
☐ HANDMAIDEN OF PALMYRA Fleur Reynolds	ISBN 0 352 32951 3	
☐ OPAL DARKNESS Cleo Cordell	ISBN 0 352 33033 3	
☐ SILKEN CHAINS Jodi Nicol	ISBN 0 352 33143 7	

BLACK LACE ANTHOLOGIES

☐ CRUEL ENCHANTMENT Erotic Fairy Stories Janine Ashbless	ISBN 0 352 33483 5	£5.99
☐ MORE WICKED WORDS Various	ISBN 0 352 33487 8	£5.99
☐ WICKED WORDS 4 Various	ISBN 0 352 33603 X	
☐ WICKED WORDS 5 Various	ISBN 0 352 33642 0	
☐ WICKED WORDS 6 Various	ISBN 0 352 33590 0	

BLACK LACE NON-FICTION

To find out the latest information about Black Lace titles, check out the website: www.blacklace-books.co.uk or send for a booklist with complete synopses by writing to:

> Black Lace Booklist, Virgin Books Ltd
> Thames Wharf Studios
> Rainville Road
> London W6 9HA

Please include an SAE of decent size. Please note only British stamps are valid.

Our privacy policy

We will not disclose information you supply us to any other parties. We will not disclose any information which identifies you personally to any person without your express consent.

From time to time we may send out information about Black Lace books and special offers. Please tick here if you do <u>not</u> wish to receive Black Lace information.   ☐

Please send me the books I have ticked above.

Name ....

Address ....

....

....

....

Post Code ....

Send to: Cash Sales, Black Lace Books, Thames Wharf Studios, Rainville Road, London W6 9HA.

US customers: for prices and details of how to order books for delivery by mail, call 1-800-343-4499.

Please enclose a cheque or postal order, made payable to Virgin Books Ltd, to the value of the books you have ordered plus postage and packing costs as follows:

UK and BFPO – £1.00 for the first book, 50p for each subsequent book.

Overseas (including Republic of Ireland) – £2.00 for the first book, £1.00 for each subsequent book.

If you would prefer to pay by VISA, ACCESS/MASTERCARD, DINERS CLUB, AMEX or SWITCH, please write your card number and expiry date here:

....

Signature ....

Please allow up to 28 days for delivery.